W9-BUO-837

Penguin Books
The Unexpurgated Code

J. P. Donleavy was born in New York City in 1926
and educated there and at Trinity College, Dublin.
His works include the novels *The Ginger Man*, *A
Singular Man*, *The Beastly Beatitudes of Balthazar B*,
The Onion Eaters, *A Fairy Tale of New York* and
The Destinies of Darcy Dancer, Gentleman; a
book of short pieces, *Meet My Maker the Mad
Molecule*; a novella, *The Saddest Summer of
Samuel S*; and four plays, *The Ginger Man*, *Fairy
Tales of New York*, *A Singular Man* and *The
Saddest Summer of Samuel S*. (These are published in
Penguins under the title *The Plays of J. P. Donleavy*.)
All these are published in Penguins.

J. P. Donleavy

The Unexpurgated Code

A Complete Manual of
Survival & Manners

With drawings by the author

Penguin Books

Penguin Books Ltd,
Harmondsworth, Middlesex, England
Penguin Books,
625 Madison Avenue, New York, New York 10022, U.S.A.
Penguin Books Australia Ltd,
Ringwood, Victoria, Australia
Penguin Books Canada Ltd, 2801 John Street,
Markham, Ontario, Canada L3R 1B4
Penguin Books (N.Z.) Ltd,
182–190 Wairau Road, Auckland 10, New Zealand

Portions of this book first appeared in
The Atlantic Monthly and *Oui Magazine*

First published in the U.S.A. 1975
Published in Great Britain by Wildwood House 1975
Published in Penguin Books 1976
Reprinted 1979

Made and printed in Great Britain by
Hazell Watson & Viney Ltd, Aylesbury, Bucks
Set in Linotype Juliana

Contents

Social Climbing

Extinctions and Mortalities

Vilenesses Various

In Pursuit of Comfortable Habits

Perils and Precautions

Mischiefs and Memorabilia

16 CONTENTS

Social Climbing

Upon Being Not to the Manner Born

When this unpleasant remark is made about you, stand up, making sure your flies are closed and announce in a firm voice.

'To hell with that shit.'

You may add, with a hint of hurt modesty flavouring the voice.

'I was born, wasn't I, and that's enough for me.'

Of course your opponent's high pitched riposte will be.

'But sir, that is not enough for us.'

Sit down and think. A valuable antique chair helps. Cross your legs and pull up your socks. Right away if your socks are white or otherwise bright you are in trouble unless you happen to be in yachting or tennis gear. In these latter equipages you can assume you are not entirely without hope.

Examine your background. If you really stare it straight in the status it's surprising the amount of dignity which can be salvaged from the unvarnished truth. Even from the unmitigated wrong side of the tracks or floor of the apartment building, there's bound to be something that will entitle you to make an effective reply to the lousy remark above. This is why everybody should research around a little in his lineage. Back far enough or out to the side, someone must have been something once.

For orphans who do not know who their parents were, this is sad but by no means socially fatal, and affords you a fresh start. If you have received a Red Cross Life Saving Certificate, riposte pronto with this information. After their first few ha ha ha's, your temporarily superior opponents will cringe at your hopeless effort to give an accounting of yourself. And you will really feel rotten. Your crestfallen demeanour, however, will make them clear off. They will not be inviting you to their parties. But you are left with a marvellous incitement to social climb.

Useful Rules in Social Climbing

Sketch out and firmly keep in mind your own personal dreams of grandeur in which circumstances you figure you will be when you finally get there. Forthrightly behave as if you had already made it. This will require you to strike various seemingly affected poses and possibly expose you to ridicule, especially in the matter of pretending to descend a grand staircase. It is entirely essential to be indifferent to those who laugh, point and smirk.

Impose a limit upon the speed at which you socially rise. This makes your ascent more graceful. Plus you do not always find yourself surrounded by a bunch of total strangers which can happen when you've sped right by everybody. Also any calm casualness by which you can proceed will recommend you to the discerning eye of other dedicated climbers.

Until you are firmly socially established, under no circumstances give large parties with fountains of good champagne and chilled marble bowls of caviar nestled on orchid covered tables. Instead indulge yourself semi privately with these extravagant deliciousnesses. When you get a lot of your folk crammed in your house slamming back the goodies, a socially demeaning conspiracy could get going against you as well as firm friendships which depressingly exclude you.

The smile ranks only after money and ass kissing as the major tool in climbing. It is recommended to smile as often as you can without appearing like a nut. Should someone accost you to say they do not like your smile. Wait. Until you are both on safari. When a lot of suitable ripostes connected with camels will rapidly come to mind and the setting will lend a helpful hand to the thrust.

Be easily amused. This is a socially superior characteristic, only improved upon by being highly amused. But for your own safety it is as well to temper this latter quality by never explosively convulsing with laughter except in the presence of established intimates. If however you are temporarily not easily amused and someone who may be of social advantage has put much effort into the telling of a joke, make every effort possible to remark.

'Hey that's really rich.'

The greatest social strides forward are always made by unhesitatingly letting people know straight to their faces how wonderful they are, especially in the matter of their apparel.

'Gee I like the roll on your lapels, I really do.'

The phrase 'I really do' offers reassurance to a guy who is not entirely certain his lapels are not for the birds and thinks you're spoofing him. Also it provides an air of surprise that you couldn't help blurting out your feelings. This is helpful when a member of the socially elite is suspicious of you. Small expletives such as 'gee', 'hey' and 'boy o boy' can always help make your remarks endearingly credible. When they might otherwise come dangerously close to gross insult. As happens when these small expletives are repeated more than once.

Don't look back. The faces are not nice to see. Your ascent will cause those whom you have left behind, below and under, to suffer a personality corrosion which will etch upon them looks of deeply grieved resentment.

Finding a Social Circle Which Spirals Upwards

Seek out the spectacularly pukka. These chaps are found in the most likely places and are easily recognized, attired as they usually are at ten a.m. in horse riding kit. Making their acquaintance can be a long time ordeal, occasioning frequent disillusionment, as more than likely on first contact they want to avoid you. Steel yourself against this.

Areas well known for social upward velocities will also be rife with folk running out of their minds frisson hunting in every direction. You can get yourself entangled with the most god awful non entities. Seize it as an opportunity to practise not letting your jaw drop when encountering persons of no account. This is helpful when you finally happen upon the spectacular pukka who is temporarily amusing himself by pretending a much lower social status. Often his signet ring and footwear is a dead give away. Train yourself to recognise these as well as the tell tale old ducks and partly stained but clean tee shirt. He'll be drinking a beer and relishing the opportunity of being away from household servants and estate workers. And remember, as he is taking time off from the corporation board room where he presides as chairman, the last thing he can stand is a stuffed shirt. But he will welcome the company of a real down to earth regular guy.

Except when spying on husbands or lovers, spectacular pukka ladies hardly ever pretend a lower social status. They prefer their gowns and leisure garments to be recently rushed from the reigning haute couturier. Featured in these creations and splendidly engemmed in their best diamonds they hit the top resorts, watering places, restaurants and hotel lobbies, knocking hell out of the opposition. Chauffeuring and undertaking is sometimes about the only entree to such women, except if you crack their country habitat.

These rural paradises are always made obvious by their great adjoining lawns, blue pebbled drives and palatial houses set with their elevations gleaming amid rare horticulture. Isolated on such estates, the spectacular pukka lady can be found reclining on down filled chaise longues, surrounded by her fashion magazines and often bored out of her brains. This however does not make the task of befriending her any less difficult. In fact, upon learning of your existence, there are some perverse enough to deliberately enjoy not meeting you. In such cases the only answer is brazen trespass.

One third of the battle is succeeding in making it over

the hedge, wall or battlement. The day chosen should be warmly sunny when your subject is on the terrace and late morning coffee has just been served. But remember you are an intruder. And prepare yourself. Because just as your more than likely elderly matron will be gasping in horror, you will be sighing with the promised sight of a person of real quality and not some half mummy anchored by gold bracelet charms and pumped up with transplant hormones.

Be sportily attired. Brazen trespass requires this. A paisley scarf at the neck is a nice touch. Obstacles must be bypassed without ripping the garments. A little reconnoitre will avoid your being accosted by outdoor servants, Doberman pinschers or, god forbid, Irish wolfhounds. Upon proceeding in an un-hurried manner and reaching your quarry, the following opening remarks are recommended delivered at six yards with an educated accent while leaning forward upon your ex-tended right foot in an impatiently enquiring manner.

'Forgive me madam, I hope I'm not disturbing you, but this is, is it not, Zanadu.'

'Who are you?'

'I was about to ask you.'

'This happens not to be Zanadu and, I think, is my terrace.'

'Good lord, what a merry puddle, my man must have taken the wrong turning. Chauffeurs these days appear to regard one rural lane the same as another. Do please, for-give me.'

Bow and withdraw immediately. Under normal circum-stances the matron, having heard your phrase 'what a merry puddle', will enquire after whom you are seeking. After first making sure your matron is not an intimate of theirs, provide a refined name of not too obvious social significance. You should be invited back that evening for drinks. If you are not, a further degree of haughtiness is required in your accent.

Accent Improvement

While accomplishing this it is essential to remove yourself from old pals, neighbourhood and hometown. By this, you may of course be doing yourself two favours instead of one. Nothing is more easily avoided than an unpleasant accent and the one you were born with, although keeping you at ease with your peers, may hinder your planned giant strides towards grandeur. Often folk's normal voices can sound ugly, abusive and threatening. This is undesirable unless you are intending work as a debt collector. Your biggest drag will come from your immediate family and their no account friends. The latter invariably commenting.

'Hey where did you get that accent from.'

'I most certainly did not get it from you, sir. Nor, I should add, from any of your near relatives.'

Provided folk upon whom you wish to make a favourable impression are not present, accent practice may be got without fatal social risks from attendants in gentlemen's conveniences. At the time of tipping, reach into a pocket to withdraw your change purse.

'O dash, what a bore, not a single bronze centime, do please forgive me, old chum, I know it sounds awfully fake, but I haven't a bean on me.'

Your accent has passed if the attendant replies.

'That's quite all right sir, another time will do.'

Your accent has failed if, upon the return of your purse to your pocket, the attendant growlingly and recklessly rips the stoppers out of the basins and then noisily slams down lavatory seats and kicks the waste basket skidding across the tiles. However, should he have the audacity while performing these tiresome antics to utter within your hearing.

'You lousy rotten phoney, you.'

Presto another opportunity is presented for accent practice.

'Sir, I refer you to your socks whose holes I am sure you will find useful in sieving out the larger of your teeth for museum exhibition after I have knocked them out of your tedious head.'

During and after accent improvement, accent slipping is a discouraging phenomenon but if properly manipulated it can be turned to some advantage in your upward velocity. In any event, having steered clear of future latrines where your practising might again be botched, it is quite permissible to indulge voluminous accent slipping in letting off steam publicly occasioned by social inferiors offering unpleasant lip.

Should the accent slip in polite company, it is of course a real triumph to have a different and better one underneath. This momentarily can hold ostracism at bay. However when a quite forward, no nonsense type of listener pricks up his ears and loudly announces.

'Sir, your accent has slipped.'

Smile winningly and slowly bow the head to regard your shoe tips shyly and explain.

'I'm awfully sorry about that but every time mother and father went on expedition and I was left with nannie I did prefer the excitement of below stairs.'

Your opponent will, if he is of any consequence, reply.

'That explanation sir I regard as a dire and an abominable tissue of poppycock.'

Before hinting of your close relatives in government tax collecting circles to this type of difficult person, take a good deep breath, blink the eyes as if you did not hear correctly and then in an offhand manner riposte.

'Well, as a matter of fact, I am of unobtrusive origins but I thought it would be skittish and amusing to presume upon your good breeding and a gentleman's toleration by entertainingly presenting my best efforts of speech to you, sir.'

The likes of this stubborn individual will no doubt continue to answer you annoyingly. And to imbue him with a peaceful civility it may require your making no bones about being prepared to tingle his ears with a firm fluffing of your gloves about his cheeks.

In the isolated but special case of Australians, difficulty may arise when your opponent replies to your accent efforts.

'Don't hand me that shit, digger.'

Respond gallantly to the purity of the remark.

'It is true that my present accent is acquired but my old one sounds fake and I should not like to do a chap such as yourself an injustice by using it.'

Upon Embellishing Your Background

Getting caught out in whopping falsehoods about your background can throw you off stride in making a big social step. People established in social status care bitterly about pedigree and position and care even more about the social status assumed by others as such representations are the very cherished ones upon which they themselves stand. It is prudent to wait a little till some vagueness has set in between your present status and your origins.

Having obscured yourself well from regrettable or unadvantageous background facts, present your strokes of embellishment in a light hearted manner and in a way that, should dangerous doubt arise, your polite listener will refer to you as 'painting with a full brush.' For security reasons distant historical figures are better than current dynastic names to attach to, although the latter if residing in a remote country may be mentioned in the relationship of first cousinhood. Second cousinhood may attach to fairly well established social figures. And third cousinhood to the society leader of the day. Descent from famous explorers, or heads of state can also nicely fit the bill.

However, when upon a gala evening you stand by the champagne punch, adorned in decorations and insignia to which you are not entitled, and this regrettable chap wearing tails, adjusting his monocle and rocking on his heels thrusts the following vowels at you.

'You are rather decorated aren't you.'

'Yes, as a matter of fact, I am.'

'And fully entitled I assume.'

'Well I do feel, as a matter of modesty, that I cannot accept full credit for these distinctions as some of them are hereditary.'

'Do you mean to say, sir, that a previous person is meriting and that you, sir, are posturing.'

'That's a rotten aspersion.'

'I say there then, from whom are you descended.'

'They got the files mixed up.'

'That, sir, is further inadequate as a reply.'

'Well, I'll tell you, you see, my ancestor was head of state at the time and because they were out to get him, all the god damn family records were strewn about, lost or burned.'

'Quite as I expected you to say sir.'

'Well, let me also say, buster, that our family motto to which I adhere is two fold and is here presented in bold letters on this card I am shoving in front of your eyes.'

SELF IS THE EMBLEM ALL

In the moment or two that it takes your opponent to make head or especially tails of your family motto, refer to his own decorations and press an index finger firmly upon the smallest and state enthusiastically.

'Ah I like that one, I really do.'

Most pomposities of his calibre will give you an endless song and dance as to how it was awarded, relieving you of further desperate necessity to appear improved from what you are.

Upon Embellishing the Area in Which You Reside

Folk in the right arrondissement know this demarcation within a footstep and will rarely venture into questionable territory. In fact they will stop and shudder in their tracks, bless themselves and retreat backwards pronto. So while taking any big social stride, it's kind of bad to be caught living in the wrong area. You're better off in a good district without a pot to piss in than one where you have a receptacle of jade. Although if you have the latter use it plenty wherever you are.

However, if there is nothing for it and you are there lurking and sneaking around on the wrong side of the tracks, freeway, or river, always refer to it by its proper geographical map name or postal district and avoid euphemisms. Provided you are within polite shouting distance of the border it is permissible to pretend you are in the better of two areas.

When no contemporary literary, artistic or show business association can be offered, you'll usually find, after historically researching the area thoroughly, that someone has had some kind of noteworthy fight there. By describing the battle sites, number of Indians and strategies employed, it's a nice touch, without stretching it too far, if the winner was an ancestor. If your bigoted listener is totally unimpressed and starts clearing his various throats, instantly hit him with your district's geology which happens to shield from the harmful radiation he's getting over on his side of town. It is disheartening if he is your usual obstinate son of a bitch and persists in keeping you in your place. Where of course, in fairness, it must be said you belong, but due to current widespread democracy you plan a change.

'Sir you are living in an unprepossessing neighbourhood.'

'Gee, I'm glad you noticed that.'

'Why.'

'Because I'm really deeply interested in self denial, although the architecture, in spite of being abused, is authentic, and much to my liking.'

'Sir, I regard that as unmitigated nonsense.'

'And you, sir, are hurting my feelings.'

Although this inflexible bugger will be temporarily nonplussed by your sudden anguish, only moving to his better district will unnerve him.

Upon Choosing Your Residence

Although in some cases this may be grossly unfair, you will be immediately classified by the approaches and front elevations. Or if an apartment house or block of flats by the lobby or stoop of your building. Every foot folk have to ambulate, motor, or limp over your property or your management's to get to you is an invaluable social exaltation and safety precaution.

If you're just making it out of lower middle or middle class, the mansion and walled private estate will in most cases have to be left for a later date in your life. However, go house hunting among the really swell places anyway. It is good practice to waltz through magnificently appointed spacious period residences of many exposed timbers, chimneypieces of character and other dignified touches, and which enjoy fine mature unspoilt views in the preferred directions with their additional landscape features. Then when you finally move into your overly boxy more modest residence and your neighbours stand around thinking you're just like them you can let them know what you nearly bought. This will also drop the hint that they should be prepared for the moment of your future socially upward departure.

As much as a dump makes them steer clear, a really nice place makes folk like you better. A leafy suburban district among the lawn mowing class with a solid yeomanry is to be preferred. These areas are easily recognised by the chaps you see in the lighter shade of gabardine raincoat, catching the train at the local station and on Saturdays pressing into service their Bermuda shorts to dump their garbage, skiing outfits to shovel their snow, or old school sports attire in raking their leaves. However, in order not to be tricked by some imitator mowing his lawn in old school equipment from a no account school, some brief interrogation may be required. But be considerate when you glide up in your suitably nifty motor to an inhabitant you spot outside his house.

'Hey, excuse me fella. Gee I don't know how to preface this but what school did you go to.'

'I beg your pardon.'

'You know, your school, I'm thinking of buying a house and I want to be sure I don't move in among a lot of phonies.'

Most folk, conscious in the extreme of their neighbourhood status, will take your forthright approach for what it is, a grossly presumptuous impertinence, and in case a deserving umbrage is taken, remain in your car for speedy departure.

Upon Choosing Your Neighbour

Right off the bat this could be fatal. You'll always know, if, when you first clap eyes on him, you can't sleep that night. His indelible boorish inelegance can really slam your social toes. And such unsatisfactory folk regrettably have implacable social confidence born of their monstrous ignorance and relieved only by a cowardly intelligence.

In addition to his merry bag of tricks, your loutish neighbour will exhibit astonishing reserves of energy and ingenuity in his unflagging resolve to cut you down to size. After adjoining your favourite flower bed with a pile of his worst garbage he invariably will hang his intimate laundry conspicuously in your view. The prominent depositing of un-

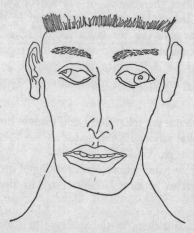

savoury human wastes and derelict vehicles will be next on his list of diabolical liberties. Followed by hooting and jeering out his apertures especially on the occasion of one of your social master strokes convening a lot of formally dressed socially superior guests. Not even aged sheep urine squirted by water pistol helps. To beat this bastard you want to get out of there fast into a dwelling centrally situated in an extensive wall enclosed deer park where your Irish wolfhounds gambol freely. Or, as a last extreme and a cheaper method altogether, hire some imported dark complexioned muscle to play dice with his teeth or, in really unimpressionable cases, baseball with his head. Words, even the most embittered, rarely suffice.

'You abominable wretched buffoon, you.'

'Ha ha.'

'You nauseous tiresome contemptible little pipsqueak, you.'

'Ha ha ha. Social climber.'

Upon Your Residence's Appurtenances

To be unerringly certain of setting your social sights straight right from the start, make sure of a butler's pantry. Knock it out of walls, squeeze it from a closet, tear it out of a hall, but get one. You can really snow the opposition with this domestic office, especially in a half assed neighbourhood.

The number of your bathrooms next sets the tone. Under no circumstances, except one, does a four bathroom guy have to take lip from a two bathroom chap. The exception being mansions and castles providing the usual closet with china, pewter or jade pots to piss in. These respectively rate as half, three quarter, and full bathrooms.

Always be aware that your more sophisticated guests are on the lookout for something charming. A chamber with full panelling will instantly put them at their ease as well as signal your upward mobility. Balconies over sunken living rooms also give you a certain stylish zing, and add that precious touch of drama when ladies, done up to the nines, descend.

In all cases the old is better than the new except where the new is much better. An original design by an architect is a distinct plus where it isn't a total minus. That is to say, when your architect is as naïve as you are.

A dwelling on a housing estate or large development needs a real enhancing boost, not only from your personal charm but by something folk can't help seeing. Night illumination of some feature in your front elevations goes a long way towards letting folk know you are not content with just the ordinary. Should this cause sneering from passersby or hostile crowds to gather, concentrate on an interior embellishment. Providing plasterworks with deliberate elements of a playful but sculptural boldness in your ceiling cornices will attract your neighbour's immediate attention when he pops in for a drink.

'Hey what's all that crap you've got up there on the ceiling.'

'Well, as a matter of fact I had first planned these frontal rooms for parade rather than for a casual guest's use.'

'Well you could have fooled me.'

'Until I succeed in having the gilt fringe form a sort of stylistic parallel with the rococo which can marry to the baroque pictorial devices I am planning, I prefer to treat the room informally.'

'Hey gee whiz I'm just plain folk, are you kidding.'

Of course this chap's ordinariness will test your mettle, but at least you become quickly advantaged in the realisation that he will do your social improvement little good. Kick him straight out of the house.

Upon Refining Your Taste

'Sir I understand you have made an impudent snob's choice of dwelling. Much ersatz outer upholstery. And would you believe it, hopeless architectural attempts at the bijou.'

'I beg your pardon.'

'And well you might sir. Because you stick out like a sore thumb in a neighbourhood whose only recommendation is, at best, its tiresome display of middle class presumptions.'

This is the new kind of lip you can expect to get just as you're enjoying the relief of being shut of the little bastard flying his vile under garments on your garden horizons. But count yourself lucky to confront such a forthright gent. Most of your folk will make their sneaky nasty references to your appalling taste behind your back. Invite the chap in for a sherry. Direct his attention away from your pornographic prints and towards your interior furnishings. Ideally your fine art and antiques should awaken his discernment.

'Well sir, not bad. No, not bad at all.'

Give him another sherry. While he notes the commercial value of your chattels. Especially your collectors' pieces. But even the purchase of these requires taste. And yours should be improving fast with the ruthless hypocrites you've been moving among. However, if you're having a devil of a time with clashing periods, stick with the medieval. It can look good anywhere. Even in your house.

As a general rule always furnish with the overtly spectacular. Should this cause doubt concerning your overall colour decoration go for sand. If you don't know what this is, go for white. Or if this is no good try beige. Above all avoid looking as if all you've got is money. The colour that makes you do this is purple.

Throughout this crucial period of sharpening your aptitude for judging the beautiful, be careful of gifts of objets d'art from friends. They like to unload the passé on you that has been unloaded on them. A gentleman with some feminine sensibilities can always be called tip toeing in to advise. And never fail to openly admit that you do not know a Regency mahogany tea-poy on a well shaped pedestal from a small rare Charles II candle stand with the base in walnut and a marquetry top.

For moments of light relief, you will find it rather fun to mark your plaster imitations 'Don't Touch'. When no one is looking your guests will ignore your signs and surreptitiously scratch your hardware to test for genuineness. The plaster should be soft so that a liberal amount will be caught under your victim's fingernail. This is a sure way to expose people like yourself.

As nothing is more socially disastrous than tipping off superior folk by your chattels, keep some rooms entirely bare or furnished with orange crates to throw them off the scent. But never say you like things natural looking. Or that a piece of furniture, unless it's an orange crate, captures the spirit of the wood. Your general attitude should be entirely carefree. Kick an antique. Lightly of course. And for the pièce de résistance, awe your opponent out of his wits with one bare room the walls of which are hung with old masters and remark as you pass between the priceless collection.

'I know what I like.'

But beware when your guest remarks.

'I think it's really you.'

And avoid the riposte.

'What do you mean by that?'

Since he will say.

'That you are a bogus brazen impostor.'

Upon Throwing Your First Large Party

This is ill advised as it gives folk a chance to conspire against your further social advancement. But if you are consumed by a relish to be seen and adored in your new dwelling among your furnishings, have one. Give your guests the best, unless you are living in an area of old established families. Where pedigree breeding allows, not to say requires, one to foist off left overs, wine past its peak or without any peak.

As they stand around on the parquet, a good mix is to be preferred for your social image at this stage. And one or two guests who are put off by the sight of each other helps enormously. A limited infiltration by a few poverty shaken and desperate social climbers like yourself will create an immense din by listening spellbound to the crap pontificated by the socially assured.

Inviting folk of importance to your party when no one of importance comes is disheartening. It may be avoided by telling prospective guests that an international name, the talk of the hemisphere and constantly headlined in the most revered gossip columns, has always wanted to meet them. To duck embarrassment occasioned by this deception your guests should be summoned out on the lawn with their drinks to witness your fountains giving a multicoloured illuminated display. As each jet of water and the height to which it is propulsed is an indication of your riches and power, be doubly careful that sewerage is not allowed to foul your pipes.

If your victims are the kind of uneasily pleased guys who flick their eyes over each other's shoulders looking for the big nob, further distractions may be supplied in the manner of risqué female marching bands and orgasmic firework displays. Keep looking at your watch and away at the evening horizon for the big shot's helicopter. This should all be happening in the summer. If it isn't and it's snowing or storming, it is only fair to allow your guests to get back into the house. That is if you can get them out in the first place. But should your folk persist to get further shifty and shirty over the failed appearance of the big timer, show your contempt. They are now social equals.

During the remainder of the evening, and the glass breakages, spillages, immersions in fountains, the liquor, silver ware and table lighter thefts, a guest may approach you not knowing you are the host.

'Who is the nut throwing this thing.'

'I believe he recently left an enclosed order of religious having endured the vows of chastity, silence and poverty for many years, and he is having a bust out. He found the vow of chastity particularly cruel. So perhaps you wouldn't mind bending over.'

Upon Not Being Socially Registered

Youthful spirits will more than make up for the mouldy rankle, demoralizing wound, spiritual maim and personality disfigurement caused by omission.

But exclusion can also be an excellent spur to your social high jumping. The worst thing being that nobody can look you up. Although it is somewhat embittering that not being listed, nobody wants to look you up. A little fair minded fraud and forgery can make the best of this situation. If the ethnic implications of your surname haven't already hopelessly compromised you, get yourself a copy of the register. At where your name should alphabetically appear you may find, if not your name, something resembling yours enough to withstand a superficial scrutiny when the volume, to momentarily fan a flame of confidence, is quickly shoved in another unlisted's face and you smile.

'That's me.'

Beware that new listees sometimes find it an advantage to change the spelling of a surname to disassociate from ne'er do well relations. Make sure you're not thought one of these.

Although this will not help you get invitations, if you're really desperate there are often gaps between names occasioned by folk's numerous club listings, and a little expert home made printing might do the trick in the space provided.

But as your son of a bitch, having actually just got listed himself, takes his brand new copy out of his faded denim yachting jacket pocket and is just about to open it, refer to it as 'O that'. Your son of a bitch will, with a mannered coolness, hungrily page towards his name which he knows in his sleep is on page five hundred and something four names down from the top. Wait till he's blowing his eyebrow hairs out from between the pages and then let him have it.

'Granddad took us out. He was kind of a pioneer in moral principles and courage.'

Upon Being Excluded from Who's Who

This is far more popular than being included. The dreadful thing about this is that it could be a permanent situation.

The excuse that there exists a conspiracy to keep you out usually provokes a widespread guttural clearing of everyone's throat. And it really is awfully mortifying. Listees are a pretty assured lot who like to play their entries down, but who will not hesitate when an uppity old pal requires them to, to point out who they are according to Who's Who and who the old pal is not. Most tomes of Who's Who are large enough that few folk can avoid being conspicuous if not downright dangerous when taking their volumes out for an airing. So usually, when you are masquerading as enrolled, you can rely upon not being looked up on the spot. The tiresome exception is the bastard charging behind a small barrow rumoured recently invented for this purpose.

By fancy semantic fencing one may completely ignore or reverse enquiry as to whether you are listed. Your adversary will as usual ever so slightly rock back and forth on his polished soles attempting to blind you by flashing light from his monocle. The dangerous time is the early moments at the start of the cocktail party when folk are shopping round for the evening's best investments in sensual and financial intercourse.

'Sir who are you.'

Boyish innocence both playful and friendly is your man here.

'Who's who, you mean me.'
'Yes, I rather think I do mean you, as no one else seems within eight feet of us, sir. And since you mention that volume, are you therein listed.'

SOCIAL CLIMBING 43

This pontificator is showing instant signs of a military background somewhat below the rank of full colonel. His dental work should, upon scrutiny, exhibit much further clues as to his presumptions.

'Well if I am the meaning of the who of whom you enquire as to who I am, and since I was already, before you asked who are you, I would enquire as to who you are before you ask who I am.'

'That is a riddle, sir, and why are you looking into my mouth.'

'Well, as a matter of fact, fella, riddles and dental bridgework are given as my hobbies in my listing.'

'Do not sir, refer to me as fella and I'll thank you to stop further looking into my mouth.'

'I was merely, in my own exercise of discovering who is who, attempting to assure myself that you are homo sapiens, you bombast, you.'

Military people get blusteringly hot and bothered when treated in this fashion and a sudden seizure of his person could occasion you physical risk if he were to fall directly forward like a tree. Without appearing to cringe cowardly, step back the usual two paces.

Upon the Sudden Reawakening of Your Sordid Background

Things are going along quite nicely now and always, in the very best of places when you're basking in front of a nice bunch of big timers, some son of a bitch out of the blue will suddenly turn around and say.

'Don't I know you. From way back when.'

Don't panic, test the guy's incredibility using your improved accent at its most stilted.

'I do not, sir, think so.'

'Sure I do, I know you.'

'I deny it.'

'Hey, don't hand me that. I mean you're getting to be somebody these days. But I knew you when you weren't worth knowing.'

Keep steady as your man reaches for his inside breast pocket.

'I've got incontrovertible proof.'

'I reject it.'

'You mean right in front of the facts you stand there and reject it.'

'Quite so.'

'Well, here's the god damn captioned picture right out of the newspaper showing you and me being arrested for lowdown lousy turpitude. Try and refute that.'

'I do.'

'For Pete's sake, it isn't enough you have to show somebody the naked truth these days, you even have to be there in history and catch them in the flesh with their faces and appendages hanging out. Can't I reason with you.'

'Certainly. Instantly get out of my sight and communicate by cablegram.'

'Hey, what is it, have you got an inability to tolerate criticism.'

'Yes.'

'Holy cow, fella, isn't god damn honour part of your makeup. What are you doing, deliberately kicking ideals in the teeth and knocking the magnetics out of your ethical compass. You could fall wobbly kneed into a moral abyss. With your parents standing on the brink humiliated and your kids shedding tears of shame.'

Of course this kind of rhetoric would try anybody's patience and one sentence of strong feeling is permissible.

'Shut up you asinine ape.'

'What, are you calling me an ape.'

'Yes, I'm calling you an ape. Plus a nonny noodled beetle brained half wit.'

'What are you looking for, a fight.'

Make sure you are not too close to large jardinieres and that your pig skin gloves are pulled tightly over your fingers in order that slack does not lessen the impact when the fist contuses your man's jaw. Your personal left hook rising from a hip position is best followed immediately by a low right cross under the heart. Under the proper administration of these punches, your man should go down in a nicely arched forward slump reaching for his brains. Lightly brush your gloves together and sniff twice through your nose. This signifies that you have only done the minimum required to deal with this tiresome effrontery. By picking up the news-paper report with a little smile and putting it in your pocket your accompanying friends will think you a man of mystery. Rather than a trumped up no account cad.

Name Changing

The world's richest families often have the names best suited to you and, with imaginatively selected christian names, they will not only immediately make you sound better than you look, but make people think they like you.

Provided you have chosen your new cognomen well, it can produce some delightful marvelment in everyday life and also smooth the ethnic repugnancies to which you might be exposed by your body colour or contours. From being the faint object of attention as eyes swiftly flash over, through and away from you at introduction time, one can arrest your opponent's gaze and watch with sheer joy his ears prick up at the sound of your resounding handle. He will, however, instantly ask if you are related to the best known holder of the name. This is sad. But following the recent large population increase, folk don't trust anybody these days. And you could do worse than to answer.

'Naturally.'

But it's amazing how many niggardly hair splitters there are lurking over the glass rims of their martinis wanting to get accurate over your harmless joy giving little presumption.

'Sir, what do you mean by naturally, are you related or not.'
'Naturally.'

It should be immediately obvious that repetition weakens one's position. But if your opponent continues his inquisition, it at least shows that he's taking no god damn chances in missing a social opportunity of a lifetime. He will therefore somewhat hysterically attempt to couch his frame of references.

'Without being pedantic, frantic or semantic, I want to know exactly what you mean sir. I just happen to be a stickler for pedigrees and that kind of thing. Are you of kindred to the family or are you not.'

While you stand soulful eyed, slowly digesting your man's utterance, it is a favourable touch to slowly extract a length of gold chain from your waist pocket upon the end of which is a large gold timepiece which at this moment is chiming the quarter hour. Hopefully a severe tropical storm is beginning to tremble the windows with heaven shattering lightning and your opponent is dying to escape into the cellars.

'Tut, tut, do you dare kid around with my veracities, hombre.'

This light perfume of jocularity with the latter foreign cognomen thrown in, serves a twofold purpose. Aside from making you sound like the life of the party with your carefree admixture of words, it appears that you are unconcerned as to the implications of your name. Anyway it's the real you that most deeply matters. And as you now lean watching your perturbed opponent cowering under the table, take a charitable attitude towards his tearful plea for clarification.

'Hey, look buster, who the hell are you.'
'Do you, sir, refer to my descent, ascent, recent jungle explorations, polar expeditions, bird watching activities or my abilities to seduce reluctant ladies. And before you answer that, may I suggest for both our enjoyment's sakes that we say to hell with the facts and let's get on with the more ebullient fiction.'

In spite of his terror in the storm, his lesson to take folk as you find them should now be well learnt. At least it shows you deserve an E for effort. And if this tiresome chap does not relent, award him right then and there an F for fuckpig.

Ass Kissing and Other Types of Flattery

This should be done lightly as well as noiselessly and noselessly and one should not linger. It also relaxes folk in superior positions to start crapping all over you. And if this gets you somewhere, look around to make sure it isn't up shit's creek.

'Gee I like the way your outfit drapes, sir. I really do.'
'Well I don't like the way yours does. I really don't.'

'Gee winikers what a lousy remark when I was only trying to be nice.'

That's the really hard thing about ass kissing. You sometimes bring the ruthless worst instead of the benign best out in people, and some, jumping to a casual conclusion, even think you disgustingly abhorrent.

But these maddeningly rushed days when personal contact has been made less than pleasant with the wholesale number of folk blatantly ignoring the fine art of social climbing, an outrageous ass kisser is often a relief to meet. Instead of these aggressive individuals possessed of the crass assumption that they have something of value to offer, and therefore, with unbelievable effrontery, assume that they do not have to ass kiss their way to stardom and other tip top triumphs.

'Are you an ass kisser.'
'Yes I am, what are you.'

Provided punching doesn't immediately begin, this opening with its forthright attendant riposte will incite spirited socially beneficial conversation. Instead of the usual glazed look interrupted only by ill disguised glances over your shoulder at the others.

'Well as a matter of fact I'm an ass kisser too.'
'Hey gee that makes two of us. Do you want to go first.'
'O no, after you.'
'Well thanks, and by the way I like the deep crimson of the carnation you're wearing, I really do.'
'Well thank you. I really like the way you said that.'

Although two ass kissers may only have ass kissing to offer each other and thereby establish an endless social plateau without further opportunities for social climbing, this should not be regarded as unrewarding in the face of today's incessantly prevalent vituperations.

'And gosh I'll bet your mother and father are really proud of you.'

'Yes, dad before he died did say that and ma stood right behind everything dad said. And had either of them lived they would have been sure glad I was frequenting people like you.'

If, however, you find that the ass kissing has become zealously over sweet, a request for a short term loan usually returns the relationship to a more tolerable level. Should this fail, some light finger stabbing upon your opponent's chest gradually increased in severity generally does the trick. Although your opponent's crestfallen cry from the heart may sadden you inconsolably.

'Hey, what's the matter, don't you like me anymore.'

'Sure I do, but can't we detest each other for a change.'

On Rubbing Elbows with the Rich

Following the sincere and successful kissing of certain multi-mounded arses, elbow rubbing with the high, mighty and splendid is a most stimulating recreation.

As you motor down their long tree shaded drives over the undulating tastefully tonsured landscape, heading for their massive porticoes, the world always somehow seems a finer place. The slobbering ass kisser, smirking interrogator, smug sceptic, bumptious begrudger and other malapert odious who have been cramping your style can seem a universe away as one listens instead to the pale blue pebbles bouncing up under one's motor's mud guards.

Converging now on this citadel, the tower of which is distantly visible ahead above the trees. On this golden late afternoon. The evening awaiting with those radiant, fine accented,

lofty demeanoured, elegantly clothed and bejewelled person-
ages of the country house interlude. This spellbound moment
that lives. Sunlight reflecting leaves on the polished limousine
windows. The green velveted vistas cutting their way horizon-
wards, each blue tipped spruce, oily leafed rhododendron,
glowing copper beech, stunning the eye. With nary a sign of
the gorpish or lout.

The fountains will of course be playing, the head grounds-
man having pushed the button precisely at four. The lawn
marquees shimmering in a light breeze. Arrow leafed canna
standing stiff, green stemmed, red flowered and rare. Pause.
Pull in by the side of the drive even as other guests are zoom-
ing by. Take in the spectacle. Nourish the spirit. This could
be the festive main chance of your life and you don't want to
shake all over with nervousness spilling drinks down the
ladies' bare backed gowns.

There they laughingly go now, mounting the series of
granite steps, real quality people. So sure of themselves it
almost makes one want to beg the honour of washing their
under silks. But remember most of those bastards inherited
on a silver platter almost every god damn thing they've got.
When all you came into the world with was a pair of over
large ears you had to have taped back. So make sure you have
your engraved invitation and that it is really you they sent it
to. Because no one of these folk will deign give you a glance of
mercy if you get caught in that vestibule horror of footmen
questioning your presence before you even get into the inner
hall. That's why you want to take in as much as you can of
the scene first, before you might get kicked out.

Your prayers have all been answered. You penetrate un-
molested or fatally snubbed as far as the inner hall. Stand
your ground here. Don't press forward to get into the formal
reception rooms but choose a little spot near the wall and
tarry awhile to regard the ceiling cornices of this gracious
vestibule. Should you come to an outrageous forgery of an

old master, don't stamp, shout and scream with quite rightful annoyance but turn your attention towards the Meissen. If this is suspiciously ersatz, further rigidly control yourself and approach the tapestries. If these are imitations then you may allow yourself to administrate a little instant justice and take the bottom hem of same and pull gently till the offending tapestry collapses.

Do move away quickly. And, as a white tied waiter approaches with the champagne, which always flows freely in this kind of house, you may demonstrate your innocence of the tapestry pulling by tasting your wine with the proper admission of air between the lips. But do beware. With all the phony furniture in this house this vino could poison you.

As the long moments tick by and nobody talks to you, this is a time to laugh lightly for no reason at all. Or for the reason that you have dumped your champagne in a flower pot and the plant keeled over. Ignore any askance looks. Continue chuckling. Someone somehow, even among the most splendidly assured, is bound to look at you twice and think you are guffawing at them, and sidle over for chat. Or fight. If the latter, this could be a good time to engage enthusiastically in a tiresome subject broached by a nearby ass kisser.

But if the accumulated wounding, as the shoulder of person after person passes, keeps you from chuckling and also totally ignored, don't give up. A deep sniff of a passing lady's scent, followed by the whispering of its brand name in her ear, will sooner or later forthwith and resoundingly identify you to some female as a connoisseur of smells. And this should bring the moment of your being completely socially accepted quite close. Therefore, as this lady stops to regard you with admiring amazement, lean over and peer closely at the signature on the grand old master hanging near you on the wall. This is a time consuming gesture, but let others rush by breaking legs to make their shallow social splash. Your immersion will be profoundly far more meaningful by being carefully plunged.

'My. You know the perfume I'm wearing.'
'It happens to be my favourite, madam.'
'Hmmn, I may come back and talk to you later.'

These are nice openers to your deepening your further acquaintance. However this is no time to let yourself get stranded on any kind of ass kisser's plateau. You may never again see a night like tonight. Keep trying to buttonhole the other ladies and gents who are exiting away from you. But reserve your most poignant adoration for the really rich who are positively incandescent in their splendour. Cast compliments freely about. To the ladies unhesitatingly state as you look them up and down.

'Gosh o me o my, you look ravishing tonight.'

To the gentlemen, even someone upon whom you have never clapped eyes before, state unequivocally.

'Hey you look real great.'

If he stops in his tracks and gives you a chillingly obtuse look. Let him have an elegantly accented riposte right in the electronics.

'Good lord, I certainly don't mean you, you amorphous slob.'

Remember, as the evening progresses with your not insubstantial social victories, not everyone is going to be quite as assured as you are. And there will be a dwindling number left ready to goodnaturedly absorb, with equal aplomb, both insult and compliment. And up close some of your real big timers you have long held in awe are going to seem pretty small fish indeed with their very ordinary vulnerabilities sticking out on their tanned faces about two miles.

By now you should have got yourself from the inner hall

into the ante chamber on your left which is, in the greater
houses, called the ante chamber because they've got chambers
and chambers all over the place. It is de rigueur to hold your
water now. By a finger's mere disturbance of the drape at
your shoulder you can take in the tortoise shell pavilion
verging the lily pond. Never mind what seems to be delighted animated groups utterly enthralled with one another
and throwing their heads back with belly laughs.

Instead watch for the kill joy. He will be walking around
with his champagne glass held like a steam ship funnel sailing through the little knots of guests trying to get their goats.
This type is usually able to fluently insult people in about
seven languages. And foreign ladies will be constantly slapping his face. Luckily this molar jarring routine sets a nice
precedent for you as you patiently stand serenely there, a
summer breeze from the nearby French window disturbing a
lock of your tousled recently shampooed hair. You have
already been through all the accent and name changing, and
those tiresome days of choosing a neighbour and residence.
Now you wait, devastatingly accoutred with that quietude
which only comes of the highest haughtiness and particularity. And then, when you most expect it, your previous
lady of the perfume returns, pointing at you between the
palms and heads.

'Ah, that's that nice person there.'

Give her ample time to near you on her delicately moving
feet. Note the way her left hand quietly suspends her gown
anklewards. Her alabaster complexion will display her few
freckles admirably and the small globules of saliva on her
teeth will glint blue white. Then whisper.

'It's me.'

These two simple words must emit without a trace of desperation. Which, with your recent kinetics in haughtiness and

particularity, should be no problem. Strike up a nice mutuality based on the questionable authenticity of the ormolu mounted marquetry side table nearby. This approach hints of much rather choice and waggish tomfoolery to follow. Provided you are not addressing your hostess.

'Ah, madam, I regard this fake as a joy to behold.'
'Do you.'

Now beware, for in those two words madam may be couching some rather hostile implication. This is your first real chance on this beguiling evening to make an impression upon an obviously established member of the thoroughbred celebrity elite, dressed as she is in the usual white Chantilly lace. She will also have the narrow racing waist and medium pear shaped bosom preferred by the speedier nobility. And will be of that marvellously indeterminate age for a woman of the extremely early thirties. Her breasts, although well covered, will be of course daringly obvious. Your next words should be chosen for their playful and carefree candour.

'Well, as a matter of fact, madam, it does rather remind me of oneself putting on the dog as one does tonight. Woof woof.'
'I beg your pardon.'
'And I, madam, beg for the pleasure of your left breast for the platform of my right palm.'

This is the kind of risqué gab the celebrity élite adore, however it must be elegantly intoned and free of any foaming at the mouth. But should this unpredictable gem encrusted, slender boned lady take umbrage and lapse into pale faced trembling anger, it is incumbent upon you to snap her out of it with a strong purposed pronouncement.

'Madam, you are behaving as if goosed by a big fingered farmer.'
'How dare you suggest such a rural nudge.'

This last remark of madam's may be taken as a pure indication of her blatant suburban superiority, and should be dealt with accordingly.

'May I then offer madam an idyll in some citified but cloistered haven where random gentle organ thrusts of largo pianissimo would temper her presently gruff tune.'
'No you may certainly not, since rather than endure your clapped out attempts in the orchestral manner you suggest, I would prefer, in the most moving style imaginable, some callow youth's vivace crescendo.'

This demeaning retort is kind of tough to deal with especially when your musical agenda has been so twisted as to imply not only your lack of rhythm but of balls. This is a time you really want to set your wits to work. And the following soul stirring riposte will instil a touch of uncertainty in your adversary's rapidly tumescing supremacy.

'Madam, haven't you ever on a still summer evening stopped solemnly in your dainty tracks and asked of the gods who, with such awe inspiring cultural integrity, was playing that saxophone.'
'As a matter of fact I have.'
'And didn't you find it refreshing.'
'As a matter of fact I did, but I find you an insufferable bore. And although you don't deserve even my pique, I shall, as a simple acknowledgement of my own distaste, slap your face.'

This is a real tough broad and the next move is of course yours as you stand rigidly there seeing stars and your face smarting. The decision of whether or not to strike ladies back is a difficult one. Some spoilt bitches need their noses broken, never mind a clout across the chops. Sound spankings, on the other hand, should be reserved for ladies who are only temporarily bitchy. In this case, this was your first real big party after plentysome discouraging social climbing and you painfully arched over backwards to be a regular guy. And where you spotted a bit of her umbrage you immediately tried to placate it with a dash of friendly verbal high jinks. She should have made allowance for your recent upgrading of class and shown appreciation for your really original conversation starter you preciously saved for such an occasion. Although one doesn't want to become too rancorous, her supercilious ball crushing conduct was unforgivable. So give her back right across her jaw one good almighty slap.

'Splaaat.'

Somewhere, when you least want that there should be, will be gentlemen who, having overheard your raised voices and the recent pistol shot smack of your above given hand, will rush to intervene in feverish aid of this lady's honour. Only those of the celebrity elite who are active polo players need really be physically taken seriously. A little threatening Kung fu and Karate waving about of your limbs will keep off nearly all types except maybe the monocle wearing ex-military and most of these have taken too much past artillery concussion to be really dangerous.

As the fight begins and the first splashing of drinks are staining folk's evening wear, the host and hostess will, this being a renowned stately home, start screaming at the tops of their lungs for the servants to protect the heirlooms. Large houses keep fire apparatus handy and, if the water pressure is good, this can really animate events. Even the cream splattering from the crystal bowls becomes pretty minor stuff when the writhing fire hose starts squirting and swinging the officious 'I am in complete control' kind of gent flat on his soaking ass. Jellies however are hard to beat for the comic touch when folk try to lick the tasty stuff missed by the water jet from their faces. If you happen to be the host, this is a time to display any whimsicality which may have been previously hidden by the awesomeness of your pedigree. From your centuries of descent take all the sense of humour you can firmly by the neck and wrench every last ounce of supreme toleration out of it. Because by god even the most sedate of your guests will be having a jamboree. After all, the upper class have a sense of fun just as strong as any lower class and they own far more stuff to break. In fact the best thing to cool things off now could be a fire.

Associating with the Bootless and Unhorsed

If you can be unmindful of the dismal lack of upward mobility it affords, it's a nice change following unenchanted occasions of abrasively rubbing elbows with the thoroughbred celebrity elite. And besides, now that you've had a chance to ride high with your accent and income at full blast among the booted and horsed, slumming around down among the old foolish pals that gained you your ambition and verve to get the hell up and out in the first place, is a good way to choke down a sheepish guffaw and take your social temperature.

Be civil and tolerant when dismounting among this swarming caste who, already totally submerged by about two new generations of go getters, nevertheless still bravely play their isolated solitary roles in failure. When confronting them suddenly on the boulevard, do not immediately suggest a handout or job opportunity. Some of these fellows may still have their pride left. Let their 'they haven't beaten me yet' spirit come to the fore. Other types of course will push their open palms out. And tell you to cough up with a giant elbow bending gratuity before they shout two miles all over the street what a big phony upstart you've now become. Guys like this might have made good top business executives.

But under no circumstances invite either gent back to the house. Where in your book lined den and leather upholstered armchair he invariably grabs a pipe from your pipe rack and puffs hell out of your aromatic tobacco while golloping down about five scotches and sodas. And all the while is deeply researching a plan for his future life like he was studying for a degree. Which is a thesis on how the hell he can get you out, and himself in, lolling around in your custom made comforts. Not to mention socks and shirts and even boots and other equine equipages.

But above all be prepared for the shock you'll get on your morning departure for work one day. Which will leave you stunned witnessing. Having, as you've just done, rushed back after breakfast for a forgotten squash racket, and the ungrateful bare arsed son of a bitch is in your own Jermyn Street shirt tails indulging to the hilt his beggarly audacity of trying something funny with the wife. Which, on top of it, the wife, hardly with a stitch on at all, is squealingly enjoying. Insurmountably bored as she now briefly is with the furs, jewels, estates, dogs, limousine and transatlantic trips you have lavished on her, not to mention the ocean going motor launch she ran permanently aground last year. Although she could now be even more of a problem than the bootless and unhorsed, it is de rigueur to remain urbane and don't let the whole god damn thing with its crushing vileness beat you to a frazzle. Because it's quite natural for ladies to think, while getting their hair done, that really lower bracketed folk can supply high jinks she's been missing with all the god damn luxury smothering her life.

Mercifully, there's another type of bootless and unhorsed you can meet. And another approach entirely must be considered. This is the guy who thinks he's going great but whom in fact you have left so far far behind that the whole spectacle of your confrontation is cruel to observe. With this type you could really have some after lunch fun with his wife Diane and not only would she thrillingly squeal and groaningly mew but, while your eyeballs revolved like windmills in a gale, she'd make lightning strike between your eardrums. To spare this chap's feelings, wait till he speaks first before plastering him with your fancy vowels. But should your intimidating presence awe him into a gasping silence, you've got then to make the first overture which is best done in the old sporty manner you used as kids.

'Gee hi Bill good to see you.'
'Why hey, it's you, Al, the real you.'

Right away note how this guy is a fighter. Pretending to put you at your ease and nearly taking up the offensive with those three latter brazen unforgettable words. Very nervy that and a nice little thing to remember later during a particularly sweaty crescendo while rogering his snake legged wife. But if his succeeding bulletins continue to hint of further blatant camaraderie, only contemplation of a wine soaked non stop harvest scented weekend with Diane's gymnastic body is worth tolerating that kind of pain.

'Why you old reckless son of a bitch, how's it going, hey your accent Al is sure something for a start, where did you get it.'

For old times sake go right along with Bill. Even though you've had enough of that 'where did you get that accent' stuff. Diane, the wife, if she has any social upward mobile tendencies at all, will adore it. But the real situation, only of course you both pretend not to know it, is that he wants to eliminate as quickly as possible the barriers of elegance that have arisen between you just as fast as you want now to impenetrably impose them. Which thank god, keep his ilk out of your celebrity riddled ken. Where his wife Diane would thrill to frolic.

'Hey come on Al, you can level with me. What happened, did you went to a charm culture school maybe.'

As Bill expectantly waits, smile frozen, make like you're your usual kind of easy going nonchalant guy just facing the unvarnished facts as they sometimes unpleasantly explode, instead of the ruthless bloodcurdling social upstart you are, putting on the dog at every socially superior hydrant, and now biding your moment for the slamming of Bill's squaw with a variety of leverages as would flabbergast major bridge building engineers.

'Well Bill, I kind of picked the accent up as I went along upward taking tea and cocktails and having picnics by the lake shore with a better class of people.'

Bill is bound to be alarmed by your candour and will now pursue a glorified description of his two bit corporate position and the bunch of really swell guys back at the office where he has, with malice aforethought, been indentured for the past four years straight. If you value your chances of putting your proud perpendicular anywhere profound in the lovely Diane, the tune to adopt here is one of incredible interest best shown by merely knitting the brows together and drawing your mouth lines straight as if resisting jealousy. But please, as you listen to him, take note, exaggeration of this expression could offend your old pal deeply.

'Gee Al, well what do you know, that's exactly what Diane keeps telling me, that I should acquaint with a better class of people. I mean my activities are already pretty diversified. The outfit I'm with is really moving along.'

'Are they going up hill, Bill, I mean really heading helter skelter for the summit.'

'Why, Al, I'm glad you brought that up and said that the way you did. You bet they are. And Diane thinks so too.'

Now Bill, because of his genuine nice guy attitude, might make it some day, but keep your eyes on him as he departs. It may be as little as thirty yards further on down the street that he will fold his shoulders forward like a bird plummeting to death and just become convulsed with sobs. If you don't want to let your psyche get caught in that kind of anguished whirlpool and end up with a jittery case of permanent paranoid tendency, hail a taxi and head pronto over to the lovely Diane and give her in the Australian manner a quick squirt. She may for a moment shed tears of remorse but in the end she'll be glad. Because poor old Bill will hardly be able to get it up for quite awhile and if he does he'll think it's his conscience pricking him.

After witnessing what happened to Bill, you will immediately wonder which one of the boys back at the office, if not the whole god damn bunch, has it in for you. And you'll be further wondering if the bootless and unhorsed instead of giving you your kicks weren't aiming these a substantial distance up your arse. So if you and the ravishing Diane have now ceased hungrily eating each other without salt on the kitchen floor, you are doing yourself no favour by frequenting the bootless and unhorsed further, unless it is to take Diane in one last unforgettable canter, when you can both decide that you don't want to be back down there footling around in the jackass latitudes even as cheerleader.

Knowing When You Have Reached the Top

Upon a chosen clement day, exercise a sartorial master stroke of impeccable taste. Don a neatly laundered and sharply pressed pair of flannel cricket trousers, white buckskin shoes, white moleskin hacking jacket with a red carnation in the lapel, silk shirt and purple tweed tie. In your summery stylish regalia, and really looking nice, poise on the sixth floor room balcony of a goodish old fashioned downtown hotel. When everyone is suitably assembled to watch you jump off to break your head, commence peeing. If no one tries to rush the hell out of the way of your pissing all over them, you have reached the top.

Failing this above public recognition of your most haughty particularity, with everyone fast putting up umbrellas, you may be forced to rely upon evidence demonstrated by various signs and portents. Such as the phenomenon of attractive ladies at outdoor sporting events being unable to tear their eyes off you. There also should be an appreciative rise in welcoming smiles received in lobbies and vestibules, even while swaggering in your chosen outfit. And a dramatic drop in the usual sidewalk insults and smart remarks from street corner cowboys.

'Hey you in the white cloud, are you raining yet.'

On very rare occasions you will still, especially when least expecting it, have the odd pissoir attendant, doorman and taxi driver giving you vile lip. But the difference is now that

you saunter past thinking that the person perpetrating the distressing lip not only has his flies undone but is jabbering without a nuance of rhyme or reason. And needs be you simply deposit him in your busy wake with maybe such a dose of unrequited rage that his testicles are left clacking like castanets.

Much will depend upon just how large your social circle is. If it includes only you as the real bee's knees, such exclusivity could result in a lot of wrist straining masturbation. However, the more folk there are poised with you up there on the pinnacle the easier it is for you to be pushed off. But if the distance you fall is really a hell of a lot further than the distance you had to climb to get up there in the first place, then as you crash on your social arse you can assume you were at the top.

But the real day of triumphal acknowledgement is the day upon which you enter your drawing room attired once more in your summit regalia, a reputable medium sherry in hand, and you refer your eyes to your chimney piece attached to a wall up through which smoke is ascending. And there heart warmingly view the engraved invitation cards edge to edge spanning the entire length of this social altar. If you do not have a chimney piece, four upended and adjoined orange crates covered by a priceless tapestry will do.

But don't jump to a conclusion. Alas, to qualify you for top drawer ranking, two thirds of these as yet unfulfilled engagements and invitations should come from at least three of the following categories listed in their order of importance.

Owners of more than two hundred acres of prime grazing
Irish Chieftains or Knights
Anyone in Larousse
Listees in The International Who's Who
Listees with more than seven lines in Who's Who

Wine merchants established over forty years
Nobles of the rank of Baronet and above
Socially registered persons

Engraved invitations to funerals rank socially above all others but, because of the infrequent singularity of the occurrence, this may be used as a lifetime indication of rank. And it is the highest of compliments to folk to extend an invite to one's obsequies.

But do not abandon hope. If you can get three unengraved invitations from persons occupying the same house, flat or apartment for three generations or more, these will qualify as one engraved invitation from one person in the category on the list. Or nine privately telephoned or thirteen pay telephoned invites from the bootless and unhorsed. Invitations from folk in any category who have unceremoniously clanked a grandparent into an institution, without so much as a box of reasonable quality chocolates to go with him, do not qualify. And, as you can imagine, the detective work this calls for could mean you'd go out of your mind not only with invitations but with the heart breaking horror of the dirty covering up tricks people are prepared to pull to stay in the social swim.

But again don't leap to a conclusion. To be on top you must have declined four fifths or more of the invitations spanning your mantel. And then you really are just about as hot shit as you can get. However, this is not a time to let the rising steam blind you. Because you really want to be enjoying the clarity as you revisit the scene of a major slight and stand there supreme in your haughty particularity with the vile perpetrator bending over backwards in an arched bridge of hands and feet to kiss your ass which, by leisurely perambulation, you have recently removed from a sensually invigorating massage, sauna and swim. Now all you have to do is be prepared for the insolence you may encounter with speak your weight machines. And these are easily busted by being pushed over and kicked.

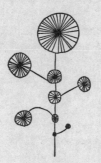

Extinctions & Mortalities

The Final Resting Place

It should in all cases be free of dampness. After a lifetime of social climbing you want to end up somewhere dry. If you do not have your own private cemetery select a good public one where the management have a sense of dignity, beauty and splendour. An hour or two with one of these gentlemen will really make your day. Choose your site at your earliest opportunity, as it lends a feeling of contentment to the intending deceased not only while dead but all the remaining days you live.

Any reputable architect will be thrilled with his commission to build you a really handsome mausoleum. And, if you've got that kind of money, will instantly inundate you with designs. Don't skimp. There is nothing worse than seeing a brand new tomb suffering a dilapidation which reflects unstylishly upon both the living and the perished. And at all costs avoid cheap ostentation or attempts at inscribed graveyard profundities. It's enough said if you're dead. Although variations of the following mildly chastising comment are permissible.

I AM GONE BUT NOT FORGIVEN

There is nothing more mind soothing than of a Tuesday three o'clock afternoon to motor by chauffeur or stroll by walking stick to where you will someday permanently rest in peace. And there stand accoutred in sporty attire having a pre death chuckle over your epitaph or casting an appreciative eye upon the linear elevations of an elegant spanking new memorial with your name prominently displayed. Throughout life everyone is trying to make your name smaller, and here finally is an opportunity to really get it big because no one else wants theirs there instead.

When your happy architect has completed your mausoleum, you of course can indulge not only the added comfort of beseating yourself to meditate in solitude sheltered from inclemencies but also to have a really nice time inciting any

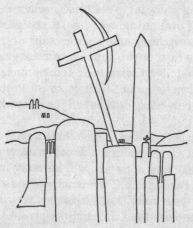

horny necrophiliac tendencies. But of course in the matter of this latter, passing snoopers, many themselves jealous necroes, might try to get you caught and arrested. Therefore, to provide for your grave or tomb in the confines of your own private cemetery is to be preferred. This may also cater for those having deep rural interests, who may obtain comfort from the fore knowledge of farm stock ultimately grazing one's grass, which is the very height of haughty particularity.

'Gee Steve, what you got all those cattle grazing all over your cemetery for.'

'Well Bob, as a really deeply committed environmentalist I want in the ultimate putrefaction to be part of somebody's T bone steak one day.'

'Holy cow.'

Upon Being Told the Fatal News That You Have Only So Long to Live and That It Is Not Long

Of course this news may enrage you so much that you start throwing things, blaming and accusing everyone and generally behaving in a hostile manner. Of course this kind of antic only shows you should have been dead long ago.

If you are the nice kind of average person, moisture in the eyes is permissible but do not burst into floods of tears. This alarms others into acute apprehension concerning the moment when their turn comes. Unless death has whispered I am here, make a reasonable effort to keep going. This is often a bleak period unless you have large assets and people around you who will benefit thereby and which prospect keeps them cheerful beyond belief. However, take strong objection to any dancing joy at your sinking. Your final will and a pen handy, plus a couple of witnesses hostile to your heirs, should make the merry take heed.

Death has the remarkable aspect of looking as if it's only happening to you. Although a sad time, it does leave more room for others. This is of course no comfort if it's you it's after. Stalking your shadow down the shrinking days. The accumulative devastation this can have upon the spirit is horrendous. But life now will begin to look so good that just living seems for the first time better than money. That is if you already have money.

Although you'd much rather be doing something else than dying, you can at least now decide to die like a man or live a wee bit longer like one. The more finances you have for this purpose, the better. But do not rush out to a night club or the latest celebrity joint and scare hell out of everybody. You've had your chance, now let somebody else enjoy. Instead, gainfully occupy yourself at this time with your funeral's invitation list, the floral displays, coffin design and music. And no small satisfaction will be yours in the timely provision of your monstrous mausoleum with its splendid acoustics.

The higher your social plateau the faster news of your impending demise will travel. And reports of your final departure may come back before you've been tucked in. But even in the face of such callousness it is not chic to complain. However, in broaching the subject the more sensitive of friends will use cowboy parlance reminiscent of the rough out of doors in deference to the fighting spirit they think you want them to think you have.

'Gee Jack, I hear you're heading for the last roundup.'

It is a pleasant gesture and a reminder of your heyday haughty particularity if you can respond in a like manner.

'Well Steve, with my shooting iron indisposed and my jewels hanging pretty low, I kinda guess an easy trot to the old corral is the way I'm gonna go.'

But if Steve's jaw drops with what he thinks is a gruesomely sickly effort to keep a stiff upper lip he may attempt to soothe you with facts you know already.

'I guess it's no consolation to you that I'm going to die too Jack.'
'Well thanks Steve, yes it is a bit.'
'Well I really am, I'm with you all the way, maybe not to the grave but I mean I could get killed in the next ten minutes by accident.'
'Steve, thanks for saying that.'
'Well I really mean it, Jack. I mean look, punch me. Injure me. I could be dead if not maybe buried before you.'

Even though Jack's muscle fibre may be shot to hell, if you

are Steve, the conversation should be terminated here as it could lead to your murder. Dying folk like company. And there are still those diehards who keep a gun under the pillow.

Dying

This is most stylishly done in your own lace covered bed, in your own beige walled room, in your own multi gabled house, on your own extensive lands during late autumn when the leaves are falling.

Dismiss from your mind as an asshole anyone who tells you you can have a happy death. When father time leaves his calling card and puts his big rough hand hauntingly up your rear end, he don't know the meaning of contentment I'm telling you.

However, in spite of the attendant spiritual tremblings, do try to make an occasion out of it. Folk watching on warmly appreciate a profound if not historic remark, should you really have a damn good one up your sleeve. But beware, the body can be stubborn and right in the middle of expiring it might go on living and your inane statement on your first attempt at dying could make you look a real jerk on your second.

For the most part your last gasp will be attended by fairly contented people since most folk prefer to see you get the shove unless you're a really good cook, seamstress, wage earner or piece of arse. The exception is if you're breathing your last on a pavement or highway in any one of the better known civilized countries in the presence of total strangers. Although their curiosity may produce some pushing and shoving, their sympathy is usually of a higher quality than that of relatives.

Once it gets going, the body knows how to die and does it all by itself. When enough bad reports sneak back through the synapses, a signal rises like a bubble out of all your troubles and your pumping station closes down. As the blood stops flowing, the light in the brain dims out. However, a not unpleasant mildly sentimental phosphorescence persists. This is the soul. It steers the way as you race towards forever land, wracked with a groaning choking haunting frustration. But don't panic, there will also be sweet waves of peace overcoming you. And you'll be shouting. With echoes fading away the names you call. And you'll be lucky if one of them is socially registered. Because most will resurrect from your discarded catalogue of the bootless and unhorsed. And then you will start running. Chasing down a familiar and unfashionable street trying to catch up to those who were closest to you of all. Don't be alarmed if your legs have wings, this is, even for the most light footed, quite usual. And there will be a few folk, mostly broom carrying women in aprons, out on their stoops who look up as you flash by.

Step carefully through the parting in the tall green drapes in front of you. It is extremely bad form to register disappointment if you were expecting something more elaborate like Grand Central Station. Anyway, inside, you won't know what hit you. When you see the number of other folk standing around nearly from here to Timbuktu. Under no circumstances get on the end of any long queue you spot. But find your bearings by gently enquiring of some nearby soul. Normally booklets are issued at the curtains and it will much benefit you to read the instructions carefully. If you can't get the hang of these rely on the conduct you have learned in this life. For those of you who are not nude avoid being in any way conspicuous in your attire and ignore the rude and quite unnecessarily diabolic comments usually made to new comers. But to persistent vile lip the brief retort of 'Get stuffed' is permissible. Or in reply to simple churlishness enquire 'Who the hell buried you.'

If you are really desperate search for a person of noble mien and give him an opportunity to inject a little clarity into one's confusion.

> 'Excuse me, but I wonder could you help me find my place.'
> 'Are you to the manner dead.'
> 'I beg your pardon.'
> 'I repeat sir, are you to the manner dead.'
> 'You mean like one could be to the manner born.'
> 'Precisely.'
> 'To hell with that shit. I'm dead, aren't I. And that's enough for me.'
> 'I regret to disturb you sir, but that is not enough for us.'

This chap of sterling demeanour may just be having a bad day but make sure that the next guy you stop to ask wasn't of the previously bootless and unhorsed past whom you may have deeply elbowed in this world. And who might now relish the awe inspiring opportunity to tell you to fuck off. However, before turning left between those two large continents of crowds you see and walking for about twenty millenniums, this could be, for those of you who were expecting an afterlife of courtesy, equality and contentment, a good time to break down and cry.

Wills, Legacies, Chattels

Keep your dignity here even though other folk are expending any amount of piranhic energy implanting their ungloved lunch hooks into the property left by another. It is of course not stylish to sue over wills but if you don't you won't get a red cent.

Lawyers lick their famished chops over the kind of litigation involving large legacies. The exercise of bloodcurdling greed, blackmail and vituperations you never even dreamt of will be the order of the day. With premises entered, desks jimmied, closets stripped, clothes strewn, trunks kicked open and pockets ripped out of good quality suits. And before somebody else does, it will be an absolute miracle if you can ever lay hands on the deceased's wrist watch. For some reason, perhaps to do with the urgent march of time, this is the first thing that gets ripped off the deceased.

Be alert during these amazing descents made by relatives upon the departed's chattels. You could get your foot broken or even an eye gouged out. And be particularly careful when approaching the deceased's stack of clothing, that upon inno- cently picking up a long scarf, suspenders, belts or braces, your opponent hasn't picked up the other end of it over on his side of the pile and the two of you stand there pulling and tugging for all you're both worth which by your behaviour is not much. Déclassé proceedings like this can quickly debase into physical violence with blows exchanging right across the middle of the deceased's tailor made suits and silk shirts. Not nice.

This doesn't mean however that you should not try to at least get a semblance of your fair share. And for the really pure of spirit and persons of the haughtiest particularity, it is ofttimes pleasanter straight away upon entering the premises to seek out some large chest of which the drawers or interior have not yet been investigated by the voracious others. Then in clear tones make your position known that you will for- sake your share provided you get the chest and its entire con- tents without ever having to disclose what's in it. You will be positively thunderstruck at the speed with which every one will drop the Chantilly lace, silverware, candelabra, first editions, Delft and other objets d'art and focus attention on the closed chest. But make sure there's something good in the chest because folk after some initial agonised soul searching hesitation are going to continue further plundering for what they see glittering in front of their very eyes. Such diabolically vile behaviour, to say the least, casts a pall of troubled anguish over those who held the deceased in high esteem.

If you think your own heirs are really swell, then upon making provisions for disposal of your own real property heap on the fair play and justice. And keep your final wishes a model of simplicity. Claimants will then have smaller legal expenses when the haggling starts. But when you know that lots of no good bastards are going to end up grappling out of their minds after your leftovers, then really have a ball with the words and legal phrases. Couch your last will and testicle in every damn hooky clause you can think of with a final stream of entangled codicils leaving your stuff to cats, dogs, and even big thriving charities who have lots of lawyers savagely protecting their incredibly honourable interests.

But there is nothing which will make you turn over in your grave faster than the knowledge of some reprehensible inlaw collecting out of your estate. Imagine the thought of that rotten lot upon your higher graduation putting their boorish feet restfully up on a tall bundle of your bonds, securities and cash. Any old cheap stove bought for the purpose can remedy this by incineration to a fatal grey ash. This carbon residue in turn when deposited in a receptacle marked private and personal and not to be opened till after my death can really get a reaction when finally revealed by your lawyers with a letter reading as follows.

As from
The Final Indisposition

Dear Folks

Upon disclosure of the contents herein contained it don't half make me groan with pleasure to hear you groan with pain.

Yours also in dust
The Proudly Deceased

But for god's sake make sure you're really dying and get this confirmed by about five doctors before you conduct a conflagration of your assets. Even so, beware, for following the destruction of these, the acute anxiety caused thereby has a way of arousing one's survival instincts so strongly that one might go on living without a pot to piss in. For the same reason never sign over anything on your death bed. Should you recover, they'll throw you the hell into the poor house or any god damn place they can get rid of you into. Without even, needless to say, your favourite candies to go with you.

Suicide

Be neat when ending it all. It is exceedingly perverse to leave one's remains in an unlovely condition or where your corpse is likely to cause distressing nuisance. Even if it means an irritating postponement or inconvenience, always plan an appropriate time and place to kill yourself. Especially avoid any impromptu on the spur of the moment leavetakings involving rail tracks. These often become impulse sites for a permanent departure. Thereby causing disquieting delays for others who with urgent deals or love trysts pending may still have a lot to live for.

On no account can it be accepted as thoroughbred to use shot gun blasts at close range particularly upon the skull where it knocks hell out of your afterlife phosphorescence. There exists a wide range of other suitable weapons and vulnerable body sites which can achieve the desired dispatch. An elegantly embellished revolver firing straight into your heart a platinum plated bullet engraved with your armorial bearings is a stylish and dignified finishing stroke. A chaise longue is a markedly suitable setting for this type of exit.

It is seemly if your method of death is in keeping with your qualities as a person. But not, however, if you are a bit of a bungler and botcher. There is nothing more dumb brained than taking a jump to hang yourself and ending up suspended under the armpits half strangling on some coat hook without a hope of dying. If this is the kind of carnival joke you're likely to perform, try free fall bridge departure over open waters. There are many architecturally fine high spans offering this opportunity but as they were not designed for this purpose make sure you're not impeded by an embellishment before hitting pay dirt or water. Additionally, some bridge sites offer the presence of sharks which make away with remains and this especially assists those without previous disposal plans with a reputable undertaker. However, if inadvertently you should execute a perfect olympic dive be prepared for bobbing back up in the water alive. Although a good punch on the nose is supposed to scare sharks away, these fish are notoriously unpredictable. And you may be suddenly glad to also be an olympic sprint swimmer.

Building jumping is most appropriately done from high up in the best financial districts where pedestrians are used to that kind of thing. It is really déclassé in other areas where it may attract a large gathering. The sense of power it incites in one is particularly unbecoming as you stand up there looking down on a sea of spellbound faces with the peanut and pretzel vendors making sales on the edge of the crowd. Even though your performance is without fee it is simply quite unchic to loll around toying with the public's attention, making yourself a socially diminished spectacle of conceit. Especially when leaning poised but teetering just that little bit extra out over the parapet with the crowd absolutely going out of its mind with gasps of suspense. Followed then by their groans of disappointment as you sway backwards to safety again. Instead of finally jumping you should join a circus.

In cases where your desire to exit this world has been provoked by many months of low down shabby treatment from the boys in the office, building jumping is permissible from your place of work. As this is your own little way of getting back at these horrid types, you may indulge to the full any parapet tricks you may have up your sleeve. And departing on your last wingless flight, be assured that it really does throw an incredible pall over the staff which can easily persist for hours on end. Although you may not be around to see it after you've been scraped up, many will descend on the elevator more slowly than you did in free flight to examine where you collided with the pavement. And they will express their surprise at how perfectly clean the spot is where hardly a trace of you now remains.

Poisons, usually of the old fashioned variety, which disfigure the facial expression, must be rated as an ungraceful leavetaking. On the whole, they make for a rather contorted goodbye. So too do the various methods of strangling which cause eye bulging and ghastly grimace. Crushing and squashing in spite of erasing one's expression should also be avoided as they leave a diabolically shocking flatness to be scratched up. Self destruction by suttee and disembowelling are dramatic but go unappreciated except in the countries where these are an accepted means of attaining your higher graduation. Although not disclosing that it is planned for this purpose, your local travel agent will be glad to arrange a leisurely trip and your heirs should be entitled to claim reimbursement for the return journey.

Requiring some self control, holding your head under water is not an unpleasant way to go. Once the first thirst quenching lungful is aboard, this initial gulp and gasp relaxes the synapses rapidly into a rather pleasant swirling sleep. Gas is another method affording some peaceful reverie before drifting off. Except of course where certain vapours in contact with a spark can incite a condition which can make yours and maybe a few of the neighbours' ascent into the last darkness take place with amazing velocity.

Although of classical significance heinous procedures such as the holding of one's nose and jumping into a den of rattlers, gaboon vipers or mambas is certain to make decent minded people in a free society wonder what the hell kind of perverted problems you are trying to tear yourself permanently away from. Dispatch in the industrial manner known as the Scandinavian blast must also be considered outré, involving as it does a stroll down the boulevard smoking a stick of dynamite disguised as a cigar usually carrying an excellent brand name. Although sending you in a lot of simultaneous directions it is an extremely unchic way of heading for the happy humping ground.

For the connoisseur, ending it all at sea is the height of particularity. A late autumn westward sailing from the old to the new world with a trunk load of tweed suitings for hurricane deck constitutionals is your man. Your moment of adieu should be chosen as that least objectionable to one's fellow first class passengers and should always be taken in black tie from the lonelier starboard side. Imbibe your usual amounts of snuff and after dinner port. Don't be afraid of enjoying these last days. They can be the happiest of your life. However do not accept an invitation to sit at the captain's table and beware of getting totally caught up in shipboard activities, especially ping pong tournaments and games, the outcome of which may delay your earthly exit till it's time to dock. Romance too should be avoided unless it is one of those heart palpitating wild mad grabbing one night stands tumbling and crashing in various frissonic crescendoes all over the state room. These fleshy shenanigans often add an aura of tender poignance to your last goodbye as well as to your brief partner's memory of you. But do avoid inciting gossip which

will make your gymnastic companion, left behind, the subject
of speculation as to what the hell she did to make you go over
the side.

As your remaining shipboard days unfold with your grave
just a jump away, continue your brisk morning walks on
deck before breakfast. The salt ocean spray on your cheeks
and fresh air in your lungs will raise a marvellous appetite.
Afternoons in your deck chair read from the minor to the
great poets and contemplate that the sea will soon be your
own private memorial. But don't allow this to make you eerie.
Nor take your dive too early in the voyage to depress everyone for the rest of the trip.

On the edge of the Gulf Stream about three hundred miles
south of Nova Scotia is the best spot. The sea temperature
will be about ten degrees centigrade and the depth plenty
deep at thirteen thousand feet. Then following a simple but
nourishing champagne meal of caviar, pressed duck, and
asparagus, ending with strawberries and cream, take a final
blast of cognac, round off with a few turns on the dance floor
with your companion pal provided you have the self control
to avoid being tugged down to her state room for another
blazing event. If she persists in hugging you excuse yourself
for a series of long distance telephone calls and take a running
hurdle at the railings just before three a.m.

Tips for your cabin steward and others who have rendered
signal service should be left placed prominently in your state
room. It is sporting to leave an amount covering the full
journey. But make sure your steward has retired for the night
as it is essential your premature gratuities do not result in
the raising of the man overboard alarm. It really is embarrassing to be rescued and fished out amid all the search lights
with the remainder of the trip a nightmare of whispers and
pointings every time you want a breath of fresh air at the
ship's rails.

With your departure succeeding unnoticed you will land

up to your scalp in the ocean. If you have avoided testicular concussion by shielding your billiards with cupped hands you will at first feel a painfree clutching sensation as you watch the liner make its way away like an illuminated fairy tale city trailing a great boiling white wake on the midnight depths. You may also think you hear the fading strains of the dance band. This is extremely unlikely but indeed you may count upon sniffing a fume or two from the vessel's turbines. In any event an awesome sense of peace will be yours paddling there in the extremely chilly water and you will be astonished as you come to profound terms with yourself at how much pleasure your own company will give you at this time.

Parting Words, Gestures, Apparel and Conversations

Proper care should be given to one's clothing at the time of one's deliberate demise. Informality is permissible for gassing and poisoning. For jumping and hanging, stick with sports apparel. Nudity, unless for drowning in the privacy of one's bath, always denotes an unpleasant characteristic in the deceased.

Final letters should be brief, unapologetic and neither sad nor glad. If you happen to have been a politically important personage in life 'No comment' is proper. Most other sentiments sound forced when they are your very last utterances. But especially sidestep the one.

'It was a good life while it lasted.'

That really is a remark of the bootless and unhorsed. Any one speaking straight from the bowels knows that life is mostly a pain in the arse. Therefore confine yourself to notes concerning various domestic matters, especially those regarding household pets who may have been your only living solace.

'Please leave milk for Esme the cat and feed Putsie my piranha.'

Political gestures, sentiments and shouts of 'Up the Republic' and 'Long live liberty' and other remarks are strictly déclassé unless you are aboard a liner travelling and jumping tourist class. Obscene gestures are also out of place except in the case of the boys at the office. To make them really smitten with your demise, an impassioned shout accompanied by a shaking of the fist is in order.

'You really dirty lousy bunch of rotten guys.'

However, one last warning concerning parting conversations. While on deck leaning expectantly over the rails, some previous pomposity may approach attempting to challenge you by first pretending to ask for a light.

'I say there old man, got a light.'
'Sorry left my solid platinum lighter in my suite.'
'Sir are you merely being painfully pretentious or have you left your vulgar valuables behind because you are jumping.'
'I beg your brazen pardon.'
'Look here old man, I saw you standing well back as if to vault the rails just as I came out on deck from the first class smoking room.'
'I was merely exercising my thighs and calves having missed my afternoon game of quoits.'
'Sir, upon my monocle I regard that as monstrous twaddle, rot, bosh and figs.'
'How dare you accuse me of arrant poppycock.'
'Of course sir, I dare. Just as I dare notice your one red

and one green sock. Witnessing such sartorial black tie blasphemy in first class is heinous, sir.'

'Those hues happen to be, if you don't mind, my racing colours, you ruddy commoner you.'

'Ha ha. If you think sir, by that remark that I would mistake you for a member of the titled classes you have another transatlantic trip coming.'

'I am a prince.'

'I venture to suggest that that is more bull, pish, tush and mummery, sir, and I would request you take your royal nonsense and person to another shipping line. Because if you think that for one muffin you are going to deliberately delay this vessel for two hours in a rescue attempt of your plebeian remains you have another jump coming.'

This is extremely irritating behaviour especially at a time during which you are tasting the last of this life. This chap has quite obviously let his monocled pomposity go to his head where clearly he intends it should set his course in history. Short of calling for ping pong paddles at dawn, a light peppering of your chamois gloves about your chap's jowls should suffice a challenge to a duel. Naturally you don't want to delay your higher graduation by getting hurt. Plus it's always difficult to jump as a cripple.

But if this son of a bitch persists in unpleasant testiness, take him by his satin lapels or cummerbund and tug trip and twist him over the rails with you. He'll yell bloody murder and you may have to sock him unconscious but at least you won't have to book another ocean passage. However it does mean a gross lack of privacy down in the waves. Especially with an opinionated prig who is likely to die like a commoner instead of a prince.

Execution

Relax and wait. Most things will be taken care of for you. And generally there will be accorded some measure of courtesy regarding your last wishes. The major part of your time will be spent praying or playing games and cards with your keepers. During this period it is extremely bad form to be caught cheating, since your opponents will, if they can, be trying to keep you happy and winning if possible.

Usually you will be fatally outnumbered and with no chance of escape you may as well comport yourself with quietude and dignity. Of course, some do attempt to present a cavalier touch with a phony feeble outburst of bombast.

'I say there, you chaps, can't we get this damn thing over with, I haven't all day.'

But wailing cowardice, grovelling and begging does stir up horror in your onlookers and makes your death not a nice thing to witness, albeit folk shouldn't be there trying to enjoy it anyway. However it is simply not done to have people have to drag, carry and tug you along to your place of dispatch.

Don't try to get friendly with your executioners or strike up poses of bonhommie. The proper posture is to be possessed of a small measure of unblinking arrogance with shoulders held well back, chin up and the arms firmly placed unflappingly at the sides. Above all never succumb to the hangdog look and allow the hands to come up in front of your person and there be wrung till the knuckles glow with whiteness. It will make everybody around you painfully ill at ease.

In cases where your keepers have wrapped your wrists in thongs behind your back, request if this restraining device can be omitted. However, in countries where they jump on you without warning while you are asleep and tie you up, you are certain to struggle at first till you wake sufficiently to find it is only the guys who have come to execute you. Ask calmly to be unhanded and walk purposefully forward but avoid being overtly military about it. A loose leg movement from the hips, as a manner of motion, is suggested.

While making your way to your place of execution do be on the look out for folk who may be visibly shaken by the spectacle. Only a passing smile or nod from you can convey poignant reassurance. Watching another being dispatched is for some people the supreme entertainment and for your own peace of mind it may be as well to avoid their sickly thrill expectant smiles. If you are of a hypochondriacal tendency it is quite a relief not to have to worry about ailing anymore, as impending execution really knocks hell out of your daily complaints like no other remedy can and it may result in your reaching the best physical condition of a lifetime.

If you are being shot before a firing squad unless the bastards have already gagged you, clenching the teeth is a sufficient way of restraining yourself from shouting out 'Don't shoot.' Tightly tensing the anus will preserve your composure immediately before the impact of the bullets. It also helps to stare at one particular gun barrel and earnestly imagine it to be the unloaded one. But do request to be blindfolded if the guns pointing at you really make you hysterical.

Special fears and anxieties are to be met with in being beheaded. Straight off dismiss from your mind the thought of your head lolling off, blood pulsing in fountains out of your neck and the rest of your body minus the nob that people recognised you by in life, gesticulating around the place. It is quite usual even for the well bred for the mouth of your severed head to emit outrageously obscene words. And it is only fair you should not be held accountable for these. However, in the case of words said, which are of major profundity, be assured that they can be properly attributed to you and protected by international copyright.

At the Funeral

Unless it is your own in which case you already will be there it is extremely remiss not to attend where you might reasonably be expected as a mourner. Keep your graveside gestures and emotions down to a minimum, especially those political. And in the case of a celebrity interment do not push and shove to get up near the coffin. Far better for the newsreel to catch you in your lachrymals at the back than in blatant publicity seeking at the front. Most sensitive people know the real tears of death and they don't go down the cheeks.

Some moisture welling in the eye which at intervals slowly proceeds down the face is the proper expression of grief befitting a gentleman. A black silk hanky should be used to wipe away any large globule of moisture collecting on the end of the nose or chin. Stand with your hands folded together just above your privates. If some lady backs up on you in this position with her posterior level with your fingers and dares round upon you with.

'Keep your hands to yourself.'

Be mindful that a funeral is in progress and murmur flatteringly.

'Madam it is with regret that I shall.'

It is quite an abominable graveside antic to pretend to want to jump in as the coffin is being lowered. If you tripped with some of the cheaper materials they are using these days, your feet could go right through the lid and your possibly muddy shoes land with the most grossly embarrassing results on the corpse. Usually this is a blatant demonstration by someone who, while the departed was living, gave him a hard time and needs now to garishly exaggerate her distress. Spear shaped high heels are particularly distressing when plunged piercingly into the deceased. If you are standing next to or preferably behind such person and want to properly take the wind out of her bereavement sails billowing all over the cemetery, a gentle shove in the small of the back propelling her towards the hole does wonders. But be prepared to find yourself in an altercation. The lady who backed on to you will certainly take this new jolt as an attempted goose. Which when the mourners are armed could produce a lot of recent funerals. Of course if you are light fingered enough this lady might turn and smile. This is the kind of contradictory behaviour you can expect from the more ill bred of your bereaved who will also later in the obsequies invariably besot themselves with drink and food.

Leave your garish clothes at home. There is nothing more annoying at a funeral than unseemly colours or Bermuda shorts. On the other hand attirement in an all black riding outfit while carrying by hand the deceased's most favourite wild flower is quite in order when attending the laying to rest of a member of the hunt whose horse may have rolled upon him with fatal consequences at some difficult jump. A couple of thwacks of your riding crop against the side of your boot is the proper gesture just as the coffin is interred, along with a low murmur of 'Tally ho' to which other members of the hunt will respond with 'Here here.' The final musical note will be the horn sounded by the master of fox hounds. These latter dogs will usually be collected together by the whipper in at a suitable distance from the graveside and will bay and howl together as the coffin is lowered. This is of course a singularly romantic occasion and there is no more acceptable method of killing yourself than busting your head, back or arse in a cross country chase on horseback. A groom leading the mount of the deceased to the graveside to paw turf in upon the coffin is another highly appreciated gesture.

At the crematorium there are many troublesome points to watch. Under no circumstances investigate or push buttons or tug on switches especially those under the catafalque where the remains of the deceased are resting. Dire embarrassment has often ensued when some inquisitive person trying to find out how things work has pushed a button and the deceased departs moving away on the conveyor towards the flames right in the middle of the funeral oration. And when some of the more athletic people present make a rush to stop the coffin, this has resulted in a melee the like of which, with the deliberately flimsy construction of the casket, can get awfully ghastly and unsatisfactory indeed. With a lot of other dead awaiting their turn to be burned, a mishap ahead of you of this kind can cause panic.

Even worse however is when premature conveyance of the corpse to its conflagration happens before any of the other mourners arrive and you stand there sheepishly having pressed the button, making helpless expressions with a rhythmic rising of the shoulders and outwardly offered upturned empty hands.

'Holy gee I'm really sorry folks.'

And if you have been impossibly stupid enough to have toppled the coffin off the conveyor on to the floor in an effort to retrieve it and now stand there where the damn fragile thing is busted right open and due to the fact of the deceased's imminent combustion he is attired in something not quite cricket or fully covering or flattering, in such cases instantly assume a precise military air. The tone of your voice should be that used for an emergency. Keep everyone at a distance, especially those tiresome busybodies and aunt sallys who encroach attempting to refold the corpse's arms back in the box with the rigor mortised limbs waggingly giving them well deserved bumps in the face.

In your expressions of sympathy to the other bereaved, a gentle tap of a hand, or pat on the shoulder is proper. In the case of a male mourner who by his rich mate's death has inherited her massive wealth one meaningful back slap may be given. However, it is simply never done to use reassuring body contact as an excuse for nudging a comely widow under the tit or gently cupping a cheek of her behind. Sexual arousal is a well known phenomenon that takes place at funerals. And if a female fellow mourner sticks her tongue down your throat in a french kiss, don't fight it, go with it, but this is not the place to overly prolong the event and stand there feverishly engripped by the graveside with the two of you grossly tampering with each other's intimate parts. That simply is not on.

People do strange things when beset by grief and their friends should steer them clear of publicly indelicate behaviour. Elegance and the proper rig out is de rigueur. Nudity, even when partial gives a particularly distressing slant to any funeral proceeding unless all present are members of a sun worshippers' group. In such case black umbrellas should be held open against the sky as a gesture to the corpse. Should a fellow balloonist be the deceased it is quite in order to have your tie embroidered in blue with an ascending balloon and gondola with the legend 'Bon voyage' underneath. If it's at all possible, unless the deceased was the operator of a strip mining excavator, some sample illustration of the departed's occupation while alive is in keeping.

Of the haughtiest particularity, however, is burial at sea. This should be conducted by life long nautical professionals. The coffin should be properly caulked and encased in a heavy lead container. For seemliness' sake those who are sea sick should keep to the other side of the vessel when the remains are being slipped into the waves. The scattering of ashes at sea is appropriate only for the remains of the bootless and unhorsed.

Cannibalism

This of course is, in its way, a kind of funeral and appropriate formalities are well to be observed. Aside from reincarnationists who eat each other for this purpose and whose motives must be classed as religious, there exists the everyday matter that must be reckoned with when taking one's seat on an aircraft. Flying over remote uninhabited areas such as some polar region, one must unfortunately recognise the possibility that one can plummet out of the sky and that until you are discovered on some blizzard swept mountain top and rescued there might not be much around to eat.

The regrettable possibility therefore must be considered of ingesting one of your fellow passengers. This you may really find foul making to contemplate especially with the type that might be sitting next to you these days on group charter flights. But here is a rare opportunity to find qualities objectionable in the living quite beneficial in the dead.

However, certain proprieties must be observed. And particularly when some perfectly beautiful creature sits next to you on the aircraft who makes your mouth water to eat. Under no circumstances is it permissible to allow any expression of this appetite upon your face. It is bound to be the most sickly visage imaginable. You may freely, however, contemplate her delightfully eating you. This can indeed quite unaccountably be exciting to a degree perceptible in your smile. Which might easily result in this dazzling babe socking your jaw loose and leaving you with an even more unfortunate leer.

When the plane crash lands in the snow and you have run out of the usually accepted conversational topics, it is objectionable and in extremely poor taste to try to touch upon matters relating to bloodsucking, fiends or group depravity.

Different rules ensue, alas, as soon as the stage is reached where if you are not to starve to death you must discuss the eating of fellow passengers including your winsome travelling partner. This is a moment for the supreme nobility of words. And those of the dead and dying who are being dismembered to become part of the larder still should be referred to as persons and never as this bit of liver, tit or testicle.

Because of her elegant leanness and lack of cushioning in the impact, your seat mate may have been killed instantly. As a gentleman some effort should be made to restrain the eagerness of the others, appetized to a frenzy by the lissome

sight of her, to eat her raw. Cooking is less blatant than gulping her fresh so to speak. Be mindful not to exhibit any relish, while ingesting the gorgeous body, hungry as you may be, and never smack or lick your lips over her dainty viands. The swallowing of her remains down your throat is a moment of profound sorrow and mourning, being that of her final obsequies. Of course, fair is fair, and some allowance can be made for the normal healthy enjoyment of a bite to eat.

Gusto is bound to be less restrained when a couple of the

other cannibals are chewing some boorish passenger whom they may have disliked on sight. Needless to say one must be aware of incarnating a devoured passenger's obnoxiousness in oneself requiring exorcism upon one's returning to civilian life again. In the matter of racial and colour repugnancies and prejudices, these should never become criteria when asking for another helping. However having a genuine gustatory preference it should be couched in requesting white, yellow or dark meat and never for a bit of Pole, Chink or Nigger.

Unless there is nothing else left, it is on the whole seemly that you do not eat the intimate parts of the opposite sex. In particular the excitingly flavourful portions of the attractive passenger who sat next to you. Even though you may feel absolutely convinced that you alone can treat such delicacies with all the sacred dignity that the masticating of these may require. The more swinish however may fight bitterly over these morsels of the anatomy and in such cases do not hesitate to make it loudly known that this is exactly what one might expect from the bootless and unhorsed.

Those who survive their ordeal by swallowing one another, often without salt or other condiments, should be allowed to lead normal lives afterwards. Harassment by relatives who may resent you for downing their nearest and dearest is to be expected. Especially the gobbling up of a chap's good looking really curvaceous wife. It is understandable that one may shrink from these folk should they approach and stare overlong at one's figure, even though you have left their relative's bones and teeth behind. Remember, in effect, you are now a walking cemetery. And it is not without possibility that the bereaved may want to kneel and pray at your feet, burn candles on your shoe tips or place a wreath of flowers on your back. Be mindful to be understanding at these times. Take such adoration and decoration in the spirit in which it is meant, it is the least you can do and you have your own life to thank for it.

In cases where in a public place a grab is made at your person and you hear a scream loud and clear.

'This fat on you is my Herbie. I want him back.'

If the lady making this not utterly impossible demand is comely enough, here is your opportunity. Repair somewhere suitably private and there on the bed or over dressing tables or upon chairs, as she might prefer, you will be able to at least tender to her some vestige of Herbie diffused in your body. However do not take it amiss, when in her paroxysms she groans her dead husband's name. But do seek immediate advice should answering shouts come out of your stomach.

The Duel

For the purpose of inciting such, the chamois gloves should always be carried on your person. Upon being affronted by the blatant instance of a chap's déclassé demeanour, the gloves are slowly pulled by the open end, never by the fingers, from the left lower waistcoat pocket. Advance upon the fellow. Raise your wrist with the gloves suspended from your down flexed fingers and flick the chamois forward upon your opponent.

The area to be fluffed and peppered is first that of the cheeks, especially the hollows, then lower your attack to the jaws followed by a final vibration at the neck area just under the chin. If your chap has pendulant jowls and other incapacitations brought on by wine, food, worry and women, so much the better. Clearly he is in need of a moral correction and there is nothing like mortal combat to excite and inspire the spiritual condition. Besides, the bevy of babes who have spent most of this guy's money will always think it is high time for his comeuppance.

In many circles these days a man's honour is considered less valuable than his hide, and often chaps will remain cringingly silent to your challenge. In such cases another glove fluffing and peppering of your fellow's tonsil area and your abrupt departure noisily clearing your throat, is sufficient disgrace. However, should you be the recipient of such glove quivering about the face don't wait till your chap is oscillating the chamois under your ear lobes but announce firmly.

'Sir make known your weapon.'

Of course one of today's wise guys is likely to zip open his flies. Let this poseur know immediately that this is a deadly serious business he has brought upon himself and dismiss his obscene overtness with a riposte.

'Sir, although an improvement upon your face, it would be as well if your flies were closed before some amputation by swinging you bodily in a circle should happen.'

Posh hotel lavatory attendants who accuse you of stealing latrine combs, unless they are possessed of a pedigree, and quite astonishingly some are, are to be merely dismissed with a firm shove on the shoulder backwards into a basin or bowl he has recently filled. The throwing of one of his towels after him completes this little bit of instant justice. Which may also apply in the cases of footmen and other menials who have the audacity to level at you some sneaky jeer or irreverence.

The subject of a duel should be to satisfy aspersions cast upon your haughty particularity or that of a lady. Of course one is always tempted to deflate some tiresome upstart's puffed up presence and certainly this is permissible in cases where a chap is foolhardy enough to sigh because he's heard the story you're telling, twice before. Especially in one's club, where many things which may be said to one while out proceeding in public may never be voiced. And certainly not without the retribution of formal combat with deadly weapons.

There are occasions when formal steps towards a challenge to a duel may be temporarily frustrated. One such is a confrontation with a behemoth, who may, before you can get your gloves out, be picking you up in his hands and compressing you to a phosphorescence in his eager fingers. And what's more is about to wring your neck in about another micro second. Naturally one does not want the elitist formality of one's challenge to be fussed by such unleashing of some towering bastard's uninhibited violence. Therefore, as the guy's size and occasion demand, keep your distance. Of course this will be aided by the tendency felt in one's toes to step even farther back. But it is de rigueur to stand your present ground absolutely. Vigorously shake and flap your chamois gloves high in the air. Onlookers will understand your first flush of cowardice while you announce your challenge. But this demand for satisfaction had better be in rapid fire word formation because the behemoth will be looking for gaps in your syllables to shoot one of his great paws between and possibly wrench you into two or more parts.

'Sir do not think for one second that I am in the least terrified by your size, or bulging muscles, or that you may be the member of an athletic club where you have skilled yourself in killer techniques. Therefore I am suggesting, sir, that you repeat your insult to me in another aspect of voice, which if I deem it less contrary to my honour, I will forgive you absolutely.'

Your little speech will more than likely be met by the behemoth's sarcastic laughter and since there is no point in dying for a lost cause which may be your neck, be ready to make a run for it. But there's a chance the monster will listen attentively bemused by the considerable elegance of your accent. Keep talking until such time as he has finished smiling.

Then get ready for his lunge, which if you are deliriously

lucky will only tear off your lapels. Your solo hope may now be if you are a slightly built lady killer whose most recent deeply contented female companion is present at your side and who will now leap forward in screaming wildcat fashion and scratch the big ape's cheeks for him till his facial expression looks like an arab israeli chess board.

At the Duelling Site

For death dealing weapons, the area chosen should be in the openness of a glade sheltered by trees and free of public traffic. The grass should not be too long so that when folk are stretched out with gashes or gaping holes, bugs can't easily jump up into the wounds. If the ground has been worn smooth by previous duels, choose a spot free of blood so that in shedding yours there is no historical confusion as to the place where you died.

Proceed in front of your seconds. One of the latter carrying a smaller sized samovar for indulging hot refreshment while assistants are examining weaponry, is a nice touch. Keep your composure at all costs. The fact that the both of you have shown up means you share at least a bond of bravery if not lunacy of mind. At dawn of course there will be some chill and some shivering will be apparent in your adversary. Do not take comfort from this. But if your own knees are knocking draw your cloak around you and recall that in the privacy of your fencing room or shooting range you have become a deadly marksman capable of springing a leak with blade or bullet in an auricle or ventricle of your choosing.

If your gun or sword hand still keeps shaking try to take in a soothing moment of nature. Some kind of a bird is bound to be around somewhere. And at least a few of these winged creatures should be melodically singing at this time of morning. If they're not it's a sign of bad luck for somebody. But the other guy if he has a vestige of sense should be scared shitless too especially as at any moment you might both be arrested.

Should your opponent be a buck of sporting blood he will have chosen rapiers. He'll also know there is an endless supply of guys like you and that he could not go on just killing them all one after another. Especially with a lot of other daily trivialities to suffer from the guys back at the office. So a few nicks here and there and a drop or two of blood from non vital parts will suffice to satisfy one's esteem. Bullets, particularly of a forty five calibre variety which go off in the breech like cannons and can send your whole liver a mile backwards ruptured in two parts by your spine, never leave much room for noble moments. Such as a stepping back when your adversary goes down momentarily on the greasy grass and maybe, if he's amateurish, getting a stick of his own blade up the arse. Although he will not be inclined to laugh along with you about this indignity he will appreciate your not swiping off an ear or two. Following this kind of blasé gallantry, and provided combatants have some class affinity, such a noble gesture can lead to the joining of strong enduring acquaintanceships.

Conduct your swordsmanship coolly. Shaking and brushing your hair out of your eyes every few moments is a sign of timidity as well as having a bad barber. And also a way of encouraging early death. Avoid the angry impetuous thrust. Parry till you get your opponent's measure. Jump way back or bizarrely to the side once in a while to see if it will make him do something really stupid. Of course thereby, you may end up yourself doing something hysterically inane. And your opponent, luxuriating in this, will guffaw. Then, by god, carve him. A swipe, fingernail thickness deep, diagonally downwards across the chest really gets the message home.

Ideally his garment should flap open exposing the flesh where the thin line of your incision slowly oozes blood. He will look down unless he is a very cool customer indeed. Then notch him again. Just as a reminder that there is a lot more where that came from. And that his fly buttons, chillingly one by one, may be the next to go.

Should the unfortunate happen and your man succeed in laying you open in a mortally incapacitating way, wait with dignity to be dispatched by his sword. It is not done to beg for mercy. Or to exhibit fear or concern even though you may feel deeply agonized about getting the chop. However, in the eventuality happily encountered, that you are to be given a gentleman's chance to come out of the proceedings with your life, do not rush attempting to shake the guy's hand. Spilling gratitude all over the place is tawdry at this time. Just a civil nod will do. Later your seconds can deliver the chap a really corking bottle of vintage port.

If your wounds have merely been superficial, following combat, always retire for a hot bath. Don't stint scenting the water with selected oils of perfume. Although you may have had some of the stuffing and pride punctured out of you, still you did not falter. A fight lost but fought with both courage and fair play is an honourable comeuppance. But beware. The rest of the world will only care about your winner's laurels. And the sooner you literally cut the shit out of some new fucker, the better, because before you know it you'll be inundated by a bunch of opportunists who now think that sticking a foil up your whammo scalammo is a nice way to pretend they're eating canapés. And they could come in droves fluffing and peppering your adam's apple till it's utterly polished red.

To avoid lethalities other weapons to be considered are boxing gloves, sling shots, pea shooters, water pistols and the testicle twisting practised by the ancient Firbolg. This latter is, however, nearly as bad if not worse than being killed, and only those possessed of elastically robust and leathery testicles should consider it a mode of combat satisfying one's honour. Underripe grapes are generally the best ammunition to be used in the pea shooter. The grape splattering on your opponent's forehead and the acidly unripe contents seeping down into his eyes will temporarily blind him thus allowing more forceful measures to be introduced for his chastisement.

Water pistols have the advantage of being able to carry a liquid varying in preferred degrees of noxiousness to suit the seriousness of the combat. One may vary from vinegar, across a whole phalanx of unpleasant urines including yak, goat, wolfhound to various dilutions of sulphuric acid. Make sure the plunger of your water pistol is airtight. There is nothing more dispiriting than the arc of one's squirt falling short of the mark and maybe, in the case of acid, only eating a hole through your adversary's flashy shoe tips, or worse, your own conservative ones. However should your opponent lean backwards laughing, hurry forward a few paces and give him a right old mouthful. This is an exceedingly appropriate basting for a lot of your fops and déclassé popinjays perving around these days.

Impromptu Combat

Although one is used to the bluff inherent in the litany.

'Come and say that outside.'

Or if you are outside.

'Come and say that to my lawyer.'

Nevertheless violence may not be far away especially when encountering the explosive rage smouldering inside those manoeuvring a motorized vehicle. Usually occasioned by some son of a bitch cutting in front of you or stealing your parking space just as you are about to turn into it. Often a highly polished blue black automatic pistol taken from your glove compartment is the only pacifier unless your opponent is also taking aim with his revolver. In which case you must silence him between the eyes before he springs an unwanted leak in you.

If matters have not already been irrevocably settled by the bang bang of see through perforations, the raising to your lips of an artifact resembling a microphone into which it would appear you are speaking and which also conveys an indication that it will summon the instant descent of a dozen henchmen with their usual assortment of knuckle dusters, axe handles and bicycle chains, can often make your disobliging adversary steer into a direction delivering him from your area of annoyance fast.

Other cases of fist flying can arise when unseemly chaps barge in front of you, take without leave your seat, churlishly demand service out of turn or put their foot over the coin you just dropped or elbows or prods while you all crowd towards some sporting fixture. Signify by a thunderously glowering look that just another hair's breadth hint of his aggression will incite to toupee ripping or in the case of a fellow with a full head of hair, the imminent need of a toupee. Your accent and cavalry twill suit aided and abetted by your demeanour of elegant fair play will also heap suitable chastisement along with the hint of your charm and wealth nicely couched in the phrase.

'Ruffian most odious.'

If your adversary stands there in his splashily cut garments shouting that he is an expert in one of the arts of self defence and has qualified to the high entitlement of a pink, black, blue, or green belt or other glorified gladiatorial status, and that you had better watch out, jeeringly protrude your tongue at him. This has a way of defusing your opponent's killer instinct by delighting him with your seeming vulnerability. Reinforce this by stepping back two paces. And then wade in doubling over this objectionable bully with a body fusillade of left and right hooks which amply contuse the ganglia of your man's abdominal viscera.

Being able to think you can give a fierce account of yourself is nearly better than even being able to. And schooling at a good athletic club in the manly art of self defence increases this illusion plus it might possibly scare somebody by lending a jauntiness to your gait. If after months of instruction you're not even able to hurt a fly and you've failed miserably with all other instructed methods of ancient jaw splintering, eye gouging, and shoulder dislocating, you may, if not absolutely enfeebled, find that perfecting an old fashioned one footer boot up the commoner's balls is as good as anything.

When attacked by street gangs, keep your wits about you. Usually the smallest and weakest member of these marauders is first encouraged forward to taunt and jeer before the gang take their more serious steps in beating, stabbing or stomping you to death. Your refined accent and clothes will further delight the kids with the prospect and their smallest member will demonstrate this enthusiasm by dancing a series of tricky feints accompanied by bizarre footwork conducted right under your very nose.

Laughingly show your amusement with this exhibition. And then suddenly without warning grab this smart assed little kid by the scruff and spin him around with your forearm choked across his throat so that his tongue is sticking out a mile and his face is turning alternate shades of purple and blue. As he gasps helplessly for breath while his eyeballs get ready to pop from his sockets like red hot fried corn, smile indulgently at the gang. They will be dumbfoundedly facing this surprise display of your ferocity with a plaintive sheepishness you'll hardly believe.

Let the situation sink nicely in. Then announce in a calm voice to your now horrified listeners that their friend gets the chop if anyone of them moves the merest degree of an inch. Don't be afraid of using freely descriptive adjectives of the heinously vile manner in which this little kid will die if the whole gang doesn't retreat back step by step while you count these off in a booming voice ONE TWO THREE and so forth until they are out of revenging distance. But leave at least a slight trace of hope in your voice. Gangs always highly regard their mascot member and hate to see his life snuffed out right in front of their very eyes.

Another method of defending against the gang is to taunt their biggest and toughest who will as a result rush you. Grab this loutish behemoth by the belt and tug yourself in to him close. In his feverished attempt to knock your head off he will land his punches on other members of the mob presently descending upon you from behind. As the melee thickens the whole gang will end up in one great writhing heap. But keep your head down while you get a really marvellous laugh out of this mad spectacle. Plus the extra amusement occasioned by the damage you can do to private parts is nobody's business. When you have the whole bloody bunch disabled, stomp a few outstretched fingers for good measure and stealthily creep away in case any other gangs are lurking nearby.

If you in the first place are carrying your sword stick, it does give you a rather overt cheerful advantage. While firmly holding the handle, extend the disguised cane end which your opponent will grab in order to wrap it about forty times round your old grey head. As he enthusiastically tugs however, he pulls off the scabbard and unsheaths your sword. Glints of this instrument wagging in the sunlight accompanied by a few whistling swipes along with teeth exposed whoops and hollers, gets a message across bearing far less goodwill than your chap might like in this particularly precarious time in his personal history. And so a little verbiage is not entirely without appropriateness.

'Now, what would you like to lose first, my fine foolish loutish friend. Your left foot, middle testicle or your right eyebrow. Or shall I give you a slashing overture with a fortissimo shortening of your various appendages.'

A prolonged silent gleam of your teeth should follow this little speech. And your son of a bitch will more than likely turn and run like the enthusiastically scared coward he well and truly is. The speed with which he will withdraw may spellbind you and in the interests of universal justice do try to decorate the bastard prior to departure with a few good arse stabs. And the world will benefit of one more diabolical bullying devil brought to book.

Of all impromptu combat that of fighting a woman presents the most peculiar difficulties. Unless for the arse cheeks, it is not done to strike ladies below the neck. And then only with the flat of the hand. But first make absolutely sure she is not armed. Or you may get your head blown off or bowel enlarged without ceremony. Women rarely defer to the niceties of sporting fair play. And being killed by a lady does kind of leave a sad image of you as a man.

Most ladies carry a pair of fairly lethal legs. So be sure to shield your privates. Tying these in a knot while you howl in agony will always be high on her list of target priorities. And absolute unconsciousness is the only thing that stops an infuriated woman. Therefore be ready to flatten her ladyship before she deranges your complexion with claws flying or permanently puts new contours in your jewels with a crotch kick. The right cross delivered with your palm to the apex of madam's chin is the gallant way to knock her cold.

Women usually rely upon a gentleman's hesitation to slug a lady and that's when she usually gets in those two good matching gouge scratches down your cheeks. In parrying these however you may find her ladyship engripped upon you. To avoid her advantage in such one sided infighting trip her backwards to the floor. While rolling there it is unseemly to feel madam up. But do guard against her biting anything she can get her god damn deep teeth into. Which could, among other delicate things, be your neck and mortal.

On the boulevard it may happen that an enraged woman is encountered who descends banging upon you with an umbrella or parasol. Usually you are accused of leering or harbouring untrue thoughts about her. In such cases seize the umbrella from her and grasp each end firmly, and slowly, accompanied by a low evil growl, bend it into a pretzel.

'Venture any closer madam, and the same will happen to you.'
'You'd dare to strike a woman.'
'Yes, if madam is a woman then I dare.'

Upon successful escape from being killed by a female adversary an appropriate chastisement is de rigueur. And spanking serves especially well in the case of nicely brought up ladies. Who although they may momentarily become viciously violent nevertheless still continue to exhibit their well bred refinement in other spheres of behaviour. To get the message soundly home it is essential to expose both cheeks of her ladyship's bottom. This may take some preliminary ripping, tearing and wrestling. But once over your knee with one of her arms bent up behind her back the subject should be at your mercy. Deliver your blows with a straight downward motion of the hand to the peak of madam's cheeks with the fingers slightly ajar to decrease wind resistance and increase impact. The smacking should mount in severity until your ladyship shrieks. Be careful to detect pleasure in these outcries especially when in the very middle of your correctional measures your subject abandons all resistance and invites you to strike even harder blows. Usually ladies requesting such auxiliary shenanigans become extremely red faced and attempt even while firmly restrained by the wrists to seek out your erogenous zones. Succumbing to such an overture is sure to negate all disciplinary effectiveness as well as to afford new opportunities and encouragements for her ladyship to clonk your distinguished temples with a series of heavy glass ashtrays. Especially at times when you have taken a leisurely moment in the tomblike peace of your library to peruse with magnifying glass your stamp or moth collections.

Upon Making the Contract for the Rubout

These expedient days when one wants desperately to live in prolonged decency there come agonizing moral dilemmas especially where one has been smothered for years in paper work involving subpoenas, writs, mandamuses, suits, claims and counter claims. As the sincere desire wells up in you for ongoing situations and to be clear of the continual lawyers' bills and personal harassment from some human odium, so that you can make meaningful progress with the pleasures and profits you have planned for your life, it is sometimes terribly unfortunate but necessary to have administered a little strong arm and in the stubborn cases, which most turn out to be, to rub certain people out absolutely and altogether.

First, avoid suspicion and never be witnessed threatening to kill someone. Especially when screaming the expression.

'I will kill you.'

And followed by the added emphasis.

'With my bare hands.'

Which shows you are angry as well. For even though you are

an old greyhead and seemingly small and frail, it is well known that tiny people when overtaken by huge angers can exert strengths far beyond their obvious capabilities and are also types who might order a murder from the many à la carte menus around these days.

However where merely the working over of the victim is required with a few breaks, strains or multi hued bruises one need only hire a couple of lead pipe hoodlums. But for such beatings to be effective it is necessary to first administer a warning in the form of your chap's car or bicycle tyres being slashed, his stoop messily decorated with gobbets of non matching coloured paint or just a bustment of a selected few of his main windows. If the victim lives high up this can be done by a sling shot artist from a nearby roof.

Give clear directions to your roughnecks as to the area of your chap's anatomy you want broken as this directly affects the duration of incapacitation. To stop him writing cheques or his memoirs, the wrists can be smashed. In preventing him preparing his own favourite spaghettis, clean break fractures above the elbow keep him away from his chopping board. Contused kneecaps are an ideal way to keep him a week or two off the golf course but to confine him to his house for three months, compound fractures administered by cricket or baseball bat while your man's thigh is stretched over a kerbstone, are normally required.

It is invariably an awesome responsibility to take the decision to put an end to a person's life. Although you would never know it, some of them have near and dear ones and may even support their community and regularly attend religious services. But they should have known not to tangle with you in the first place. No matter how you try to reason with them, such folks who fuss you always tend to stand oozing smug justification and remain implacably right smack bang in the way of one's profit or maybe even a dazzling female pleasure one seeks. Often this rubout is humane for the victim who is only going to spend the best years of his life piling up monstrous lawyers' bills and vituperating your name to all and sundry around him plus spending endless wasteful hours shivering with rage fruitlessly trying to dream up some new scheme to get you when he could instead be happily resting in peace with his heirs delighted by the calm following his final departure.

Confidentiality is of course a must in the planning and execution of the rubout as you do not want to have a nosy finger pointing directly back at you as the accessory before the fact, after it or in it. So carefully choose the man for the job. Deal only with the genuine underworld. Avoid shoddy impostors who offer bargain basement rates. A cool professional is required and for such accomplished experts one must be prepared to pay. These skilled reliable chaps, with their established track records, have at their fingertips the right kind of suitable send off for your chosen obtuse persons who, although you want to get rid of him at all costs you nevertheless want him to meet his end in an efficient manner without leaving a whole bunch of ghosts around.

But in all cases it is wise and proper for you to decide whether you wish the total disappearance of the victim, afforded by providing him with cement shoes to walk across a river, or to let his corpse be found after giving your man a bunch of electrodes to hug while they're made lively enough for a gavotte too strenuous for your victim's slowed down heart and he is deposited somewhere unbruised in his rigor mortis. And of course it is well to remember that no matter where your chappie is vanished without trace, one is always wondering if at some future date the son of a bitch's soggy remains are going to be turned up and a whole new investigation ensue as to who did that. When you might be nervously surrounded by a bunch of avid crime solving bureaucratic people insinuating that you did. Even incineration in a guy's private crematorium always runs the risk of snoopers claiming they know who the embers are. Or who the gas was if they're watching the chimney smoke with a telescope. But such embarrassment is usually prevented by syrupy sea burial from a fish entrail and tail mincer. The flow from which the seagulls and fish are ravenous for.

At some stage it will be necessary for you to speak with an intermediary to deal with the contract. In doing so couch your words in a manner which allows for your conversation to be overheard or bugged. Be patient with the overly classical usage you may encounter and always include all the other parties' nicknames.

> 'I'd like to speak to One Fingered Legs Apart Vinnie.'
> 'This is he that speaks. Pray tell who dat.'
> 'I have a proposal for membership of the club.'
> 'Ah vouchsafe and behoove how soon does this individual wanta join.'
> 'He's dying for membership.'
> 'In dat case we assure you of every convenience and dignity for his rapid election.'

Upon Abandoning Ship

Sea disasters have a way of happening in the most unsuitable weather. And it could be for this reason that crews made nervous by the high waves behave in a singularly disconcerting manner, especially those of nationalities without a great seafaring tradition to uphold. Some of these ruffians have been known to come on deck after rifling first class staterooms to commandeer the lifeboats exclusively for themselves. And don't be surprised if you see kitchen hands mounting the davits stretching your good woman's diamond bracelets over their wrists while waving a magnum of crystal brut champagne in one fist and gnawing on a chunk of smoked salmon held in the other.

It is quite understandable that no matter who you are, when a ship is sinking, folk want off with a degree of speed commonly referred to as in a hurry. Adding to this distress is the lack of the ship's company's diligence to the usual protocol and courtesy shown first class passengers. Especially now when this is most needed in the face of cabin and tourist type voyagers invading precincts reserved strictly for first class. So do please be prepared for these previous people to behave just as if their lives were absolutely as important as those travelling in the top privileged condition. It is further quite disconcerting when you remonstrate with those clearly elevated up from the bowels of the ship and making merry free in one's luxurious preserves when they answer you with.

'It's everyman for himself, squire.'

However, in such emergency, the casual if not boorish regard paid to you from the more plebeian members of the vessel's passenger list, although it often leaves much to be desired, should under no circumstances be the cause of your losing your perspective in providing for your own survival and that of your loved ones. And you may even venture to employ the otherwise forbidden behaviour of rudeness expected is to be rudeness given and simply shoulder these clodhoppers out of the way.

Nevertheless make it a habit as you leave your stateroom to always take with you a few fistfuls of your more excitingly enticeful valuables. These are awful handy up on deck in the milling and mêlée when it may be necessary to bargain your way into a lifeboat past a bunch of vintage wine consuming seaport hardened cut throats. It is no joke that a small pouch of uncut diamonds cuts the most ice for this purpose. Especially as you can whisper a description of the contents to your adversary and it won't make you look as crass as the whole slew of folk tendering outright handfuls of vulgar ready cash which even at that moment may be being critically devalued on some international bourse. With the ill luck attendant at such times this whole scene is bound to be during dinner and if so, your evening clothes and natural silk shirt will help vouch for the genuineness of the pouch's contents. And it is a wise precaution to be continually splendidly attired at sea.

Some of the most wretched and heartrending moments of human trial however, have taken place in the wee hours of the morning following the alarm to abandon ship. Again it must be stressed that your clothing should at all times give immediate recognition to your haughty particularity. Your choice of bed wear therefore, must be most meticulous. Attiring yourself in a half arsed manner when you think you are out of sight simply will not do. You will of course see others in slipshod sleeping garments revealing their true and perhaps humbler status than the superior one they were pretending while playing bridge. And to you this display of tattiness should not matter. For as a person of finer feelings there is no doubt as to where your duty lies and social distinctions should not be imposed where children, mothers and other ladies' lives are concerned. Should you suffer any momentary hesitation in this respect, forcefully remind yourself that it is simply not on to save your own neck while ignoring the desperate pleas and cries of help from those weaker and beseeching the safety of the lifeboats. If a ruffian is barring the way use strong words.

'Remove yourself you bounder, before I strike you.'
'Take it easy on the apoplexy pops and you won't get hurt.'

Under no circumstances let this kind of riposte deter you. It is understandable that only a minute or two previous, you may have been relaxing in the clubby atmosphere of the captain's quarters following dinner on the veranda deck and now over port and cigars you are enthralling a specially selected group of your fellow first class travelling mates with a rollicking yarn over which the ship's chief engineer is hammering his knees in helpless laughter. At that moment back there all the world was yours. Precipitated, savoured and enjoyed as only a vessel underway on the high seas can make it. And now rushing in a fuss in your life jacket which the captain himself chucked to you, you confront at nearly every turn of the corridor some son of a bitch escaped up out of steerage with a bottle of Napoleon brandy to his lips having a whale of a time as he sinks his unsavoury lunch hooks into the elegance of other people's property. This is only the beginning of the heinousness so steel yourself.

If you have no knowledge of seafaring ways the ship's officers especially those of the higher ranks must be looked to at this time for guidance. They will issue you with instructions and if necessary assign you appropriate duties befitting any well known responsibilities you may have held in your terra firma station in life. But don't think because of this, that you know it all. As the ship lists you may start directing your upper class passengers to run appropriately to the highest side and there enjoy this privileged area. It is in this blind pursuit of elite supremacy that many of your patrician folks drown. Plus you look pretty stupid and sheepish with the bunch of your exalted gullibles marooned standing suspended high on a forlorn bulge of hull. Which at its present angle of elevation will make a head busting distance for you all to dive from.

Be mindful also in encountering embarrassment in having to take on your authoritative position. People with whom you have established a passing recognition if not a friendship of happy equality over quoits and backgammon may take it upon themselves to absolutely ignore your commands and rush past lifebelted and clutching their emeralds as if they had never seen you before. Don't hesitate to take action.

'Madam. Stop.'

'Who the hell are you suddenly telling me to stop.'

'Madam I have for the benefit of passengers' safety been put in authority by the executive officer and there also happens to be a celebrity gold star next to my name on the passenger list.'

'Well the purser has put me in possession of this famous make of pistol from my safety deposit box and I hope there'll be a rest in peace next to your name after I shoot you.'

Such unthoroughbred behaviour is deeply troubling but should not be taken personally. Not everyone is able in times of stress to adhere to the simple niceties. Especially ocean voyaging dowagers with vast private incomes. In any case ladies carrying pistols do not need your assistance as a firearm is a great aid in securing a place in a lifeboat. And the one this lady is about to board you would do well to keep out of.

Upon Abandoning the Aircraft

Upon entering an aircraft one must immediately suppress the tendency of the mind to conjure up the inside of an undertaking parlour with its soft lights and music. Such mournful reflections not only make you unduly nervous at take off but also can alarm another passenger sitting next you who, bug eyed, is planning a sinful happy spree at destination. Such funereal images are further upsetting as you get buffeted about with the engines billowing smoke and spouting flame and the fuselage descending out of control towards some unpremeditated spot on the earth's surface. This is the time to insert a pillow between your seat belt and belly to prevent the former from snapping you in two and also to put on your gloves which will protect you when grabbing red hot handles on emergency doors.

There is nothing quite like the relief felt when one puts a gentle foot on solid ground after difficulties encountered staying up in the sky. And there's no end to the resolves and gratitude you're willing to give to anybody to get safely delivered from a big stricken motor bird. At such times it always helps to hold tight, but it is often distracting to other passengers to pray too loudly and above all don't grab your fellow passenger's arm, leg or neck for comfort as he's got his own limbs to think about and is liable to struggle unscrupulously. But god knows if a charming female is next you, it's easier somehow to die in her embrace. But be sure it's going to be a non survival crash otherwise you could be later hearing from her lawyers concerning the matter of assault and battery. And your only crazy chance of a counterclaim may be the damage her screams did to your eardrums.

Much debate accompanies the premise of whether it is safer

to bring your own personal parachute with you and jump out of a crippled aircraft or come down with it on the off chance of a miraculous landing. It is argued that as the worst happens, folk with their own parachutes pushing and shoving to make for the emergency exits, might end up in the aisles struggling with jealous unparachuted passengers which with angry hair pulling would incite to a chaos of bloodcurdling ferocity. Coupled together with folk's frantic efforts to retrieve top confidential business papers flying all over the cabin, the whole scene could be most disagreeable. And many is the man who because of the last second pursuit of a business file never required its need again.

Exiting into the slip stream is the next mad horror. Accompanied as it may be by the possible loss of every stitch of clothing on your back even including your long winter woolly underwear. Landing like this out of the sky right on the podium at some outdoor religious convention could really set you as an unholy cat among a lot of devout pigeons. That is if you manage to miss being segmented by the rear tailwings of the aircraft or sucked in and expelled as a gaseous mince by the jets. In which case your suffocation from the lack of oxygen in descent is no problem. But landing on a crowded highway and having to dodge a bunch of speeding cars is. However, providing you miss high voltage electric cables, one of the lousiest pieces of bad luck of all is coming down on top of an oil refinery chimney and getting your arse scorched. For all these reasons it may be, just as the good people of the airline usually suggest, prudent that one descend along with the motor bird.

Fortunately in most air disasters you don't know what hit you and you'll hardly recall even being out of the comfort of your seat. Yet this does not deter those unpleasant people you meet in plenty who feel their lives should be saved before anyone else's and who desperately seek certain seating accommodation in the fervent belief that it will ensure their necks in preference to the expendable necks of others. And my god how they can be spotted in the departure lounge before boarding the plane with one foot kicking their brief-cases ahead of them edging a sneaky way into position with their revolting pretence at nonchalance.

Make these kind of folk suffer. Sweep them up and down with glowering obtuse glances. Don't, when they are sitting next to you as they usually are since it's only sensible to take a safe seat yourself, let them read over your shoulder or borrow your latest magazine. Their heinousness is to be shunned with glacial implacability. And in the case of an emergency when you really do see an opening, make for it first before this bugger does, with a headlong lunge. Resting on ceremony often provides that sheer agonizing instant in which you get landed into heaven where you eternally regret ever having let that son of a bitch get in front of you. And you might warn him.

> 'Would you mind awfully, my good chap, if I sat here next to the emergency exit, I tend to gouge people's eyes out if they get in front of me.'

The Drunken Lout Loose in the Aircraft

First make sure the lout is not an insane person. These latter need sympathetic treatment as they react badly to flying and are apt to shake, tremble and rub their noses or beat their knees in paroxysms. Generally the drunken lout can be identi-fied by his loud declarations and behaviour prior to his finally getting up roaring out of his seat to go lurching and shoulder slapping down the aisles, leaning on elderly ladies, knocking over folk's cocktails and generally giving acute displeasure to other passengers as well as looming right up to their faces asking each if they have any objections.

It is quite proper for all able bodied passengers in the vicinity to jump him when his back is turned. However, wait until he's heading up to the cockpit to take over from the pilot and on the way momentarily pauses to lean in towards some feeble mild tourist persons in order to scare the wits out of them. Don't be afraid to put plenty of fracturing umph behind your kicks and punches. If the boor has hair, pull it goodo out in lumpfuls. Due to the tight squeeze of seats your footwork will be restricted but since your adversary is footloose this will slow his movements so that you can get in some deep punishing body blows at close quarters.

The more your chap is pummelled and confused the sooner the fight in him will be quelled. In his final subjugation it is best to get him spreadeagled on his back in the aisle and put two passengers standing on each one of his limbs. A wet towel stuffed in his mouth usually shuts him up. But always make sure to rip the lapels, pockets and at least one sleeve off his shiny blue suit. This helps keep him identified for later when you want the glowing satisfaction of witnessing any relatives meeting him. Which alas, is unlikely.

Such airborne incidents although irksome, build up a nice little camaraderie among those who successfully landed kicks or punches on the poor devil. And really shorten the trip. But the other worse thing about such lopsided louts is they always choose to sit right next to you. And it's best to say straight off.

'Shut up you gorp or I'll bust your face.'

Upon Being Hijacked

Should the passenger sitting next you exhibit any suspicious behaviour such as rapidly turning the pages of a magazine without being able to concentrate on any one article, keep your eyes on him. This is not a time to take chances and if his curious behaviour continues with him examining a second periodical in the same manner, jump him, making sure to stifle his cries in case he tries to alert any accomplices. You'll be amazed by the effectiveness of this out of the blue surprise attack and at how fast the chap is subdued. Although you run the embarrassing risk of beating up an entirely innocent person it certainly will be understood when it is remembered that an explosive device can result in instant depressurization of the cabin and that you and a lot like you, could be sucked out the resulting aperture eyeballs first. And that is far more humiliating.

If the hijackers are really cool customers you will never be sure you are not sitting next to one of their accomplices. As a precaution keep your eyes open slightly wider than usual, this popeyed look will convince the jackers that you are well and truly alarmed and not likely to do anything foolish for which they might have to kill you sooner than they might like. Jackers respond well to healthy respect but dislike ingratiation and fawning. Especially when they are impatiently awaiting payment of a ransom from a lot of haggling cheapskates who don't give a god damn for your safe deliverance.

As minutes are prolonged into eternities there is no question but that hijacking is hard on passengers' nerves. Especially as before these aerial highwaymen appeared, everything in the matter of reaching one's destination was going swell, even the boredom. Although you may be sorely tempted to do so, never single handedly attempt to subdue the jacker unless for certain he has absentmindedly laid aside his guns, grenades and knives. After removing these out of the way, retain a knife and execute repeated swift underhanded jabs to the jacker's belly. This is often a lonely task as none of the other passengers will normally lend a hand. But above all keep stabbing. Your bravery in performing this disagreeable dispatch will add lustre to the history of aeronautics and you might even find an airline to let you ride free foreverafter.

Upon Your Dog Killing Another

Plenty of shouting of 'Stop Rover Stop', when your dog is winning is essential. People always take it to heart when a huge killer canine comes right up to their obnoxious mutt and without so much as a condiment, gobbles him right up off the surface of the earth. Of course the owner will fly into a lather of heated protestations. And with these usually lousy kinds of people who even try to kick your dog while he's putting the finishing touches to theirs, it's best to endure silently.

Although fights between dog owners have a way of being quite enfeebled it is still likely that the owner of the dead dog will be right up under your nose, the spit flying, the fingers congealed in trembling hooks and his whole being shaking. Usually it's only necessary to give him a few shoves on the shoulder but always be ready for this small minded loser to attempt taking a lash at you with his departed dog's leash.

In cases where the owner of a vanquished dog has got so hysterical that he is even unmindful of your Rover chewing his billiards off, try reasoning that his grief is utterly blinding him in seeing the sporting side of things and that besides his little woof woof insisted upon attacking but was hope-lessly outclassed from the start. But don't let him catch you smiling or later laughing like hell when you are out of sight over the grassy knoll. This son of a bitch could come rushing after you with accusations for the rest of your life. Especially if he gets a chance to read your address on your dog's collar.

Upon Your Dog Being Killed by Another

To instantly squelch the deep purring satisfaction of this dreadfully unchic dog owner whose mutt just managed to get in a lucky but fatal bite, immediately put your hands to your face and in your most elegant accent repeat over and over.

'O my god.'

Then as this bastard approaches with all the wind of vic-tory slowly seeping out of his sails and stands entreating trying to placate you, ignore him. Until a crowd has collected. Then if the ground is dry and not too dirty, slowly crumple in a heap repeating in even louder tones.

'O my god.'

Continue to lie silent and utterly forlorn. The killer dog

owner will stand wishing he hadn't been born or having been born that he didn't have his horrible big mutt shot dead for evil long ago.

Your silent prostrate bereavement will of course elicit an offer to pay for your dog. And don't move till it does. At this point groaningly and slowly recite your dead canine's Kennel Club socially registered pedigree right back through its fourteen generations of acclaimed international champions. If this dirty insensitive commoner doesn't faint by the time he imagines the price you could sue him for, especially with the special casket and undertaking trimmings plus the monument your dog is going to get, then rise to your hands and knees. First making sure someone is holding back his killer canine. Then let out a blood curdling growl. And lunge snapping at his ankles.

In front of all the people collected and in view of your immeasurably inconsolable loss, he wouldn't dare kick you. Even when you manage to sink in some teeth. But if by some outrageous evil chance he does, grab his foot, dislocate his hip with a violent twist and flip him. The gathered crowd will applaud your little demonstration of justice in a case of dog eat dog.

Upon Being a Victim at the Hospital

When summoning attention, with everybody these days hysterically obsessed with their own problems, they are bound once in a while to impatiently reach for the wrong pill, bottle or cylinder. But it really is a hell of a terrible feeling to lie there suddenly or even slowly getting the axe instead of the cure.

To keep hospital employees on their toes and their hands on the right remedy you must alternate between being highly irritated or generously polite. A little of each following plenty of the former is the recipe. Require the nurse to sniff, taste or sample whatever it is she's treating you with. She'll give you a lot of raised eyebrow back talk but this is preferable to being swabbed with paint remover instead of a liniment. And in cases where they start amputating or taking out something healthy you still need, don't hesitate to shout blue murder and jump straight up from wherever they've got you immovably strapped down. Previous practice getting out of strait jackets really helps in these situations.

In a busy hospital when you are one of plenty of patients it is essential to make an impression. It helps to have your coat of arms largely and colourfully emblazoned on the sheet covering you. Wheeled into the operating theatre under the doc's nose, it will make him glance up from sharpening his scalpel. It also brings looks of awe from folk watching you carted by down the corridors. And provided everybody isn't doing it, this harmless pretentiousness always makes staff think you're someone different and special and it stimulates dim witted minds.

Show the doc you're a sport by winking and grinning up at him. This gives you a personality instead of being about the thirteenth bloody mass of shivering belly he had had to hack through that night with it now a god awful four a.m. in the morning. And if the doc is red eyed and seems, as you stare up from the table, to be a wee bit unsteady on his feet, laughingly offer the little reflection.

'Jesus doc, don't kill me will ya.'

Carefully watch what impression this makes on him. If he is unsympathetically unamused and turns away to take another drag on his cigarette, or worse, cigar, it is more than high time to add further to your remark.

'And by the way doc if you do kill me, I've left instructions with my lawyers to slam you and the hospital with a multiple series of malpractice suits that will make the trustees of this hospital and their endowments tremble as well as your scalpel shake so much you couldn't cut your way out of a cardboard built barn.'

It is essential that these words have the desired effect of making the doc pull himself together. It would never do if when the doc's cutting through a particularly difficult area criss crossed with major nerves and blood supplies that he mulls over your threat and his scalpel goes into a spasm of tremor on the spot. This coupled with his tense cautiousness plus the pressure of hours of operating, he could completely panic and instead of a few minor little gashes here and there, you could end up needing to have your parts listed and labelled before they could be stitched back together again. And it just might, even at this last minute, be best to change docs.

Shun physicians who have berserk tempers. Especially those heavy drinking ones with somewhat eccentric reputations. Who have been known to throw artistic tantrums in the sweat of operating when trying to get their hands around something slippery to pull out through the overly discreet opening they've made to impress colleagues. As the ruddy item keeps escaping from their fingers, they have been known to take a back handed swipe at the tray of instruments. The sound of these surgical steel tools tinkling across the floor tiles generally gets a laugh. But is often followed by the doc storming out of the theatre shouting 'God damn it', having ripped the oxygen mask off the patient's face and then sneered at the protesting anaesthetist. Although there are a lot of eager experience seeking final year students to take over who thrill to this kind of robust display of temperament, it can produce acute pessimism even in the most optimistic of awaking patients.

After the long arduous endurance of being cut, clipped,

staunched and stitched and then heavily billed it is a painful feeling to wake up and sense that a lot of operating utensils may have been left in you. The awareness is even worse when you feel around a bit and find that they have. Never take this uncomfortable situation legally lying down. Complaint should be immediate. But little will be gained from heaping bitter rebuke on the doc who will already be sheepish enough, as they hate doing things like this especially as he has a batting average, based on the number of folk who die under his knife, to keep low.

If you've decided because of the risks attendant to hospital care to instead enjoy a nice natural death in your own cosy home, remember to make provisions to stop the smart arsed relatives who are going to think you can get better treatment far enough away from their daily inconvenience as they can get you. To prevent them suddenly jumping you at all unsavoury hours of the day or night to shovel you into an ambulance usually requires the secreting of firearms.

Upon Dying of Shame

With the advent of the latest in morals this is such a slow process that it often never fully takes place. However, in some of the better class communities, decency has become so prevalent that shame can still be a hell of a burden. The first moment of disgrace normally begins with a sudden horizontal parenthesis in the neighbours' venetian blinds or twitch in their curtains. Especially when you come out with the garbage or to tonsure your lawn.

Whatever you do never try to sneak anywhere. But don't start shaking your fist back at them or revving your car engine mornings till it wakes the damned. And then with a whoop and holler honk your horn three times going out your driveway with a roar of smoking tyres plus three more honks for good measure. Instead keep your shades down for three days' mourning or, if you have that little added luxury, your shutters closed. This at least is a sign that you are soul searching as to how the hell you came to the moral crossroads, went wrong and what's worse, got caught.

It will astonish you at how slow folk are to conclude that you have paid your debt to society. And they will spend years continuing to intimidate you with their fish eyed looks. Till sometimes you've just about had enough. It is time then to set up on your lawn a sign illuminated by night with two large lettered words on top and two very tiny lettered ones underneath.

FORGIVE ME
you fuckers

This plea really shakes the neighbours and especially the ones who crawl up close to read the small print. With shutters open and shades raised again, they'll soon tire of watching you read the newspaper over your martini as if nothing had happened. And throwing your head back with a few guffaws every time you turn a page, will send them rushing to read their own papers. When they come back to stare at you again, be standing at your own window making a mute screaming face. Although this mock drollness will suggest that your ego has been kicked into total disarray, nevertheless the neighbours might believe that from the pieces, a brand new ethical correct person could emerge.

These antics of course are not possible living in a block of flats. However, luckily, you can cast such a contaminating moral pall over the whole building that it will make everybody coming and going look bad and you'll hardly as a result seem much worse. But no matter where you are the neighbourhood kids go on jeering you. Be understanding about this.

It's always such a relief when kids find someone else they think is an even bigger shit than their own pop.

If the community is giving you the silent treatment you might try sounding a few ear piercing shrieks on a boatswain's whistle as you pass by. This only momentarily makes them think thoughts of your possible mental instability. But confirmation comes when you run your remote control lawn mower right clean over a goodly section of your neighbour's gladioli. Not only will the resulting plentysome verbiage breach the silence but it will also provide you with a chance to get in a few cutting remarks.

If all else fails to reestablish you in the community, a few medical practitioners followed by funeral directors gravely coming and going from your house while your curtains are drawn and you hide, is a good touch and shows you are well and truly dying of shame. And nobody likes to kick a man when he's down unless it's the only way of keeping him there.

Euthanasia

To work in the proper spirit this painless putting to death of the suffering incurable requires folk to be at hand who genuinely like the subject. But it is not nice to assume that someone needs this without asking them first if they'd like to try it. Otherwise you'd likely find in a hurry that a lot of your unsuffering people were getting it incurably in the neck.

Once having agreed to your demise, it is not then done to resist at the last moment, as this puts a person doing you this favour into a very awkward position should others not in on your extinction walk in the door. Just make damn sure that in being put out of your misery, you are not heading for even more in the hereafter.

Posterity

Is that conception where less of you is now than you hope there'll be later when you like to think now there'll be a lot when more than likely there will be even less than fuck all. But do all you can for the sake of it because there will always be plenty of low down shabby people blackening your name.

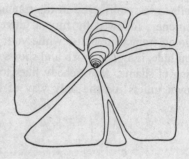

Vilenesses Various

Farting

In ancient times this feature of personal metabolism was esteemed an expression of the conscience as having just let off steam. And with so much artificial air around these days one would have thought sending forth wind from the anus was at least a bolt of something natural if not fresh. But this stinkingly difficult habit is sometimes a noisesome one as well. And in most haughty circumstances it is not nice to be caught at. But provided you keep it quiet one is not normally ostracized from good society.

There are however awkward environs for the sounding and the fuming of the fart. Namely during lectures on art, largo passages in symphonies, high points of religious ceremony, or when another is spiritually transported in the rapturous delirium of orgasm. It is however a reprehensible act in airless conditions encountered on tightly crowded public transport as well as stationary elevators. Not to mention saunas which can occasion the dreadful stifling phenomenon of the Baked fart. In supersonic aircraft it may be regarded as an extremely revolting and tiresome form of aggression, especially coming from businessmen in a hurry who should know better. But emanating from a breathtakingly beautiful woman you might, if so aromatically disposed, make no effort whatever to stop breathing.

Never admit to farting even if there are only two of you. If this is going to really make you look like a liar, a flustered pretence of searching for an imaginary gas seepage between the floorboards with the attendant turning up your own nose in disbelief at that horrid smell is a proper demonstration of innocence preventing blame and embarrassment. This ruse will of course be understood by other fair minded farters.

Who know what it feels like to be the object of unflattering attention.

The silently emitted fart has some advantage in that it gives no prior warning or instant identification of the guilty party. But such meekly brought forth fumes are, in some informed circles, held as being more odoriferous and can, as folk unmistakably grimace, produce an atmosphere of greater inelegance than those which come out with a bang. But it is never done to deliberately blast one with a window shivering report in the hope of its being less ill fragrant or that the detonation will beguile folk into thinking so.

Which brings one to those boorish and unscrupulous farters who plead that their rear fanfares are a sign of welcome and friendship. Some even going so far as to imitate the rare wailing love call of some musk secreting invertebrates. Of course in some primitive climes this form of personal gas dispersal is indeed regarded as a demonstration inviting of intimacy. But these are far off tropical places not subject to the tight squeeze of the modern up to date world where it can result in a whole bunch of people crying out in plain accent.

'Hey holy cow I want pronto out of here.'

Or in pukka.

'I say, this is uncommonly foul.'

For parlour games the fart may of course have a truly entertaining social use. There are the few who through the fine adjustment of certain muscles can use the anus as a solo instrument, even to rendering syncopated chords. If you are gifted in this respect make certain that your audience is musically sophisticated enough to appreciate this rare form of concert instrumentalization, otherwise you might be superficially regarded as being merely a filthy disgusting person.

Those possessed of the singular ability to send messages in anal morse code should in playing any guessing game devised to suit this knack, always avoid transmitting anything, which when decoded, is offensive. And there are still others, who can, by the use of a match, create minor explosions with attendant flames whose colours can be varied from blast to blast. Should this latter be your métier do please temper the discharge in a manner so as not to tremble your host's windows or injure one of the guests who of course will be put to the temerity of having to explain the origin of the hurt.

Upon initial intimacy with another, one naturally attempts a standard of fastidiousness which upon prolonged and better acquaintance one may tend to relent of. However, in the early stages one is frequently confronted with having to battle a bottled up fart. Leading as these can, to an unconscious irritability, there is nothing worse than this kind of discomfort. If unable to remove yourself from the company you are in, it is best to take the bull by the horns and effuse a ceremoniously loud one with pride. If followed immediately by the expletive

WHOOPS

which also smilingly should escape from your lips, your personal audience who hopefully will be cultivated and stylish will present you with an appreciative response, and perhaps a little patter of clapping.

In times of social distress, especially occasioned during introductions, some persons of extremely shy nature cannot for the life of them control emitting a wind upon the mention of their surnames. This is a well known disability. And for those so stricken the only defence is to continue looking pleased and brave your way through the agonizing period during which everyone is wondering who the hell it was who laid that one. Should the latter gas disperse these tentative friends, you would be well advised to find yourself a more socially confident crowd.

Farting upon meal completion in the confines of the dining room is another unfortunate moment. Further fermented by previously consumed ingredients and topped off with vintage port, brandy and cigars, which calorifics, in concert, have a way of adding not only impact to the concussion elements of the egress but also to the acerbic fustiness of its fume. Which put more forcefully means that from a full fed gentleman of long term epicurean indulgence, you could be gassed stupid and reeling before you got as far as the withdrawing room to join the fortunately absent ladies. The host should brook no delay in opening a door or window as air conditioning systems often abet the noxiousness. And as it's damn sure not a life giving elixir, the usual normal nicety of sportingly tolerating the post prandial vapours may be understandably forgone. Indeed chaps, still with their wits about them, have been known to take to hand a Meissen figurine to smash a pane or two. Menthol inhalation is suggested for those already collapsed.

Deportment concerning lovers' and marital farts will frequently depend upon their place of emission and upon the degree of emotional harmony between the parties. When an uncontrollable one threatens to let loose under the bedcovers, it is de rigueur to turn immediately upon your side which allows your trumpet to face away from your opponent. Gently lift the covers to make an opening to the outside air. Silence the fart by pressing apart the cheeks with the longer index fingers. Then with these precautionary dampers in force, let go as inaudibly as you can. Unless there is a breeze blowing, the lukewarm fume will rise harmlessly to the bedroom ceiling and if lethal enough, will there usefully asphyxiate the mosquitoes. But should you accidentally let off an uncontrolled bomb which awakens your sleeping opponent and they are maritally abusive of you, openly referring to your filthy disgusting habits, it is permissible to classically riposte.

'My soul speaks when my mouth knows the moment is too divine for words.'

In mixed drawing room conversational company where candlelight helps incinerate the fume, the fart to be preferred is a ladylike fart known as The Nert or Chirping fart. This backfired cheep, high pitched in frequency and resembling that of a small bird in song, not only can be an endearing feminine feature, but should, like The Whispering or Purring fart also practised by well bred ladies, be emulated by gentlemen who may in all their other activities be robust but prefer a refined indoor demeanour.

Out of doors, with the world abundance of leafage greenery which absorbs human gases, shrinking, the fart is now a far more significant matter than heretofore. On rural roads on windless days when you know other walkers are following, one should, on the pretext of examining a plant, release gas well off the road. For this purpose an interest in botany should always be part of your pursuits. Farting is fine while shooting but not while stalking. However fox hunting serves as an ideal milieu for the release of almost any kind of fart you care to mention as most mounts galloping across fields or jumping hedges bang out a barrage various during which ladies and gentlemen alike may let go with abandon their own prized ones.

For your own safety if not edification it is best to have some idea of the various types and brand names of wind releases which are, in circles of the most haughty particularity, always referred to as personal breezes. The Percolating fart is of little distinction except that it should never be confused with The Stammering fart, the former being popped from folk who haven't a clue to finer farting and the latter being a fart practised by folk whose personalities are predominantly amusing. The Stammering fart will mostly be met along with The Morse in diplomatic circles, but the latter is greeted with some suspicion as it is often a method of communication between spies. It is most easily perfected by those capable of The Stammering fart.

Other farts, whose names speak for themselves are The King, The Blaster, The Flash, The Fake, and The Farewell. Except for The Fake these are all fulsome without being overly frouzy and are normally met with at weekend country house parties. Especially where an interesting cross section of people are gathered from the more rakish walks of life. Take note that the high pitched Beep fart denotes someone extremely fit.

The farts to be avoided are The Foghorn, perpetrated by the boorish, and The French, this latter being only exceeded in objectionability by The Swiss and Austrian which farts are individually extremely soul corroding fetid depth bombs. The Sleeper, so called because of its slow permeating somewhat suffocating quality, is also a rough one. But nothing anywhere matches The Requiem, or The Royal, which usually silently creep out upon the atmosphere with such immense lurking lethality that one should instantly seek egress from the area and not return until someone in gear suitably protective has given the all clear especially where there has been the copious eating of sauerkraut, onions, garlic or aromatic meats and care needs be taken to protect the eyes from smarting. Needless to say the perpetrators of these, the 'R' farts, are persons of the very highest social calibre and you may find yourself in protocol difficulties when trying to withdraw from them but if you don't you may be facing medical problems instead.

Among the upper echelons of rank where haughty particularity is often times utterly dehumanizing, farting can bring to relationships a heartening reassurance of some basic equalities shared by the most privileged down to that of the most humble. But again even in this eruptive capacity, an inequality exists. For should it be a contest of gaseous lethality opposing that of mere rear obstreperousness the upper classes can, with their caviar fed pungencies, knock hell out of the cabbage stuffed commoner herd.

Bodily Stench

Persons who sally forth in their daily pursuits especially those attempting advancement among the semi executive gang around the office should try to avoid stinking to high heaven. For after a preliminary sniff or two most people will not stand near enough to you to listen to what you're saying and you could end up getting not only hoarse from shouting but also fired.

The worst fumes are carried in continually worn undergarments which absorb rancidities from the vaporous areas under the arms and between the legs. In warm enclosed places these reasty gases finally rise up through the rest of the clothing. However one can by prolonged fermentation carefully cultivate an acceptable odour out of one's overall fulsomeness which resembles the not unpleasant smell of new mown hay.

But, except to maybe some insanely deprived and perverted yokel, a stranger's reeking armpit is usually not a source of pleasure to another. Pits shaved of hair which then have deposited upon them chemical deodorants can without malice aforethought literally gassify anyone who may have been merely in pursuit of a little sexually stimulating musky fume. Where the pubic hair is shaved from the pudenda either for laughs or lust it too should be kept free of artificial smell killers and, in general, like all the body bifurcations, should be rinsed clean more than once in a blue moon using only the purest of soaps.

If you are happily possessed of such endearing and entertaining eccentricities that others will suffer your stinking aerodynamics for the sake of the love of your company, then it is only fair and reasonable to warn folk when the socks covering your feet have long since gone stiff and green through continued wear. It is well known that seating such persons in front of the drawing room fire with their shoes off and their footsies toasting has produced a stench which can make a Requiem fart seem like a tea rose. As this often necessitates the redecoration of the room as well as a revarnishing of the furniture, don't hesitate to heap abuse on the vile, low, shabby, inglorious perpetrator. If you do have the nerve to bring a wash bowl for such feet make sure after transporting the socks on the end of a shovel, to bury them deep.

Bad Breath and Toothpicks

Vile odour of the mouth is a feature of folk greedy beyond belief and generally deeply obnoxious in other respects. And far away from such sorts you should be delighted to keep. However, sweet breathers may communicate to the unsweet by megaphone in the following manner.

'Sir, forgive my timorous approach but I know you would like to forgo the litigation attendant upon my injury occasioned by fainting backwards when close up blasted by your exhalation.'

Although there is no reason to avoid breathing on people who have, in other multiple respects, just finished pissing and shitting on you, nevertheless if you just so happen to be a nice guy who is stricken with unwholesome breath which sends everyone you meet reeling back ten feet, your fumes can be disguised by chewing down plenty of raw onions and garlic. The reek of these strongly scented root fruits delights certain folk when detected on the breath. Should you end up being crowded with a gang trying to lean a nose into your face, the taking of curiously strong peppermints will help deter these admirers.

Foul mouth conditions are also incited by putrefactive aggregates in teeth fissures which can also lead to your being one hell of an ordeal close up. And this is when your toothpick should be brought into play. Avoid exerting leverages with the mouth gasping open thereby permitting the sudden springboard effect of spitting out debris which may strike another intently dining nearby right smack bang on the lip or eye. In which case, instantly proffer your regret.

'Hey gee fella, I really am sorry, let me wipe you off.'

Expect however, some unappreciative folk to respond as they gather themselves up to beat it.

'Jesus, stay away from me.'

Or in pukka.

'I say, good god, you tiresome person, don't you dare.'

But often the whole nauseous spectacle of your digging around in your oral area can be pardoned by the slow removal of your gold toothpick from its monogrammed ebony case. This ceremony can often stimulate your onlookers to a moment of appreciative awe. As they figure you out to be a really hot social item. But beware this useful instrument doesn't get hysterically jammed into a deep cavity where it ends up sticking out of your feeding aperture in the manner of a worn vampire tooth.

In cases where your mouth can be opened like a mountain cave, it is permissible to reach in a hand and by neatly exerting a long fingernail, hook out foreign matter. Do not however screw up your face with loud sucking noises of pleasure following such engineering feats. All fragments so removed should immediately be very sprucely catapulted off the thumb by the index finger into an area hopefully free of people or polished antique surfaces. But most folk now, having seen you in action, will have enough sense to duck.

Other Orifices Ears and Enemas

Nose picking is a highly satisfying habit mostly practised by folk of high intellect whose further sterling qualities are indicated by what they do with the pickings. Although the eating of these is the quickest method of disposal it must be regarded as off putting to others. But nonetheless, your possession of superior brains is thereby demonstrated.

As a practice it is worst regarded at meal times and least while on safari. But the practice of dirty little habits like this one only serves to entrench one class while severely demoting another much lower one. For nose picking by the haughty and particular during important board meetings, conferences and dinner parties will be looked upon as a not too unseemly eccentricity whereas for you it will undoubtedly result in your being stumped in a social strike out. And the corkscrew use of the index finger with the elbow upraised will further expose your humble origins and hopeless future.

Nostril disgorgement by a gentleman should if outdoors be done at the kerb, bending over and placing the feet apart with the left foot slightly forward. Take a deep breath while holding one finger across the left nose hole and mightily explode the contents of the chamber into the gutter. Repeat with the right chamber taking care that the matter flies out and does not land on your fabrics or drip down the wrist where it causes discomfort under the cuffs. Upon both nostril barrels being discharged, stand upright again and take in several deep breaths of fresh air but make sure some son of a bitch isn't about to roar by through a puddle in his roadster after a recent rain storm and leave you drenched in spatterings of mud.

To rid olfactories of blockages indoors, a plant pot may be used. Both your aim and discretion can be improved by putting your head in under the plant leaves. If your host is one who wants you to feel really at home you could start hocking and spitting all over the place but it is only fair to confine yourself to using his table and bed linens. At other times, and especially when you'd like to signal your presence or make mild protest at a polite gathering, a prolonged noisy blasting away into a beige silk monogrammed hanky although unhygienic is effective.

Sneezing is one of the best ways of widely spreading your germs if this is what the people around you deserve. And may explain the distinct suffusion of pleasure felt. It is also the moment when one is closest to death as most of the body's involuntary actions are temporarily suspended. Your beige silk monogrammed hanky is again the rag to be brought forth here. This kept slightly secreted and gently scented beneath the shirt cuff will be a sign of your elegant particularity as it is whipped out to arrest your nasal tempest which suddenly makes you the centre of attention.

Ear and arse holes are places into which people look after they know you well and want, somewhat earnestly, to know you even better. The condition of these chambers may indeed be regarded as an indication as to how folk's other holes are, if this is something you want urgently to know without wanting to pry. Therefore these places should be kept up to scratch. Especially your arse hole which will often be referred to throughout your life, either as a place you are speaking from or where it is suggested something might be shoved.

Enemas are normally taken to improve the buoyancy of the spirit and to render patently false that frequent accusation that one is full of shit. And there are far worse ways to spend a half an hour. Ideally the undertaking is administered by buxomly attractive smiling ladies and a penile erection at this time is regarded as an unavoidable reaction to internal water pressures and no apologies are necessary. Although some regard it as thrilling, the procedure should be taken seriously and giggling and risqué remarks avoided. Crested or monogrammed bathrobe and slippers are de rigueur. Under no circumstances should games of discipline be played at these times.

Hocking, Spitting and Throat Clearing

Although ladies object to these noisome operations first thing in the morning when you are bent double with lungs rattling like the shutters of a haunted house, nevertheless it is essential for you to void all dross, dottle and drast from your breathing system.

Hocking should start with an inhalation of breath together with robust snoring sounds well back in the nasal passages. These acoustics when made with practised purposefulness will lose their normally disgusting overtones. With the phlegm thereby nicely rounded up and compressed, it can then be expelled by the puffed out cheeks with an explosive force which, along with the optimum angle of elevation, can send the missile great distances. Accuracy may be improved by the mouth being curved in such a manner as to resemble the rifling in a gun barrel. And a thrilling sense of personal achievement is felt when you can land spit in the most amazing places and spot hit various targets or narrowly miss others.

Indoors, firing into a silver or gold plated and crested hand-cup embossed with your usual or latest crest is to be preferred.

A spittoon similarly decorated is not without playful advantage if filled with a ringing bell when used. But outdoors as a boulevardier it is de rigueur you aim for the gutter always and high over the heads of any pedestrians.

Throat clearing is an excellent method of signalling your presence or demonstrating your impatience or boredom and invariably denotes a man of action. But concert soloists and stage actors abhor your attendance in the concert or theatre hall with a life endangering insanity. For your own safety and so that some temperamental artiste doesn't come vaulting right at you over the footlights and orchestra pit to throttle you right in your pricy seat, wait till you're back safely in the lobby where you can freely indulge your oesophagusical pontifications.

Smoking

This is the most laughable thing yet done to the innocent. Who keep paying to do it. And except for gentlemen in black tie with port, taking a puff of their cigars after dinner upon the ladies' retiring, it is a most offensive habit. Smoking denotes a weakness in, if not a total collapse of character, which is enfeebled even further when you stop smoking.

The desperate spectacle you present as a smoker may be countered by sporting stylishly elite smoking accessories, which can be popped dazzlingly from your person and flashed before folk, who, when eyeing the platinum, golds and embossments gleamingly enclosed by amphibious animal skins, think you're really the very latest in human delectability not to mention hot shit.

This agreeable aura, when discussing high finance, or even low, at least lasts till your opponent lights up, using his own old fashioned box of matches, which, if you have even a particle of sensitivity, ought to make you feel like the really awful snide person you are. But there can be propitious moments in the confines of a first class hotel with its first class staff which might redeem you when you take out your cigarette and hold it aloft a moment parrying in your conversation and which weed as you place it to your lips is instantly lit by a hotel servant's match. When this happens it is permissible to blow your first smoke ring right around your opponent's head. He will think you really frequent big time hotels like this one all the time.

Even though you don't look tanned, healthy or self assured the manner of your taking out, selecting and holding your cigarette and disposing of the ashes can nearly make you so. Flicking the thumb up at the mouth end is less elegant than the discreet tapping of the forefinger on the ash end. But doing the latter when you feel like doing the former will turn you into a suspicious looking person. You should also beware where you drop ash or snub out your cigarette especially in the people's houses who have their secretaries secretly taking down the names of people seen dropping ash or dinching cigarettes on antique surfaces, carpets or parquet floors. If you do this contemptuously it is a sign of small time shabbiness and you may find a nearby bombast taking you to task for it.

'I say sir, you've snubbed your cigarette out with your heel upon the carpet.'

'What's it to you, you meddling old fart.'

'Nothing except a gentleman uses his toe.'

Plate and Knife Licking

This is a satisfying ritual and is not only to be resorted to when one is not able to get a further helping. Although widely ridiculed as bad manners, it is permissible if delicately executed and demonstrates more than anything else your enjoyed appetite as well as your thrift.

While holding the plate surface vertically in both hands well up to the face, licking should begin from the bottom upwards with long perpendicular strokes and never from side to side. Make sure not to cascade gravy all over the place and it is not done to take bites or allow your teeth to make clashing sounds against the crockery. Also do not attempt to talk to your dinner partner while lapping. Unless you are merely grunting replies to her long discourse on gardening. If your partner however, is wide eyed at your antic don't panic. Your host and hostess, as formal etiquette requires, will, as the opportunity affords, also lift and lick their plates. Should less well bred folk show surprise at you and ask.

'Where the hell were you brought up.'

Come right out with it.

'Sir I was raised in poor and humble circumstances and

I regard your question as an insult to all those still in the sacred embrace of deprivation.'

If you are still around at another meal time you will find the guests sneakily looking on all sides wondering who the hell should start licking first. And as an example for the hesitant to follow, take up your knife and making sure the cutting edge is blunt, wrap your tongue around it. This warms the blade for the easy cutting of butter.

Shaving

This daily repeated ritual of symbolic castration does help to keep chaps in their place who might otherwise become roaring out of control gorillas. Those who have the audacious vanity to let sprout side burns, moustaches and the like only call attention to their self advertised symptom of testicular curtailment. Pressing a sharp blade or other cutting contraption close over the facial and throat skin as well as across the jugular vein is even more hilarious than it is barbaric. Although the cuts and abrasions regularly caused thereby serve as a nice series of distractions of a morning.

Being yourself a bellowing hairy ape accosted by some clean shaven rube who comes bleating at you with his bare face hanging out with the question.

'Hey why are you growing that beard.'

Always reply in pukka.

'I say, you unpleasantly unfortunate radoteur, I'm not doing a thing. You're shaving every day.'

Baldness

This shiny head top condition is highly prized by some ladies. However it is true natural baldness which counts. If you are not blessed with this it is abhorrent to fake it.

Upon sporting a toupee always disclose the fact. Not only will the revelation overcome people's desperate grabbing urge to see what you appear like without it but also will remind folk that the rest of you is indeed alive and living. Of course there are those perverse mummies whose phony hair is the most vigorous looking thing about them. And these obnoxious, as they sidle up, are usually attempting to find out if the conversation promises a profit.

In church and while changing motor tyres, the toupee may be used as a kneeling pad but in cases where a waiter's sleeve

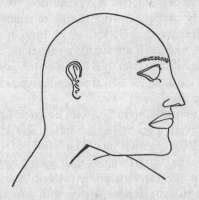

pushes your custom made hairpiece down over your eye or it is knocked off into your caviar, always have ready your response.

'Eureka, you've uncovered my gold.'

Dentures

These are awkward appurtenances often leading to embarrassment on wedding nights and sometimes fatal choking in folk who cannot control their amusement and swallow them backwards laughing. And to those who know you best with your dentures in, it is an affront to then appear toothlessly smiling broadly without these brightening up your mouth interior and puffing out your cheeks. Even though certain people delight in regarding naked gums while imagining the naughty antics that therein can be played.

Although it is not too nice to use your tongue to lark loudly with your removable teeth, it is permissible for persons who are extremely comic in telling stories, to remove full upper and lower dentures and clack them by hand in order to imitate another mouth in an amusing exchange, the words of which are supplied by your own jaw operated toothless orifice. However, some acting school training here will help prevent your looking a real nut.

When eating scaldingly hot soup be careful this does not make you spit out a denture with a splash. Should this happen the false teeth in question should be fished out with a dessert fork and dried in your napkin, as their poking up presence left in your soup dish can look positively evil. And always turn immediately to your dinner partner with an apology in case she has suddenly been ashenfacedly transfixed.

'Do forgive me madam exploding out my fake masticators like that, but the soup is deucedly hot.'

Dandruff

Is the sign of indoor folk who through scruffy hair habits provide themselves with something to scratch while they are thinking. Although in plentitude this brightens the hue of dark fabrics across your shoulders it is not nice when given off in a choking cloud when someone claps you on the back.

Promiscuous Pissing

Piss pots, which previously afforded great convenience as one was able merely to roll just a fraction out of bed and pee without hardly leaving one's mattress, are sadly disappearing the world over. And where less than splendid living conditions prevail, the abominably filthy English habit of using wash hand basins and sinks is often resorted to. In such situations, ladies, who as they climb up on these to squat, have often been known to bend many an hotelier's and host's toilet fixtures right off the wall.

However there is some quaint pleasure to be had from convenient peeing and upon being interrupted by your host in taking such relief infelicitously in his sink or out his window, do avoid the conciliatory words.

'Gee I'm sorry you caught me doing this.'

Nor should your feeble reply be.

'I sort of was bursting at the seams.'

Rather come clean with the more charming.

'Gee John, this is just a dirty little habit I've got left over from my unprivileged background and damn if I can correct it.'

But as a host who may be long troubled by the secretive unpleasantly shabby habits of guests, it is prudent upon occasion not to mince matters when catching a visitor red pricked peeing in your inappropriate plumbing or in other areas not requiring such wettings.

'Why you filthy sneaky son of a bitch.'

Or in pukka.

'How utterly thoroughly vile of you.'

If he is anywhere near normal, your unhappily guilty guest will greet your spoken chastisement with nervous laughter, and may even, while still streaming pee, attempt to rehouse his penis. But as most of your indiscriminate pissers are usually colourful personalities and are disposed to believing their company highly valuable, they will consider you blessed if they piss anywhere they please in or around your house. To early dissuade him of this fervently held opinion, advance menacingly immediately. But if he foolishly remains in the throes of peeing do be careful that his flow does not go in a more damaging direction. Some folk's urine can really be corrosive, especially those chaps of extrovert demeanour.

Other perpetrators of urinating indiscretions are usually introspective insensitive guys who upon taking exception to their wives' guests gathered at cocktail or dinner parties will, without preamble, pee in full view of all present and sometimes, should he also take disfavour with the music, visit his urine upon the gramophone turntable. Such pissing behaviour may also be witnessed performed by the aesthetic in spirit at office parties as a way of letting business colleagues know of one's deep mercantile dissatisfaction. And if you have peed óff or on to a high executive's desk, will generally result in your being fired.

Although relieving oneself upon a prostrate drunken friend with a view to restoring him quickly to a sobering upright position is permissible, and albeit that this method achieves remarkable effect, it also invariably arouses the pissed upon to an insane anger and you run the risk of being chased for miles with an unbelievable hostility.

Pimple and Black Head Squeezing

Upon inviting your companion to peruse parts you present for squeezing, it is not then done to cry out in pain attendant to these activities. And such satisfying pastimes should normally be confined to folk who know each other well although it is also one of the fastest ways to get to know someone better.

Those who upon sizing another up, feel that with their applied effort, their opponent's blemishes could be remedied, should never then and there encroach to start contusing the area with fingers without first asking.

'Do you mind.'

If one wants to take advantage of such treatment offered, it is only fair that one swallows any umbrage felt in this bitch's suggestion of one's blatant scruffiness.

In all occasions upon exhibiting the results of such squeezings to the squeezed, do give them adequate time to scrutinise such as it is extremely irritating when these exudate extrinsics are whisked away prematurely.

Discarded Hairs and Nails

Unless left for the purpose of finding if your room has been adequately cleaned during your absence, cast off body ingredients such as toe and finger nails, head and pubic hairs, are gigantically off putting to others who come upon them sprinkled on or stuck to toiletries, carpets and the like. Always summon the management and point to the offending particulars as confronting such is always a reliable sign of second rate accommodation.

Discreet and comely people carry their usual crested small silver caskets for the deposit of their done with horny sheddings. Other less equipped folk may use appropriate envelopes. These must not, however, under any circumstances save the most dire, be mailed and then only to the most detested of enemies.

Solitary Masturbation

One should guard against interruptions which the silence prevailing during the enjoyment of this habit frequently occasions. Always have ready a quip to offer the person looking for you so that he may exercise an unembarrassed discreet retreat. Avoid however, the phrase.

'I'll be right with you.'

As it leads an intruder with the intent of loitering, to reply.

'O no, that's all right, please take your time.'

Upon coming upon someone engaged in this practice,

always demonstrate your broadminded urbanity with a smile and the brief comment.

'Ah you're in good hands.'

In cases where you feel you may be of assistance ask politely.

'May I help you.'

And when you do not want someone's aid, respond.

'Thanks but no thanks, I'm nearly coming.'

Or in pukka.

'How extremely kind of you but I do believe I am already about to piquantly shiver my timbers.'

As the deposit and stain and accumulative stale stink of masturbatory deliquescences is not of the nicest, all good chaps having a pull should be mindful to provide napery to dispose of same. To leave grume upon one's host's sheets is a chink out of one's haughty particularity, unless one hints next morning at breakfast of an unrelenting night of stormily sailing across a sea of wet dreams.

The Vicissitudes of Clap

With so many of your varied folk these days vicariously engaged in the clearly discourteous activity of unceremoniously clapping others up, some preventive prudencies are called for as it is often too late when partners the morning after have the audacity to hand out doctors' prescriptions. However always accept such offers instantly as the microbe in question is eager to set up house, and therein, amid brand new luxuriance, be long termed entrenched.

If you are guilty of clapping everybody up and news of your activity gets around don't expect to be greeted with effusive delight on the rialto. Especially from a victim who has in turn dished out a dose to an unsympathetic spouse. However do be civil in the face of such acrimony and bow back your condolences.

If you are contentedly not yet clapped up, it is wise not to let clapped up people ramble round your house. Even the lurking thought of clap you can't catch off a doorknob unless you are overly intimate with it, and with which you are damn sure not about to be, is unpleasant.

Upon Being Clapped Up

Take solace that a whole host of historically prominent folk precede you in suffering this annoyance. But once it is medically confirmed you are in this condition, the feeling is unmistakably not nice. Besides having to release one's evil doings to a doctor who must, for the sake of protecting society from you, record such facts, you are conscience confined to cohabitation with others whom you believe, to the best of your knowledge, are chronically and hopelessly clapped up and to whom another dose will make little difference. However, this continual friendly little extension of hospitality to your respective microbes which, through interbreeding, pathologically improve their species, can keep you both clapped up forever.

Naming Names of Clapper Uppers

A moment of embarrassed hesitation will normally confront you upon releasing identifications to public health authorities of folk who have clapped you up or whom you have clapped up. This is always a sad occasion except for those unprincipled enough to relish throwing in a lot of innocent names for good measure.

There is of course nothing quite like the tension encountered when a stranger confronts you with a notebook upon his knee taking down your details of this embarrassing disease. Be calm when innocently accused, and treat it as practice for the day when it might be true and you can release your own shit list of folk who although they might not have the disease, ought to have it.

Upon Confronting the Clapped Up

If you are yourself presently free of the troubling condition, try not to overtly wipe off door handles or drop utensils just touched by folk branded with this venereal ailment. But when in greeting a hand is offered by the clapped up for you to take, do then prevail upon your courage to state your position unequivocally.

'Gosh if you don't mind I'd prefer to shake hands when you're cured.'

Or in pukka.

'I'm frightfully sorry but I cannot possibly allow myself to touch those morbidly infirm.'

If the infected lady is devastatingly exciting and you cannot overcome your ardour this presents an awkward situation. Before you jump her and hoplessly contaminate yourself, do ask the victim to sit down to see if you can work out a medical treatment schedule during which, with a suggested proper employment of prophylactics, you can meanwhile nearly wholesomely enjoy her body.

Now and again you will meet certain tweedy ladies who may not take well to such a proffered tactic and your face may suddenly be stinging from her instant slap followed by her challenge.

'How dare you.'

And it is permissible to riposte to test their effrontery for hollowness.

'Holy cow, baby, I don't want a dose dampening down my one eyed snake.'

Or in pukka, using your most soulful manner.

'Madam, I do beg not to displease, but it is you I am after, not your disease.'

If madam still fumes with umbrage and takes lunging swipes at you with the broadside of her patent leather handbag, plus screaming and scratching and trying to kick you in the balls while drawing everybody's attention as she chases you all over this elegant hotel lobby, you may then safely assume that she is not harbouring the affliction.

But it is quite possible that her moral outrage will continue even after you take her to bed, where just as you are nodding off to sleep after succeeding in giving her a ruddy royal rogering, she may, being close up, leap fist pounding and face ripping upon you. Following all this if you do get the gleet, at least you'll already have a recently familiar doctor near at hand to treat the additional affliction.

Upon Placing the Blame for Venereal Infection

Do this as soon as you can and admit to nothing. The first person getting in their accusation stands a better chance of appearing innocent. This finger pointing game is extremely ancient, with folk and races accusing and reaccusing other folk and anybody and races right back across oceans, continents and even further back into the dawn of time. Where indeed there may still stand some poor bastard at the mouth of his cave

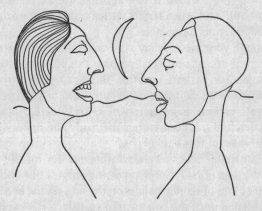

with his limp prick bandaged and hopelessly too Cro Magnon to point the blame even further backwards at a guilty looking bunch of passing orangoutangs.

It always sounds better but alas is no better to have caught the clap from a social superior. However there is no need to be selective of the social class to whom you give it. But venereal disease does quickly lower your social tone when the rumour goes abounding that you've got it. Although movement in elite circles is no certain protection it does lower the risk of gleet, merely because the unsavoury news of your having contracted it travels faster. And you may suddenly be left standing utterly alone toying desperately with your canapé at your next and perhaps your last refined cocktail party.

The Syph

This bug can by slow corkscrew propulsion, move either backwards or forwards, turn on its axis, or stand on its head nearly wagging its ears. It can also tolerate all kinds of inclement chill. And when it gets settled nicely in your tissues, its dislodgement is formidable.

Although your income may avail you of the best treatment, neither your accent nor social position can prevent infection. With some Far Eastern varieties, these can even thrive on your huge arse given injections of cure. And to kill them you might just as well make your will as seek further prescriptions. Therefore it is deeply ungentlemanly and unladylike to hand out doses of this kind of pox.

Upon introductions, keep a weather eye out for the moth eaten type loss of hair. Sores appearing chronically unhealed and other kinds of reprehensibles on the skin should be viewed with suspicion until the opponent has satisfactorily explained their harmless existence. And then make damn sure they haven't been out to and recently returned from some no account wog land in the Far East.

When pieces of arse are requested from persons who actually exhibit chancre, immediately refer to your appointments diary and exclaim with disappointment that you are unendingly booked solid. And direct them straight out of your house. Poxed up folk, principally of the loutish races, like the whole world to be poxed up with them. Be particularly careful of scruffy persons who are unmindful of their appearance. Impromptu gang bangers, holy orgy rollers and others looking for frequent and varied pieces of flesh interminglement are especially to be treated with caution. However if you don't have long to live these admonitions may be overlooked.

The Crab Louse

Sometimes these little monsters in profusion about the private parts and hooked into the skin at the roots of the hair, can wreak more havoc than all your enemies formed into a well financed corporation the whole purpose of which is to get you. Because of their incredible engripment and optimistically prodigious reproduction abilities together with their slow crab like deliberate movement whenever they feel like a stroll, these infuriating little bugs can really settle in for the long haul upon your person.

If as you lie there with this sweet thing in your arms and you begin to itch where you have not itched before and you wonder what in hell is chewing around your pubic hair follicles, it may already be too late. These bloody bugs with their nearly unbelievable migratory tactics can travel like trapeze artists right across her hairs to yours. And even though you only hesitate for brief additional seconds before leaping to your feet to dump mild methylated spirits all over your privates, these buggers may have already established their vice like toe holds in your crotch ermine.

Increased itching will now be profound evidence that these mighty little mites are presently abroad on both your persons and grazing away. And unless you are still jumping all over the room with your prick and balls scalded by meths, severe silent embarrassment will exist between you and your partner. If your present life style happens not to be of the best, it will now suffer such a thoroughly despicable mortification that it could socially relegate you for good and always, especially if these considerable creatures get up into your eyebrows where others without any optic assistance can see them crawling around.

Do not stupidly try dilute acids or hot baths, scorching yourself in the process. And aside from the disenchanting greasy handful this presents to another, do avoid the long term attempts to smother them with vaseline. It takes real he man chemicals to make these diminutive parasitic brutes pack up and vamoose. Your persistent scratching or undergoing a generally intolerable fidgitiness around your pubic parts is usually a dead giveaway. Watch carefully for such folk and although you may take comfort from the fact that this noxious animal is feeble at jumping, it is nevertheless prudent to stand well clear of infested persons.

Since the most efficient remedy stinks to high heaven you will now find it necessary to come clean to all within smelling distance that you have the crabs. The fairminded will of course allow a moment of grace before their departure to acknowledge your explanation that you are under the speediest first class treatment for these beasts' removal. Some callous folk however, ignoring nostrums, have been known to try to deliberately shift the entirety of their creatures onto someone else and astonishingly this sometimes works with the result that entire office staffs end up having to be fumigated.

As low standards of hygiene are favourable to their multiplication, the pubic louse can be found in more groins than you can shake a stick at. In its epidemic form whole armies have been reduced to a bunch of scratching idiots unable to man mortar or cannon, with the opposing uninfested enemy able to charge unhindered to cut the loused up to pieces.

The Flea

If you do not detect this fantastic leaping animal by feeling its distinct assaults in a rising manner up and down the legs which immediately leads to scratching, then you will certainly notice the parasite's presence as it drills for blood. And anyone, even those of the most haughtiest particularity, may be guilty of harbouring these little buggers.

If, as with some hosts' mutts, you suspect these ready to send a cloud of fleas upon your person, don't hesitate to let fly with a boot in their direction. In the case of Irish wolfhounds or other monsters who might bite your foot off, make a run for it. But when taking tea with an elderly old lady who may sometimes unavoidably have these jumpers skittering about, it could be mortally wounding to her to withdraw. Rather pretend your discomfort as an old recurrence of piles. And a long vigorous walk later through the countryside will often rid you of the heaviest infestation.

On aircraft or trains when it is obvious that it is one of your fleas which has jumped straight onto the open clear page of your winsome fellow passenger's fashion magazine, immediately call the insect by the name, Igor. If your highly attractive seating partner hasn't screamed or clawed her way over you to escape down the aisle it will astonish you how this conversational opener may get you places. Even into bed where, if you suspect it wasn't your flea who jumped in the first place, it is recommended that you become immediately beware of the crabs.

The Sneaky Doing of the Reprehensible

Aside from the permissible brightening up of your day with merry pranks played on others, such as replacing shave lotion with vinegar and cat pee for perfume, there are also the moments when your own wilful choosing to do the decent or indecent thing to the weak and unprotected is at hand. This is the supreme testing time of a gentleman's thoroughbred nobility.

Secretly kicking small kittens up in the air or giving little children continued thumps on the chest till they cry are things which although they deeply satisfy your rotten inglorious inner nature, do mark you as a bully. Although better folk agonize in an effort to arrest this weakness of the personality, there are those who, presenting themselves as the dignified quintessence of respectable trustworthiness, still persist with relish in committing these unseemly vilenesses.

Therefore when about to do something dastardly cruel and immeasurably sneaky especially upon a defenceless creature, double check that no one is looking. And further make sure there is a good supply of helpless victims before you allow this to become a deeply ingrained habit. It can rapidly be cured by taking up bullfighting.

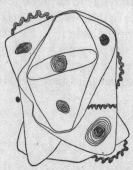

In Pursuit of
Comfortable Habits

At the Breast

It is here that one first picks up many principles not to mention bewitchments that later become impulses of a lifetime. Pinching, punching and pulling at the breast and then swinging on the nipple as one gorges down mother's milk cultivates one for future daily routines which can be full of pleasure, charm, delight and gladness. And it is permissible for the infant to screech and sock away baby bottles or other mammary substitutes. For not only do such imitative contrivances blunt the palate but they can addle your digestion for a lifetime.

In the Cradle

In your first private domain, don't just let anyone come and rock you. But if it is your mother always try to acknowledge her presence with a smile. When feeling discomfort from crapping and peeing in your diaper, howl until you are properly cleaned, dried, powdered and freshly attired. Remember you did not ask to be born, but having been, you now require certain civilized comforts.

In Your High Chair

In addition to your silver spoon, the first thing folk will try to put in your mouth is food that you do not like. This unpleasant practice stubbornly insisted upon by mommies who think they are giving you what's good for you, can later in life make you forever insensitive to exotic foods. It is therefore allowable to push this unwanted grub away and should attempts to make you eat it persist, to then knock the purée of spinach all over the place.

Upon Throwing Objects Out of Your Perambulator

Many of your adult pleasant pastimes such as tennis, baseball, hockey and cricket not to mention lacrosse, golf and skittles, are first indoctrinated in this manner. But in unloading various objects over the side of your pram, elders do not seem to understand that this is your way of first learning and then exhaustively testing the laws of gravity. If you lack objects to throw or if those items already thrown are not returned in a reasonable time, it is permissible to bawl loudly.

Beginning Your Daily Adult Day

Start with a good night's sleep which is usually made more restful by hanky panky with the old lady or in wrestling with some new carefully selected piece imported for an occasional change. But be careful a thunderous finale with the latter does not knock the pastoral peace out of your bowels.

Your cheerfully decorated breakfast tray should be served as near to eight a.m. each morning as possible along with one upper class and one lower class newspaper to get a balanced view of the news. The fare should be ample, slowly consumed and accompanied by melodic symphonic music. Honey, whole-meal bread and delicately flavoured butters do much to enhance the light breakfast, whereas buckwheat cakes, maple syrup, sausage and bacon act as centre pieces for the more robust repast. Coffee, tea and other beverages should be of their natural best and in no circumstances ersatz.

Beauty in the forenoon prolongs life and benefits one to stomach annoyances during the rest of the day by putting one in better mien which in turn tempers acrimony elsewhere in the world. If park lands, fields and cattle are not available, then breakfast should be taken while overlooking a garden or flowered terrace from which people other than those tending it, are excluded. In utterly restricted urban circumstances a tastefully illuminated screen with a suitable scene will do. Especially where deliberate unsightliness has been provided by your nearby thoroughly loutish neighbour.

Toilet

Breakfast should continue until the gentle stirring of the bowel beckons. This ought always to be the most profound moment of your day. With your entire body corporate at total ease. It is expedient the crapularium be provided with selected reading matter concerning one of your more favourite subjects. And have close at hand a cool taint free glass of water. All household noises should either be extinguished or kept to a minimum. Do not let telephones, tax returns, marriage partners or spirited offspring interfere with your utter calm at this time. It is essential you or your servants make sure all doors and entrances to your quarters are closed and firmly bolted. And until one is bathed, showered, dried and dressed, no displeasing matters should be allowed to infringe one's attention. A bell of course can be provided to be rung for the all clear when household activities may recommence.

Your bath anointed with suitable oils must be drawn with the temperature just allowing for some additional hot water. Your immersion should always last until such time as you feel inclined to shampoo your hair. Following which private parts are then washed boisterously fore and aft. Dry yourself vigorously starting with the toes and then upwards over the rest of the body. Conduct this in the manner of a robust daily exercise.

If abroad from your premises and suddenly forced to seek a crapularium available to others always carry an easily affixed OUT OF ORDER sign to avoid the horrendous aggravation caused by someone either banging to gain immediate entrance or getting down on their knees to start staring up at you from under the door at where you happen to be sitting shitting.

Upon Clothing and Appearances

The preservation of peace of mind should be foremost in providing for indoor or outdoor social intercourse and there is nothing more devastating to one's optimism than being present in the right place in the wrong attire. But if sufficiently possessed of your own personal significance, you can make a whole bunch of other people at the gathering collectively feel wrong. Especially when they have the presumption to patronize you with overtures to make you feel right by approaching you at that magically convivial moment prior to heading in to dinner.

'Hey I like your suit. Where are you going, to the races.'
'Presently perhaps, but immediately beyond this point in time, you may find yourself wandering dumbfounded in search of your jaw.'

Impertinence, cheek, nerve and sauce must without pre-amble or argument be thoroughly stamped upon. And in order to highlight your true gent's disposition in meeting with such insolence, always instruct your servant to provide some small blithesomeness, such as a nosegay, when laying out your day's toggery. Polish your pate too with a soft cloth and if you are inconvenienced by hair, this should be vigor-ously brushed and a parting, which worn on the left during the day, should be worn on the right during the evening. This always acts as a test as to how observant and ultimately fond your friends are of you.

With the single exception of when it is worn by a cattle breeder, the coloured bow tie although a nifty neck item should give cause to view the wearer with suspicion as a parvenu, a know it all and an extremely slippery customer. And all throat fripperies are to be avoided by any seriously intentioned chap taking up the position of long term gentle-man. Flamboyancy however is not altogether to be forbidden, but ought nevertheless to be confined to one's hanky, a mere contour of which should be showing. Anyone caught adopt-ing a recent fashion before it is sufficiently abandoned as old hat is not to be countenanced. Nor are those who sport various tightnesses in the middle anatomy of their tailoring and take up wide footed stances right in front of one's offended good breeding as if they were the bee's knees instead of an ass's arse.

Upon Having One's Ultimate Kit

The fortified castle ranks first in residences as providing the last word in the matter of one's appointments. Your draw-bridge, moat and battlements put the loutish on immediate notice as to your wherewithal to dispense much what for to any of their let's try that. However, more modest abodes containing certain principal prerequisites can still allow for the best in the pursuit of one's comfortable habits.

All estate walls and fences should be man proof. Folk whom you do not want to see always like to make themselves known nonetheless even to the extent of being chewed up by your hounds. For poachers, interlopers and the plain nosy who attempt a last desperate grab to haul themselves over your barricades, a load of buckshot tickling their fingernails can make them awfully nervous. Plus they begin to regard you with a new kind of hatred based upon look at all he's got and I've got fuck all and he'd even kill me for less.

It needs to be that your acreage is secluded by evergreenery so that neighbours cannot witness you dressing, undressing or handing your wife a deserved fist in the gob. Your front entrance should be flanked by gate lodges and your drive laid with suitable small stones of a blue grey tint which bang up under a vehicle's mudguards. This gives your guests a sense of arrival and expectation which exceeds any disappointment felt when you send down word that you are not at home. Strategically located spying slits will provide a view of your rejected callers as well as a place from which to discharge fire and shot when required.

It is an everyday essential that you are not importuned with tiresome matters till after you have sufficiently taken in the beauties and graces of your estate. The morning hour of ten thirty is a proper time to venture forth from personal chambers. Descend by the main staircase and pause to take in the seasonal floral displays on the landing. Following a stroll through the main reception rooms, observe the barometer readings in the front hall and take note of the wind direction from your wall indicator. Choose your walking stick, and with your secateurs in your pocket, exit and stand in front of your door. There you may remind yourself yet again of what fun it is to have such a lot of money.

Beware to provide small pavilions where you can hide and meditate when finished taking flower cuttings and walking your forest pathways and gardens. And now with your appetite for lunch quickened, your first social intercourse of the day should take place. With music of some pomp and pleasant circumstance, your guests should be summoned to convene to a major room suitably outfitted with armour, trophies and even bogus ancestral pretensions. This not only awes visitors but allows you further chance to take your sense of self importance seriously. Nor is anything more exciting for a host than to hear from newcomers entering.

'Jeese get a load of this.'

Or in pukka.

'I say, it's too enchanting.'

At guests' arrivals or departures station your butler in the hall. Two servants should attend outside at the mounting or dismounting of vehicles with one assigned to door opening and apparel arrangement and another to load or unload appurtenances. And upon their requirement, extra footmen ought to be taken from their weeding chores in the garden, as it is aggravating to get entangled reaching for something you cannot find in an enclosed small area of a vehicle or in pitching head first out of it with an umbrella or ski pole up where you do not want it.

Nor is anything more inhospitable than letting a guest risk a rupture toting the big bags he's brought. Unless of course the bugger is preparing for a long stay to test your largess to the limit or upon leavetaking is planning to remove a sampling of your silver as a memento. In which case your properly goggled and gaitered chauffeur presently tabulating mileage or scrutinizing his map for new scenic routes, should, as you do not want yourself to be fussed with such trivialities, slap a pair of silver handcuffs on the bastard and slam him down into your cellar dungeons to reflect upon future better manners.

The tableau of shooting parties smashing woodcock out of the sky can ameliorate your lack of haughty particularity if you are not in the possession of white forest cattle for your parklands, or moorlands to provide deer stalking. Having a horse or two provides an excuse for your making an occasional socially worthwhile appearance in riding garb. However these creatures are notoriously unpredictable but with luck you'll perhaps avoid the odd disagreeable experience of being thrown through your orangery windows with cacti spines intruding up your whammo scalammo.

Although they encourage trespassers, small ponds, lakes, rivers and streams well stocked with bird and fish life add immeasurably to the elegant upholstery of your estate. Disconcertings do occur in climes where snapping turtles gobble down your prize ducks or the latter quack quack and shit all over your swimming pool. But except for venomous reptiles, the sight of rare or prized animals taking their ease will always get a stream of praising emphatics from your guests, in the avalanche of which you can be self effacingly modest.

Indoors, make sure each wing is staffed fully and that there is ample athletic gear, and surfeit of towels, and facilities for squash, real tennis, ping pong and fencing. Roll the red, scare the squeamish and other daring nightly entertainments should also be catered for. A small theatre with footlights where charades may be played will thrill guests deprived of acting careers. Also encourage activities which call for a frequent change of clothing throughout the day. This not only allows for lecheries but prevents guests' boredom with each other as they ornament themselves in new exciting colour changes and sartorial settings.

Large roasts groaning on sideboards look well in country houses as do heapings of salads, fruits and vegetables. And dining off different dinner services plus your chef's triumphs will keep visitors' palates appetized. And in this respect do not overlook changes of your table silver and match covers. But no guest should be allowed to stay long enough so that he falters in the expression of his constant delight at the repeated splendours. Although it is to be permitted that between his outpourings of superlatives, he can, for the sake of seasoning, mildly inject a cautious word.

With a frequent fresh new change of people, you as host can spout your same old stories and hackneyed statements, without unduly disorbiting your neurons in the search of something different. Accumulated years of this finally make you sound utterly endearing. Which in itself becomes yet another perfection. And it is but left now to make sure that the collective impact of impeccabilities does not obtrude to become an imperfection which in any way is the least bit tiresome.

The upshot of your splendours in life reaching their zenith in this manner, is not only for the trembling pleasure to be had when guest book signing time comes with all the happily written signatures, but also the relief enjoyed in knowing that about you it may never be said, as it is often said about the poor slob who, in trying desperately to preserve appearances, has merely ended up with a broken social arse with the statement after his name.

'He was rather without his kit, you know.'

Visiting Your Banker

At executive level your banker is a judge of men. And in order to present yourself as a credit worthy man of power and purpose it is necessary to demonstrate the proper respect due money, the source of so many pleasures. It is an occasion for simple conservative dark clothing. It is also worth all the discomfort and fuss to wear garters. You will realize this when you see your banker's eyes frequently deflect downwards to assess the evenness with which your sock is pulled across your ankle. In addition to your shoes being black and plain and your laces leather, your suit ought not to be tight nor too striped.

Always avoid the cold grey sweat on the forehead and upper lip as well as quivering and quakes. When hand-shaking, keep it just a jot less vigorous and not overly pro-longed. And immediately seek out an architectural detail of the building to comment upon. Most better banks are rife with structural embellishments, and your banker who spends much time indoors, often enjoys a little informal discussion regarding his daily surroundings. Especially in these days of swindles, computer frauds and robberies which continue to keep banking a hazardous occupation. And it is wise as well as more gratifying, that before finding out how you stand finan-cially, you first convince yourself that matters must be hope-lessly appalling.

One note of caution. Do not take your banker to an ex-tremely expensive restaurant to there discuss an even bigger loan than you already have, as when you are finished lunch-ing and have paid the enormous bill by cheque, your banker may in prudence upon his return to his office, stop payment on this.

Visiting Your Bank

At teller level this can be a distinctly uncomfortable habit as you can end up facing some smart aleck behind his or her shiny counter that you may have taken some time to reach after waiting in line. And it is now and again a rather nice touch to make these folk gasp at the astronomical amount of a deposit or withdrawal.

Insist upon your bank notes being crisp and clean and supplied in denominations which can provide for their convenient disbursement. In this demand be careful not to disturb the peace to such an extent that other tellers think there is a bank hold up in progress.

At the Barber

An unavoidable intimacy exists in the cutting of hair and your barber therefore should be carefully selected. Done fortnightly with warm moist anointments this is a nice way to spend a semi cloistered hour of late afternoon. And along with an attractive lady's delicate hand fondling manicure, it allows for a spirit boosting pampering.

It is your hair and head. So take immediate command of the situation from the beginning and announce your requirements in a firm unquavering voice. If you are desirous of a certain length of forelock or fullness about the ears, state these exactly. But remember it is very unchic to yell or scream should the barber take an unscheduled snip or cut into your surface skin. And it is just as effective to simply announce.

'Jesus Christ Almighty, will you watch it please.'

Or in pukka.

'Good Lord, do be careful, you cunt.'

But, many a further ignominy has been perpetrated due to overt nervousness of an hysterical kind occasioned when a barber who has taken an instant dislike to you momentarily thinks you may have underworld criminal connections. And you will get wind of his feelings if his automatic clipper suddenly slips and makes a gleaming highway right down the centre of your skull.

Prolonged low growling is the most effective response to barbers who think they have all the very latest suitable styles for you up their sleeves which in ten minutes will make you look better than the stupid way he infers you've been looking all your life till now. But should the son of a bitch go so far as to intimate that he has cut the hair of numerous people better than you, this is heinous. And you are quite justified to assume your full standing position to straightaway bare your teeth and continue growling. Barbers on this kick are usually looking for an opening to further get smart and sassy with a patronizing sniff down their nose.

> 'How do you want it styled, sir.'
> 'I should like it styled to look as if I did not just have a haircut given me by some inept bastard just cashiered from Barber College.'
> 'Hey what an attitude. Would sir then like the most recent style.'
> 'An old style will do.'
> 'I see, well if that's how sir wants it.'
> 'That's exactly how sir wants it.'

As many murders have been committed by scissors and razors and with your jugular right there at his elbow, it is essential that a barber be watched for quiver, stagger, wibble wabble or other telltale signs of mental instability. A mere slip about the ear or a trembling indecision across the throat could spell if not the end, then a particularly unpleasant maiming. And do not be lulled into political or religious discussions. Which, since you are sitting there stupidly enveloped from the neck down in a white sheet, or worse, adjusted backwards reclining and ready for a close shave over the adam's apple, really places you at a terrible disadvantage.

However, despite the fear that one might inadvertently awaken any manic tendencies in one's tonsorial attendant, be not so intimidated that you do not insist upon proper precautions being taken to prevent clippings seeping down your neck, shampoo being smeared in your eye, waters too hot or cold being doused on your head, the hair drier scorching your skull, your scalp sproutings being loosed in handfuls with an application of the barber's own special preparation to cure your dandruff, or your ears being burned in attempts to singe your hair ends with a flame to stop them splitting. In the end it might be better, if she values your life more than your appearance, to let your presently enjoyed female companion cut your hair and not risk the temperamental whims of an artisan clique notoriously prone to being set off in explosive bouts of butchering mayhem.

At the Chiropodist

Footwork is always of the utmost importance and most often needed when least expected. And it is essential that your tootsies proceed upon all surfaces without discomfort. A professional should always be consulted upon the toenails being required to be shortened. At the same time, corns, callouses and other bumps on the foot may be dealt with and it is de rigueur that you feign interest while you hear a discourse concerning the skeletal structure of the foot. As you will usually receive attendance in their little cubicles your hosiery should be fresh and your feet free from stink.

The Shoeshine

Where this has not already been given by your hotel, man-servant or wife, it should be undertaken as soon as possible following your stepping out of doors in the city. Seek a practitioner who takes pride in his work and avoid those who smear unmatching leather lacquers and waxes along your socks. To encourage the best from the artist, look admiringly down at pleasant intervals to assess the progress of the shine. Providing you are wary not to walk smack into an obstruction, the perambulating appearance of your gleaming shoe tips as you put your best foot forward is yet another way in which the spirit is uplifted and attests to your gentleman's haughty particularity.

At the Porno Show

When this is a film, be careful upon entering the cinema to see that your flies are securely closed and then wait at the back until your eyes are sufficiently accustomed to the dark so that you can see where you are going. Your behaviour here is important as you will be surrounded by college professors, corporation executives, members of the peerage, celebrated society figures and socially registered folk. To brush up against someone, perhaps a member of your country club, stimulated beyond control, could lead to an embarrassing engrapplement blocking the view of people sitting behind. When such a confrontation does occur, it is proper for you both to remove quickly to the back of the cinema where, under an exit light, the two of you can stand fervently in a prolonged dialogue of explanation.

Upon finding a suitable row of seats, preferably where no one else is sitting, make your way slowly into this. Avoid rows where someone appears to be playing with something in his lap. Keep your eyes off the screen until you've actually taken your seat to escape being suddenly mesmerized by an extremely saucy antic. And make sure that all roving hands and other people's fingers are absent from where you are about to sit. For even your attempt to twist an appendage painfully back out of your way in the direction of its owner can be misinterpreted as an invite to a little furtive sadism. For single folk who do not want to be annoyed or otherwise interfered with, a big spoon together with a large carton of ice cream is an ideal cooler when dolloped upon some interloper's head.

It is not nice to groan loudly with pleasure at a particular scene which especially excites you. Others who may not be lusting in the same way will openly resent it. Plus, your groans instead of being recognized as genuine sexual craving, may instead be taken for a heart attack, the frequency of which is quite marked in porno shows.

During live dirty exhibitions on stage, the performers should be accorded the usual courtesies given legitimate theatrical actors. One should not talk in the audience, chew gum loudly, make a noisy entrance or leave before the final spectacle. Such disgustingly filthy theatricals require immense emotional fortitude and craft where a lack of sincerity can lead to a total collapse in performance. Do not demand excessive encores or curtain calls as these sometimes can so exhaust the leading man that he finally needs a stretcher to get him off the stage.

There is a time and place for everything and when accompanied by a companion, don't grope in each other's lap no matter how uncontrollably stimulated. This is unfair competition to the players whose own caprices may at that moment require an audience's undivided attention. And your nearby fellow socialites, many of whom will abhor this behaviour, may also look upon it as being very bootless and unhorsed. Leading as it might to a wild grabbing clothing tearing mêlée, with the entire audience losing not only their modesty but any patrician demeanours they were seen to possess on admission. Needless to say, such occasions become pickpockets' jamborees.

At the Massage Parlour

To make what otherwise might be an embarrassing outing into a pleasant one, it is as well, as with most things in life, if you keep your place in respect of attending these. And do not go if it means you are travelling some distance upwards or downwards out of your price or social range.

The best time to choose for an excursion, especially as it makes for a striking contrast, is following a black tie dinner at your club. Upon digestion being complete, take with you only as much money as you think you will need. Upon removal of your club insignia and decorations, carry yourself purposefully and erect into the premises and do not be furtive nor apologetic. As since when was it a crime to get your rocks off.

Where there is a choice of ladies, don't dilly dally changing your mind about five times. Before any stripping occurs discuss terms and services. Drive a firm hard bargain. As you undress, although you should relax and enjoy, do not strew your clothing all over the place or behave in an obstreperous manner. But as you are paying a fee for services don't vacillate in demanding the full degree and nature of the sauciness you have negotiated for. And never accept a bored tired couldn't care less attitude, even though you may be your hostess's forty fourth client that day.

To start the ball rolling, especially if you're unbearably nervous and shy, it is permissible to use the old fashioned inquiry.

'What's a nice girl like you doing in a place like this.'

Although considered hackneyed it is always a hopefully flattering way to begin your conversation. But should she reply.

'Making money out of hard up jerks like you.'

Don't hesitate to show your injured feelings, following which you will often get a further response usually describing the support of parentless younger brothers and sisters back home. Or the pursuit of her own studies in the fields of zoology, anthropology and the fine arts, that is, if she is not helping her husband to get through medical school.

In your physical graspings, behave suavely. Do not paw her but instead inquire with a civil tongue.

'How about a feel baby.'

Or in pukka.

'Mademoiselle, may I in a prehensile manner familiarize with a choice contour of your arse.'

Should she shrink from your suggestion.

'Don't take liberties with the merchandise you old fart and speak English.'

You are perfectly entitled to plaintively plead.

'Come on give the boy a treat.'

Upon the lady flattering you as to the considerable dimensions of your engorged private appurtenance.

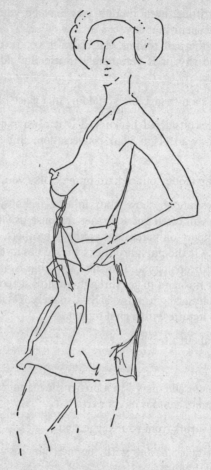

'Gee dad, yours is really something.'

A gentleman umpires such compliments by a referral to known authorities on the matter.

'According to Gray's Anatomy I am only modestly over-sized.'

In surprise confrontations with a relative or someone you know from back home who may be plying her trade and is assigned to you as a customer, much spiritual distress can be prevented if you both recognize immediately that you are just two human beings caught up in a very human situation. And who knows, by letting come what may, this nice little additive of familiarity may breed more satisfaction than it does contempt.

Upon Saucy Assemblages

Although the quality of the enjoyment can be best estimated when the frivolity shows signs of sweatiness, it is proper when invited, to come well bathed.

If the naughty consortium is happening in a climate where the folk are not already nude, then upon the other guests' removing their clothes, it is to be preferred that if your body is not beautiful, for you to wait till the gathering is sufficiently roused by bodies that are, and then disrobe in as tantalizing manner as possible. If your clothes in the process are ripped from you, consider this entirely flattering. But naturally everyone will make a bee line for the most beautiful bodies. Do not be dispirited by this. Merely tarry till there is general engripment and then make your approach and have upon the part or parts you fancy. Should someone else be using it, firmly squeeze in close and await your opportunity. Do not grab, shove or tear. This can cause pain if not injury to someone elsewhere in the mêlée who in turn could maim another especially by biting. Remember that for the most part the cohesiveness of the naked entanglement is achieved by the most delicate of interlockings, the abrupt breaching of which could result in a wholesale cacophony of pain.

During these gratifyingly humanitarian conflagrations of

lust a sense of total involvement with everyone putting their backs into it is at all times to be desired. But when something highly distasteful is being perpetrated upon you, it is permitted to object.

'Hey cut that out.'

Or in pukka.

'O my god, how horrid.'

But show your sportsmanship with a little fake laughter which will also prevent your opponent taking offence. However, should this be interpreted in the heat of the moment as encouragement, a hard sock of the fist is usually required to knock some kind of courteous restraint into your antagonist, especially where the latter is already driven wild by the debauch.

Upon attaining your orgasm, it is ill mannered to simply lie back luxuriating in your own selfish purple contentment while someone somewhere is still desperately struggling to reach theirs. And always be ready to good naturedly lend a hand or the appropriate part of your anatomy where needed. Often this can have the favourable effect of reexciting you. But do try to recognize when you have had enough. There is nothing more unflattering than to see someone gormlessly groaning and flapping about still seeking one last thrill which is quite beyond them to enjoy.

As such intense paroxysmal group excitement admits to much physical invasion of privacy with the attendant risk occasioned thereby to jewellery, cash, bonds not to mention other movable assets, folk are advised to confine their orgiastic shenanigans to people similarly socially situated and where possible, restrict themselves to the confines of their estates. And to further make sure that their household policy fully indemnifies them against guest injury which is bound to come from the abandoned antics and all kinds of wild negligence present especially in swimming pool frolics.

Indoor servants in attendance upon these foregathered caressings should wear livery if not attired in their usual household garb. But in undertakings where their nakedness is required, a suitably identifying mask decorated with your racing colours may be worn covering the face. But a note of warning here. Undue familiarity with members of your staff in the pursuit of such prurient doings in large households can lead to a chronic breakdown in servant discipline. Especially among the better looking of your retinue who may on becoming a sudden object of attraction turn shirty and take signal liberties in the most outrageous ways throughout the mansion and in their final insolence will sometimes stop working altogether. When such a situation obtains do not leave your wine cellar keys or cheque books lying around.

In the Proximity of the Horse

Horses are dangerous creatures and should be treated with respect at all times. Never stand near their heels trying to show how used to horses you are. It is a good way to take a fast gallop to kingdom come. Keep your face, shoulders and hands out of biting distance. Not only can this quadruped remove such appendages but also by rearing skywards give you a fatal trouncing with forelegs.

But upon this animal you can ride into and enjoy almost any indoor or outdoor society, and those into which you can't canter are only worth considering if you've got some intellect. Having the replica of a horse on your tie, cufflinks, motor car or head scarf helps lend you a nonchalant air of superiority which can be further enjoyed when it infuriates those bootless and unhorsed.

As your obsession with the equine animal continues to develop, along with increased indulgence of the allied sports of racing and riding to hounds, you can finally even become totally intolerant of folk who profess other interests in life. Which should give you plenty of time to oversee the polishing of your tack, the cleaning out of your stables and the grooming and foddering of your horses.

By buying the world's best steeds you provide not only very racy social pursuits in various members' enclosures, paddocks or bars but chaps who would otherwise not give you a smell of the steam off an infrequently worn sock, will upon your having a winner, nod and smile to you after the race. And when your mares foal you can expect many appreciative and expectant oohs and ahs from your friends.

Horse induced injury entitles you to a kind of unforgettable fellowship from your other horsey folk. It is not unknown for a chap on his crutches to give your crutches a friendly bang with his. And there is nothing more approved of than the sight of you departing a great country house with your equine bowed decrepit legs feebly carrying you tottering down the front steps followed by the admiring glances of other presently uncrippled members of the hunt in the doorway. It is also a nice touch if the one or two hounds you constantly keep in the back of your car, howl with welcome at your infirm approach.

At the Stud Sale

This auction arena requires one to be suitably dressed and wool in the form of cavalry twill or tweed is the customary fabric. Any flashy recent urban style will, as it ought, be the object of silent ridicule.

Having taken your seat around the sales ring, two matters

require attention. Firstly, when a horse being paraded in the enclosure manures, it is refined to look down at your catalogue. But upon the man so assigned coming with his tray to collect up the droppings, it is permissible to witness this skilful process.

The second matter is in regard to stallions' erections. Often as these temperamental creatures are led in they pick up the stimulating whiff of a muskily beautiful woman seated ringside. And it is not done for a gentleman at such times to overtly stare at the lady to see if she is watching the massively huge engorgement. Although it is permissible to glance over the upper rim of your sales catalogue to see which other ladies are looking. And since stud fees earned by these horses are often far more than can be obtained by most chaps for similar duties, women who turn their attention away at such times are advised that this may spread not only the impression that they have a distaste for one of the most important parts of their husband's or boyfriend's anatomy but also that they don't know what horse breeding is all about.

At the Races

It is highly unchic to be late for the races. Always dress, shower and cohabit in time. Providing a private box for yourself and friends where you can all drink, eat and cavort in comfort is stylish. As are visits to the paddock prior to each race. Where you can make sure the horse you are placing a bet on shows no overt signs of sleepiness or incapacitation, and also this little excursion gives you a chance to rub shoulders with other less affluent race goers who love to gawk at the horse proud likes of you giving last minute instructions to your jockey.

Betting should be done in an offhand manner and for the

fun of it. It is rude to gamble and attempt to gain thereby or to get hysterically enraged or thoroughly dispirited when you lose. But if you are one of those lucky persons who come up with one winner after another this can cause severe resentment among your friends especially when you can't muster the self control to not guffaw in their faces as they consistently are taken to the cleaners.

Upon overhearing any rapidly spreading unpleasant gossip about a certain lady at the track, this is your moment to be elite. Raise your eyebrows, and if you are wearing a fedora, put your head back so that more light reflects upon your face and state in no uncertain terms to the shabby cad disseminating the vile lip.

> 'Sir I don't know how you come to be, but you are in polite society. Please don't therefore give me cause to knock you down or, should we, protocol forbid, ever be too close for me to punch I shall then tweak your nose.'

Upon Choosing Your Racing Colours

As these hues can have social ramifications do be careful about your choice. It is preferred to be practical rather than ultra stylish. Although there are lots of your upstart yaboes who will attempt to make a splash brandishing their dyes. And thereby outrage old established racing families whose colours have graced the better tracks and public horse events for many years.

Upon being accosted in places where you are sedately sporting your colours upon your person and a disdaining irate dowager finger points with the accusation.

> 'Sir you are wearing my ancestors' racing colours.'

You may, since this is quite an untoward reflection upon you, reply in rough house.

'Get stuffed sister.'

Or should you feel the complainant so entitled, respond in ultra pukka.

'Forgive me madam, but I am hopelessly colourblind and upon your pointing out in detail the offending chromatics I will tear same if not suddenly from my person, then most immediately upon the first most decent opportunity.'

Upon Entering Your Horse for the Derby

Do not do this unless your nag is really ready for the big one. To have your horse lag hopelessly about eight lengths behind as an also ran, last to last, is a heinous bit of mortification certainly deserved and certainly increased by the many of your racing friends who will never forgive nor forget this piece of arrogant albeit mettlesome wishful thinking.

If of course you have done this vaingloriously embarrassing thing out of desperation for a little current turf recognition,

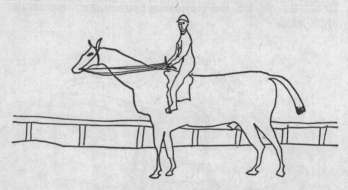

then be sure to have a high powered binoculars and be the first to know when your horse drops hopelessly behind. And make your way quickly from the stands. Your programme raised to the side of your face will allow you to pass un-recognized by other race goers of your acquaintance. The safest place to seclude is often the parking area where on the floor or seat of your motor you can lie low under rugs.

Should your horse have shamed you in the last race and you are unable to slip away unnoticed in the exodus, the gentlemen's crapper may be your best hideout till such time as the course clears. By bringing with you an enthralling thriller to read you will also be able to skulk long enough to avoid those owner winners who tarry in champagne celebra-tion. But beware, horse racing being what it is, there may always be some nosy bastard hanging over the transom trying to get a look at you sitting in your sins, or to see the tears streaming down your face. It is advised to stay away from any major horse sale for at least six months and allow nothing sartorially to hint of your racing colours.

But if before the race, your jockey takes the diabolical liberty in the green elegance of the mounting enclosure to cast an aspersion upon your entry, and as you are aware of your horse's sensitive nature to know when folk profess little faith, it is permissible to remonstrate to his cavil.

'Why the derby.'

By pausing with your riposte till you have laid a firm tap of your shooting stick upon his knee cap.

'Please keep your lightweight opinions to yourself and out of hearing of my horse who clearly finds you gravely distressing to listen to and will have you to thank if he runs last.'

Polo

Whamming this willow root about, watched by admiring parasoled ladies, is an invigorating way to spend an afternoon. Make sure that your ponies are at all times well watered and fed and kept in the absolute peak of condition. It is extremely bad form if during play, any of your mounts drops dead beneath you. Unless of course you have just scored three goals in succession.

Never flaunt your high rated handicap. Nor on the ground of play, swing your mallet in such a fashion that it could wrap around your opponent's neck and clean wipe him right out of his saddle. Side swiping is acceptable but charging your pony broadside onto an opposing player easily leads to disputes. And while dismounted during pony changes rigidly control your temper as it is never done to be part of a punch up along the sideline.

The expense of this sport will throw you into the company

of hale outspoken, hard drinking but eminently socially acceptable chaps. But do beware of impostors who frequently are to be encountered unhorsed and unashamedly wheedling invitations to the intimate but dazzlingly splendid dinners held by the partakers of this ancient game. Such mountebank adventurers and chancers are often recognized by their proclivity for too obvious tailoring, ornamented shirtings and shoe buckles. Never hesitate to accost these bogus straight off, even though they pretend to dance attendance upon you between chukkars by making themselves useful proffering sweat towels or holding reins while you mount. If you can start a fight with one of these Joe Superficials, so much the better, someone of course will always hold you back but the gesture is sufficient to publically register your fatal disapproval.

Recreational Amusements

Depending upon your physique many happy pastimes can be indulged which not only keep you chipper but make you admired and envied among your weaker and more decrepit friends. For increasing lung capacity and broadening the shoulders, water polo has few equals although this aqueous contest is constantly interrupted throughout by referee's blasts of whistle occasioned by constant fouls, which if you are a real tiger might frustrate you.

However, for those able bodied but of weakling appearance, one of the easiest ways of giving a sporting image is to be frequently seen with an armful of tennis rackets to which you refer as bats. Armed with these and with your sword arm in a sling you can even show up at a fencing tournament and make a virile impression upon the splendid looking curvaceous ladies who are usually thick in attendance. And whose acquaintance can be made by inquiring as to who was just penalized for corps à corps.

To indulge your devilish, sadistic and brutal tendencies there is nothing quite like croquet on a sunny afternoon outdoors. This simple lawn amusement will cause much disagreeable rancour especially from players who like to keep strictly to the rules and proceed about their officious little ways. And one can gratify the disgustingly pleasant delight in banging their ball a mile out of bounds.

After which you might want to rush indoors to some ping pong, otherwise called 'pingers' and by some 'pongers'. The really big guns at this game make it impossible for just average players not to be blasted off the table. But don't whatever you do resort to shuttlecock whose participants display a most disagreeable self importance and will often let doors slam in your face. As an antidote to such types, squash will put you amongst fellows who shoot straight from the shoulder. And except for an odd chap with an unhealthy amount of unreleased rage, which may require you to be well practised at ducking, it is a healthy activity.

Should your frond like physical condition restrict you to seated table sport, remember that chequers is a good game with which to make the unpractised look stupid if you know a few basic stratagems. Chess, however, is a friendship breaker but does keep the mind agile. And although this pastime can make momentary giants out of quite ordinary folk who can succeed in little else in life, it also produces people who with an overinflated opinion of themselves as players have been known to upset playing boards, punch opponents and attack onlookers.

Gaming

This dissipation should only be undertaken in the evening and requires the company of a beautiful woman in whose adoring smiles you can bask as you collar in vast amounts of winnings. If you want to appear at your best, chemin de fer and baccarat should be chosen. Sit poised, head held up. Do not slump in your seat or give any impression of sneakiness. Gather up your winnings without smiling. Nor does it do to leave a casino laughing your head off after breaking the bank as it can give the impression to all the crowd watching that you are a rank amateur who has never won anything before.

In divesting yourself of huge sums in prolonged losing streaks which you can ill afford, it is time for you to be, above all other things, urbane. Show not a trickle of saliva from the corners of your mouth, or when you are really skint, let your jaw drop in utter humiliation and defeat and walk cowering away from the tables. The loneliness after losing is something which can disembowel the soul and never at such times have firearms near at hand.

Greed being a most intractable desire, gambling for gain demands vast reserves of self control, and so while standing at the slot machine waiting impatiently for it to dump jackpot coins on you and while sporting the incomparably stupid look that has overcome your face, it is not done to try to cheat this machine by the use of devices or tricky little shenanigans to thwart the honest performance of its mechanism. Especially is it bad form to pull the machine over and as it lies floored and helpless on its side to then rain kicks into its glass and metal areas.

Those who oversee gambling enjoy a very nervous occupation. And if their constant facial tics, jerks and spasms put you off your game, don't hesitate to request such chaps to stand a little outside your range of sight. But be careful of giving offence to these habitués of this profession for they go nearly out of their minds at the merest slight and instead of just a tiny distracting convulsion or two in the background they may end up shaking and quivering all over the place.

When high rollers hit town watch out. They displace small time gamblers even to getting their bookings in hotels. Stand clear of these big spenders at the tables. For it is here that they reign as kings. At craps they are ebullient, and real regular guys. And throw the bones with suitably accompanying words.

'Come on baby, buy daddy a new pair of transplant balls.'

You might if you feel particularly robust of the moment, suggest.

'And you need them pop.'

At the Arena

In frequenting contests where blood and gore is likely to splash the spectators, do contain your enthusiasm. There is nothing more disenchanting than seeing a lust thirsty onlooker at a dog or cock fight wildly gesticulating and sweating or indeed adding to the stench by nervously breaking wind during these battles to the death. Therefore do not eat odoriferous methane makers such as sauerkraut, garlic, hot dogs, peanuts or beans prior to or during attendance.

To lend an air of daring to your appearance, always carry prominently upon your person up to date appurtenances which identify you as an aficionado but do not overdo it so that you look like an itinerant snake oil peddler. Be aware of the proper way of showing your pleasure and displeasure. It never does to be singled out in a refined crowd for having committed a faux pas, such as letting go with a loud squeal in the hear a pin drop silence of a prolonged cliff hanging rally during a championship tennis match. But if you really make it a good old fashioned scream, your outburst will help relieve everyone's tension and they along with the players will be grateful. You may even be applauded but don't count on it.

At major boxing contests there is much to be recommended in being seen arriving ringside just before the main bout and trading mock uppercuts with former heavyweight champions and backslapping promotors. But never climb up through the ropes and jump uninvited into the ring to shake the gloves of the pugilists who in their pre fight tension will usually pleasantly accommodate even though they don't know you from Adam. A further boorishness is to wipe your feet in the rosin of a neutral corner and then raise your arms hopefully for cheers from the crowd. These antics, however, will instil caution in your neighbouring onlooker, who at prize fights, is usually itching himself to get into fisticuffs.

At the bullfight, to increase one's enjoyment as a spectator, it helps to know the intimate workings of the corrida de toros. And this is best done by taking a little private practice yourself. Rehearsals can be had free of charge walking the streets pretending matador status with quick sidesteps and a little cape work with your top coat trembled provocatively at the more rapidly oncoming pedestrians. Some of whom will immediately catch on and in a suitable crouched position will erect their arms and hands in a pair of horns for you. When this makes you utterly fleet of foot you can try your moments of truth on passing cars, even to skilfully crossing a speedy many laned highway with a series of passes. And if a motorist has sufficient nerve to stop and get out and accost you for being a risk to other road users, you may by further inciting him with verbal abuse, be given the opportunity of improving your agility by having to dodge a few fists. Following which you should then be fully capable of jumping the barrier of a bull ring to distract a totally out of control bull who has grievously gored the matador. But on no account await toro's charge recibiendo.

The Season

Wherever these rage, involving as they do, regattas, steeplechases, boulevards, festivals and spas, take in as many as you can since it is always congenial in a suitable setting to let people know you are alive, and if not smiling, at least kicking. The pageantry occasioned by the sunshine on ladies' large hats and bare backs plus the throngs of toilet watered people flowing to and fro without boor or lout anywhere, can inspire one to feel that all the world reposes rich, nicely mannered and safe from harm. And quietly inviting you to pursue a deserved longevity.

Be the day mud deep inclement, the spirit still can soar provided you have your boots and umbrella. And to give yourself a sense of belonging, if you don't belong, it is an advantage to sport the garb appropriate to the day and to make sure your binocular case is not plastic. If it is, get rid of it as soon as possible. Even though folk may look mesmerized by who's winning, they have a naughty habit of allowing one eye to tabulate the quality and origin of your various accessories with the wholesale purpose of relegating you good and proper to your social station with as much prejudice as their eyeballs can encompass. And this can make you feel unseasonably rotten.

Reunions

Seeing all those passé clapped out dead beat faces from yester-year can sometimes make you think you're on a roller coaster to the grave. And if you've really made it big, these get togethers of the old gang can become tight lipped occasions of resentment. It is rare that bygone comraderies can do any-thing but tempt you to drink more than you should or make you utterly teetotal with distaste.

But if you have suffered failure and defeat and have mustered the courage to crawl out of your little niche where you've been hibernating over the years cooking with your lonesome skillet while hearing of the marvellous things your long past peers have been doing, here is your chance to make up for it. Straight off get laughingly stinking drunk. You'll make the assembly a happy one by letting everyone refer to you as look at that poor son of a bitch. Especially if you choose to wear only the old school insignia upon your nudity while stomping your war dance hullabaloo and singing the old school song. It will of course be your farewell reunion.

On Safari

In order to get entirely away from it all for a stretch during the year and between the de rigueur international dates, this kind of outing does the trick. Rakish informality should be the key note. Without of course looking like something a big cat dragged in. Make sure to have all your guns overhauled at the hands of a good gunsmith and pack the proper quality khaki and the essential pith helmet. Indeed take several of the latter which will, while you wait en route on piers and train platforms, give you the admired air of the long practised professional jungle explorer.

The sharing of hardship and lust while on safari brings either a deepening enrichment of friendship or a life long detestation. The latter often occurring when a member of the expedition party keeps borrowing your wife or other custom made crested utensils and equipment. But even though sorely pressed you should not forgo observing civil behaviour. And following the day's kill and photographing of trophies, in which it is extremely bad form to smile, always appear showered and spruced in fresh bush regalia at your host's tent for dinner. This prevents what is commonly known in the jungle as going native. Which is only permissible when you are captured by a hostile tribe.

During inter tent itinerary keep a weather eye out for the sudden appearance of revenge seeking man eating beasts.

Nothing is more galling or makes you all look more like a bunch of amateurs than when someone gets bitten or mauled just as everyone is convening for pre dinner drinks. In the case of dangerous snakes be aware of these at all times. It is quite an unsettling experience to be confronted in the middle of one's personal toiletries with a death dealing serpent, particularly while crouching to defecate, when it could be curtains for you to move the merest muscle. While asleep special precautions should be taken against the constricting reptiles as these can wrap right around you and while you may dream it is a loved one, it can quickly be too late to find it is not.

If you have a tendency towards cowardice in the face of savage rampaging wild beasts make this known early to the guide or your host. There is nothing more inglorious than when, with your safari colleagues enjoying a leisured moment as an unarmed party of spectators, you have been appointed and are expected to divert a charging herd of marauding elephants or water buffalos with a single well aimed shot and instead you drop your gun, turn tail and beat it. It also makes your appearance absolutely painfully unhappy at the evening drink before dinner. That is if any of the other members of the stampeded assemblage escaped.

Having attended one of the better educational institutions it is possible you will come upon an old dark complexioned school chum who has now taken up his hereditary position out in the bush. Observe protocol and remember most jungle chiefs and potentates dine black tie at a high table, bush or no bush. They are usually seated before a large gathering of their own people who perform erotic dances and other gyrating entertainments to the rapid beating of tom toms. Never clap to demonstrate your appreciation but it is polite on these dusty occasions to look up from your plate and smile whenever the rhythm of the drums noticeably changes. Nor be overfamiliar with His Royal Highness as you had been accustomed during undergraduate years. An inadvertent gesture lacking proper respect could get you a spear from one of his loyal subjects without warning. Especially upon your refusal to accept some nice morsel he has selected for you from the chorus line to wrestle the night away with in your tent. Otherwise behave as you would back home at an ordinary banquet.

Upon a Gent Marrying a Lady for Her Money

This really is a hot one and a subject which regrettably must be treated at some length. As more wily guys than you think do it. But getting the spondulics in this manner is an ancient well tried method requiring aptitudes which, if applied elsewhere, might even make you richer.

Make absolutely sure that the lady has the assets you think she has, then woo her assiduously until the knot is tied. You will get all kinds of impedimenta especially from other guys who have tried or are trying the same thing. But your most embarrassing moment will come when you are confronted by your future wife's advisers, guardians and trustees who will insist you sign a forfeiture of any future ownership or benefit. This ordeal can only be made easier for you should your pedigree be quite superior to that of your wife's. But should it be inferior, good lord, it's terrible what they make you go through. And no matter how much you express in heartrending tones the simple sentiment.

'I adore Sarah.'

Everyone will know, attractive though she may be, that it is her money you are after. You could of course brazenly declare this but it is advised instead to remain silent. And don't, immediately following the ceremony, attempt to obtain information concerning the enormity of your wife's wealth or be caught trying to gain access to her bank vaults where a lot of this news you seek may reside. The little pride you have left can really be entirely extinguished by such encounters.

During your wedded bliss and to keep it that way, certain rules should be scrupulously observed. Under no circumstances whatever, fart in your wife's presence, except where at a distance she sees you from her own window early morning cantering booted and horsed across the park lands. Rise early, bathe daily, be alert, dapper and spring to do courtesies at all times. It will be found that a wife who has all the money requires the utmost in bedroom decorum and deportments. Do not be found standing hairy belly revealed without a dressing gown. Three paisley silk ones should always be ready at your grasp at a moment's notice. Nor be seen by your wife in under shorts or garters or cutting a ridiculous and ordinary figure. Therefore it is de rigueur that you have your own bed chamber and dressing room. This also prevents your marriage partner from witnessing your more irritating and perhaps sordid little habits which could needlessly mar the normally debonaire cut of your jib.

When your wife signals you to attend upon fulfilling her carnal cravings, drop immediately what you are reading and appear in your pyjamas, dressing gown and slippers. Depart the same way. Do not stay the night unless invited to, as extremely rich wives least prefer the sight of their husbands in the morning. But if she should surprise you in your own apartments as you tipple your night cap, greet her appearance with a robust stream of superlatives and as she advances throw open your arms to her. Any hesitation here could kick you right off the money nipple.

At home, always mix her drink. Never allow a servant to do this. And of course be aware that you will sometimes experience vague shirtiness from the household staff as they figure you as excess baggage on the same gravy train. To them always speak in a firm but low tone of voice and make sure to never countermand your wife. Have at your tongue tip the best jokes you can dredge up from among your friends but be careful that these are not needlessly sordid. She will of course appreciate the exercise of your well timed and placed wit, which can often momentarily make her forget you are a parasite hysterically dancing attendance upon her.

While out in public do not take admiring notice of other ladies. And never be without your weekly haircut and manicure or wear any undergarment twice, remember your wife can afford that you have a good supply. And if she is at all fascinated by you beyond your stunning looks and physique, it is permitted to laughingly suggest to people that it is your brains combined with your wife's money that makes you such a swell couple.

To further entrench your hooks and secure your sinecure it helps to be engaged with a multitude of altruistic projects. Hire a renowned architect at the earliest opportunity who can accompany you to your various town houses and country retreats where he can cause to amend or provide new embellishments. The more lavish and fantastic and long building these are, the better. Provided you have romantically kept up to scratch, such as bowingly opening car doors for your spouse when the footmen are otherwise engaged, your satisfied wife will write strong letters to her trustees to overrule their advice not to appropriate such money for such purpose.

Always profess satisfaction with your allowance. And even though your stingy wife has put you on a restricted sum, don't stamp your feet and throw your polished leathers all over the place. Remember other guys, even some less smellier than you, are always sizing up your personal gold mine wishing they were in there with their spoons digging too, and are only just waiting for an opportunity to jump champagne splashing in. It is even a nice touch once in a while to demonstrate your own frugality. Don't for instance charter an entire aircraft when first class seats will do to get you on the spur of the moment to a favoured watering place. Remember rich people love to keep their money carefully regulated, and you too can enjoy to stand by adoring to watch the steadiness of your disbursements.

Your wife will at times seem selfishly fussy and demanding and may suddenly want to go off on strange train, plane or boat trips by herself. This is your chance to show you are a man of the world. Rich women delight to pursue secret horny travels where they can indulge to the limit their fantasies of erotically getting to know the whole globe. Even to the point of gross multiple assignations with fly by night gentlemen some of whom may be extremely dark complexioned when your wife herself is distinctly not. About these private experiences you are advised not to inquire. When the servants cluster to welcome her back home, behave as if nothing had happened. And don't crowd her for a few days. She may feel reluctant that you should see her bruises and bites of love.

In attempting to permanently cement your position regarding your wife's fortune, it is of some concern to produce progeny. Give the old girl plenty of you know what. If for any reason you can't get it up, rush to your oysters and wheat germ until this makes you can. And feign slight rupture whenever disgraced by a hopelessly flaccid penis. As nothing will get you thrown out of the house quicker. Not even the lazily acquired habits of belching, teeth and nose picking, ear digging, pudenda scratching, or constant twenty one gun salvos from your rear portal.

Along with daily luxuriating in your wife's easy circumstances, it is essential you give to your life an air of busy efficiency. For this purpose supply yourself with a desk and a few ledgers. And even though she waves it away, show concern when bringing a questionable expenditure to your spouse's attention. What the hell it doesn't hurt to at least appear to carefully check tradesmen's accounts. But avoid her seeing motor fuel bills for your specially designed hand made many cylindered sports car, which, among other things, requires a resident mechanic and footman to keep in a high state of performance and polish. Well to do wives seem to find this kind of consumption particularly irritating especially when it is your pet indulgence. But always refuse to stay in a cheap little room in a crummy part of town because this is what your rich mate thinks is so quaintly romantic. Such predilection can bring back the chronic memories of your pre-nuptial impoverishment and put your spirits in such a slump that you may reveal to your wife a dark, alienating and probably evil side of your nature.

However, you will normally meet with her encouragement in lavishing opulent hospitality on a large circle of friends, hiring where necessary steam yachts, hotels, restaurants and even entire spa towns to entertain. Guests who attend will say behind your back that you must sing for your supper. But never let it be said you sing for your breakfast. Although an astonished if not pleased reaction can be had from a not only rich but cultured wife if after dinner and on your hind legs you can knock off a well phrased aria from a classical reper-toire while colourfully ablaze in your pyjamas just before bed time.

Should your golden squaw make a pig out of herself and grow fat and lazy, go with it. But you at all times must keep thin and sprightly. And do not be caught deceiving her. Or arousing suspicions by spending too much time abroad on trips or at your club. But do maintain to cut your usual swatch through good sporting society. And in the event of not being able to stand the sight of her, call upon all your re-serves of compassion. Try to see something spiritually bene-ficial in her aside from her precious metals. Remember it's worth a lot of mild discontent to continually know where your next meal is coming from.

Alas, however, the day may come when she has had enough of you. Do not take it on the chin like a gigolo. And when you are turned out into the cold with only your silks and leathers, do not agonize in long commiseration. Remove yourself with dignity despite the anguish of leaving motor cars, estates, yachts and other substantial elegancies behind. Suggest, however, that along with all your haberdashery you be allowed to take your horse. And where real pan handling hardship may confront, it is not improper to request a modest temporary emolument to give you a headstart. But above all, do not attempt by ruses to get back into the house. Or upon departure create a scene in front of the servants. Lying prostrate surrounded by your luggage on the lawn beating your fists into the grass is a shabby demonstration which only further confirms good reason for your banishment. Although some chaps pulling this sordid stunt and adding to it with an immersion in the gold fish pond, have managed temporarily to get back in the house. And what a humourless hollow little victory that is.

But upon your final irrevocable ejection and after a suitable period spent in regaining your composure, get to the nearest spa fast. And don't in your eagerness to avoid working for a living give yourself away as a fortune hunter. Nor be seen, because of your recent deprivation, eating chocolate bars or other sweet candies. As some experienced rich ladies know that this is a sure sign you intend gobbling up their riches next. But remember another wife, more affluent than the last, may lurk somewhere, provided you keep your pomade on.

At the Club

These are, at their best, exclusive sociable places where the food and wine is cheap and where a member not only can practise the exchange of the barbed innuendo with other members but can also feel the cosy quality of belonging. Depending upon whom the club keeps out, and these days there is a nice selection of people around to exclude, it can add comforting human ornament to your day and even sometimes, solace to your very life.

Do not harbour disillusionment when you find that after years of waiting to gain membership you end up among chaps hardly any better than yourself. Which is why there is always the urgent need to admit members overnight who are important and influential. In cases where a member procures membership for an undesirable with whom he is doing a deal, harden yourself to such shabbiness as otherwise it could ruin not only your digestion but also curdle the esteem in which you hold your fellow members. Such blots on the club are regrettably as flagrantly frequent as they are heinous.

Be careful to abide by club deportment and rules. Never mount the steps of your club quickly but lift one foot solemnly in front of the other. Similarly in descending, do so slowly, not to say majestically. Remember members lurk everywhere trying to size you up in order to make and foster convivial friendship. But it is never done to sit peering over the edge of your periodical desperately ready to jump up with a handshake to meet some famous or distinguished personage or to stare at such chaps close up when they are in for a quick lunch. Rather it is suave to deeply occupy yourself in reading and then, if you are really that hysterical to meet a celebrity, forthrightly go over and introduce yourself. However, be prepared. For upon disengaging from you he will ask who the hell is that, and hear the reply.

'The club bore.'

Clubs which include members of great intellectual and political achievement frequently dine communally in order that the free exchange of ideas can flow. This does upon occasion cause a member whom you detest to come sit next you. There is little that can be done about this but if for the sake of good manners you listen silently to his damn stupid opinions you are entitled when you have had enough of them to display your distaste. By stuffing your napkin in your mouth in a gesture of stiflement and to there chew angrily upon it, you will not only momentarily shut up your adversary but will also render the entire table speechless for even longer.

In harbouring intense amusement over a joke it is permissible to exercise your friendly camaraderie by repeating this to another member stopped in the club lounge or lobby. But on no account confront others with your uncontrollable mirth in the latrine or library. And in this latter context, any club member who monopolizes several periodicals at once and insists upon keeping them all after being requested to unhand those he is not reading, should immediately be put on notice that he risks not only odium but challenge to a duel. Minor inconveniences demand major remedies in the private confines of one's club.

Be careful playing cards. And especially avoid the club cheat if you are an easily angered straight shooter. To sit with a chap who has just removed an undue quantity of club stationery as well as combs, brushes and hair tonic from the lavatories and who is now peeling cards off the bottom of the deck, is dangerously provocative. And it does not do to have a trickster defending his honour to his accuser while both are engripped by each other's waistcoats and end up tumbling down the main marble staircase into the front lobby. Although a demonstration of instant justice, this behaviour does upset other tolerant members who may have become fond of this chap's cheeky swindling.

Where a club elects only the very haughtiest of haughty chaps, a deportment annex invariably exists to tone up a member's character when slack. Such facilities however remain among a club's most guarded and treasured of secrets. The healthful practice of taking a little bit of the whip now and again to improve the inner man has been long recognized as a means of purging accumulated guilts. Which get mountainous because of members' usually high and mighty station in life lording it as they do over their world at large. Such lashings are usually administered by specially tutored employees of the club and painfully shy members are naturally accorded use of a private room.

In taking your chastisement it is not done to piercingly cry out. But screams and grunts within the normal range of pain are permitted. Enjoying obvious pleasure from such thrashings is frowned upon. Nor is it proper to borrow another member's personal whip. And in the rarely permitted case of one member administering punishment to another, this, as it can encourage unseemliness, must be witnessed and duly recorded in the log for the purpose. Until you are a member it is extremely bad form to request to be advised of a club's whipping facilities.

One last but important matter. For some unaccountable reason club entrances attract the deranged. And members should always quickly pass until they are safely inside the premises. To delay while some nut to whom the hall porter has just summarily refused admittance, not to mention membership, makes the usual declaration.

'Hey I don't give two hoots for the members of this joint.'

Is looking for trouble. And although many members die safely inside their club lobbies from natural causes many another has met an embarrassing death at the hands of a violent lunatic on the front steps.

Athletic Clubs

Although less socially elite these sporting precincts are where allround regular guys really let their hair down or have it clipped extremely short for wrestling. In among the agile muscle men will also be found the more physically sluggish leading bankers, stockbrokers, investment counsellors, judges and politicians, who, if they aren't daily huffing and puffing to slough off their fat, at least convene at the annual dinners to yell, hoot, throw rolls and rain sugar cube bombardments on each other. This provides a delightful way of purging the year's accumulation of aggression which stems from making big decisions when your neck is at stake and other people's opinions are in the way.

It is seemly never to flaunt your athletic prowess or to bulge your biceps or act in a fashion which makes it obvious you could tear another member's arm out of his socket or even kill him if he tried something funny. Always comport your-self in an unassuming manner and do not while in the corri-dors or social rooms of the club burst into practice paroxysms concerning your sport. With every member doing this it could fast make the place look like a mental institution. Nor is it becoming to express yourself with erudition in these he man confines, even though it is well known that mental alertness is increased by physical workouts. However some discomfort must be taken from the fact that the dangerously insane are rarely recognized lurking at athletic club entrances due to the difficulty of distinguishing them from the more eccentric members.

At the Theatre

Although the theatre attracts a rather culturally senile lot of folk, the worst of these being those who arrive late for curtain up, it is nevertheless a way of treating yourself and a com-panion to antics which should make you think you are think-ing and feel you are feeling.

During the performance, if someone blatantly misses their

cue or the wrong piece of scenery descends from the flies onto
the star's skull, don't laugh unless it really is damn funny.
Following a poignantly theatrical nuance it is always stylish
to clap heartily for the actor who has made such scene work.
But remember there is always some little bastard in a side
aisle who has money in the show who is leading the clapping
even for the on stage silences. Don't be tricked by him.

In telling your partner of your personal first hand information concerning scandal involving a principal player always
whisper this flagrant tidbit in order that nearby folk in the

audience will not find it more interesting than what is going
on behind the footlights. But if you violently disagree with
the drama, farce or histrionics on stage, don't hesitate to get
up and protest and make your views loudly known. However,
do then sit down promptly so the play may go on. And be
tolerant if the players stumble over their lines a little before
they fully recover their cool after your heated outburst. Also
be ready to be slugged by the author.

At the final curtain if you are pleased with the performance, be generous with your applause. There is nothing quite
so moving as repeated waves of clapping which yet again

bring the players to bow, genuflect and make obeisance bathed in the beams of many limelights. And when the entire audience are standing on their seats shouting bravos you can depend upon getting some free drinks from the actors backstage who adore to be appreciated in this fashion.

Wear your finery. That little extra frippery you were saving for a special occasion can make all the difference especially if you've got the gumption to make an entrance. It is haughtier to be seen attending extremely early or extremely late in a play's run. And it's positively allround aristocratic to be present at the last performance of a loud flop. Current hits attract an unsavoury type of person, and it is always a dead giveaway when you are caught at these that you are just as ordinary as what you are watching.

Artistic and Literary Circles

Time spent swimming in these can be extremely entertaining as one constantly encounters folk manfully maintaining that money is not everything. But do make sure you are surrounded by persons whose manuscripts, paintings, sculptures and musical scores are genuine works of art sincerely and originally created and only awaiting recognition by the world at large. There is nothing quite as disappointing as when you find, after your long feverished manoeuvrings to enter this rarified sphere, that all you have encountered are just a bunch of sneaky devious jerks trying to avoid working for a living.

Upon introduction to bona fide artists, always knowingly grasp the varied number of fingers they offer for you to shake. This greeting is common among the intelligentsia and should not cause you to think someone is signifying something regrettably untoward. But prepare yourself for the waspish and wounding epithet or deflating epigram. Literary and artistic people are constantly attempting to reduce each other to tears with these. And it is as well to have in riposte a stream of playful impudences up your sleeve. Such should be spoken in Latin or Greek but don't for god's mortifying sake be caught administering these to some brain who speaks such languages fluently.

In approaching literary and artistic giants, in order that they will think that you are somebody, present yourself forcefully and ask them straight off what they are working on now. This clearly shows you are not overawed by what they have already done, whatever utterly forgotten thing that was, which anyway you have never seen, and if you had, you wouldn't have thought much of it anyway, and that unless their answer is satisfactory, you may take two steps backward out of their inflated reputations. But be careful, some of these titans of art are stubborn bastards indeed. And if you get no reaction from the question.

'Do you think you are resting on your laurels.'

Then it is time to inquire, provided the esteemed cultural figure is not big and strong.

'Do you think you have shot your bolt.'

But step way back if the reply comes.

'I'll shoot yours for you, you little fucker.'

Patronage

Although this supplies many an hour of amusement it is of course a way of providing someone else with a means of seeking comfortable habits out of which they the patronized would like to see you their patron early dispossessed.

Usually your charge will be a bachelor who has sybaritic tastes and likes to eat, drink and insult you out of house and home. Not only will he require to have his patron's undivided attention as he points out your failings but also that of your wife and as much of his benefactor's income as he can persuade him constantly to part with. He will especially demand the best of the great wines along with heaps of hot exotic foods while recounting his major problem which is that no one will let him put his dong where he wants it put. He meanwhile will maintain that the more nobly he is treated the more noble the patron and he shall become.

At the Fine Art Auction

Do not overdress for these usually dusty places. And even though they occur in the morning, carry yourself in a mild afternoon manner. It is quite becoming to wear your coat draped across your shoulders in the manner of the shop lifter, and this together with your bending to look behind or kneeling to look under furniture or sniffing at the surface of paintings will demonstrate your erudition as well as add authority when at the viewing you drop and smash a priceless piece of porcelain and loudly proclaim it a fake.

Be forceful in signalling your bid. Especially in view of the millions being tendered and that you are previously unknown to the auctioneers. Raise your walking stick and shake it vigorously should the broker appear to disregard you. But do not let it interfere with toupees or ladies' hats. Watch also for the mentally unstable who make a habit of bidding you up insanely high, but possess enough brains to laughingly leave you stuck there.

Voyeurism and Other Peeping Toms

It is widely held that gentlemen do not avail themselves enough of the ready opportunity to watch others in the joyful pursuit of their outdoor intimacies. Especially when this is done in a manner giving the victims some sporting privacy.

Firstly cruise at an even speed until you find the kind of indecency you prefer. Then having assured yourself that it is developing nicely select your spot from which to view. Do not perch in trees nor approach conspicuously in parks and glades closer than fifteen yards and then a newspaper must, as a usual decoy, be raised between oneself and the victims or victim. Your journal should be one of the more erudite financial periodicals which can be read during periods of totally unstimulating action when of course you can also eat your lunch. It is not done to peek under the newspaper but just above the upper edge. Peeking to the side is not only disadvantaged by making your view lopsided but also should be discouraged as making yourself obvious.

When employing the use of binoculars a minimum distance of forty yards must at all times be adhered to. This should be merely estimated and not paced off. As approaching right up to an active display of ruttish lasciviousness has a way of provoking the viewed into an angry protest and quite embarrassing fights have broken out between the observer and observed. Such embranglements are extremely distracting for other peeping toms so engaged who may be just rising to the very apogee of a delicately shivering piquancy which suddenly is quenched by a loutish hair pulling mêlée of half undressed folk entangled and strangling to defend themselves. Should you have provoked such an unnice situation it is de rigueur you retreat to another area of viewing in as unshirty fashion as possible in order that other courtesy abiding voyeurs are not brought into disrepute.

The use of the telescope and tripod is not thought sporting unless secluded by natural cover. Of course this allows employment of even more elaborate equipment right down to providing for the daredevil delights of hair splitting definition. But if your lair, harbouring a massive complex of instruments, is detected, this goes for making subjects self conscious for miles around. Avoid such thoughtlessness. And remember most couples will upon being discreetly viewed find the attention stimulating and will increase the ardour and tempo of their performance. And be fair, when you find proceedings of really splendid viewing possibilities, signal others. But do not allow a conspicuous crowd to collect.

Ecclesiastic Thrill Seeking

This brings to many a deep abiding sense of well being and if such diversion does not already run in your family you're really missing something. Although very much a deviation of the advanced devout of the northern latitudes, it is gradually being practised more widely especially by discerning pagan misbelieving backsliders.

Ecclesiastical garments can be obtained in most major cities. Remember these are religious vestments and should be handled with respect. Provide a proper place for their keeping and an appropriate chamber for their wearing. Some practised performers prefer to furnish dais and throne with spot lighting and these aficionados will, when attempting the heights of hierarchical high jinks, sometimes assume the rank of supreme pontiff which does of course call for having your own tailor. And although expensive, a mace is a must.

Before reaching the rank of bishop, and for special occasions, archbishop, the warm up ranks of verger, sacristan and deacon are of immense interest. But it is always permitted to immediately provide yourself with the prelatical status you prize. And often sufficient kicks are experienced in simple

surroundings by merely seating yourself in a high backed chair facing a large mirror.

Should you be desirous for discreet observance through your windows by your neighbours, it is advised to pretend reading a breviary even though this be nothing more than a movie magazine. Mostly such behaviour awes folk into deep respect. But a note of warning. This kind of make believe, harmless though it may be, has headed many a practitioner on unintended trips to the institution especially when attempts are made to imitate various saints in either dress or behaviour, particularly St John the Baptist.

Transvestism

As both a saucy and pleasant way to spend a Sunday evening at home this is in elite environs regarded highly. But do make sure when proceeding beyond your immediate household confines and especially onto your front porch that you are well enough disguised so that your neighbours don't, just when someone is calling you Jane, suddenly nudge each other and say isn't that Tom.

It is essential to avoid altercations when so attired. And this often happens between the very best of friends when least expected. Fathers who have dolled themselves up to give the kids an amusing treat can, for some crazy reason, suddenly get incited to quite hysterical jealousies as they sally about the place. The sight of men fighting and landing haymakers while dressed as women is not at all edifying. But if you do punch your opponent do so cleanly. To start ripping at his dress and him at yours, does make things look extremely unsporting and sets a bad example for the kiddies.

A Further and Better Particular of a Frisson

It is well known that in search of a normal nicety an amputee or other variously discommoded person has but to enter some little morsel of suggestion in the agony column of a reputable newspaper to reap an amplitude of suggested trysts and offers to fulfil any special refinement in the yearnings stemming from his or her missing or discommoded part and often age as well as beauty is immaterial provided the required portion or items are missing and the more absent the better.

Although it may make you highly desirable to those in the know, it is not done to flaunt your maim or disabilities in the presence of the uninitiated. There can be something quite unnecessarily hurtful not to say untoward about a whole gang of folk rushing to seek and seize upon the favours of a total invalid while agreeably handsome able bodied people are left standing idly by, ignored. Similarly it is not nice to impute that someone is not sufficiently incapacitated to awaken your interest, or indeed that because they are entirely in one piece, lack attraction altogether.

Stripping and Streaking

Although sometimes a symptom of someone who is trembling their lid before flipping it, this is a diverting and delightful pursuit which lets the world know you have nothing to hide.

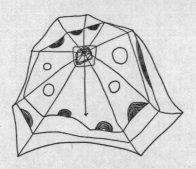

When stripping do not fling your clothes in all directions or attempt at saucy stimulation. Streaking should not commence until totally nude and all erectile tissue is in full rigid tumescence. If, while under way, you tend to overly flap due to largeness in the appendages, reduce your speed.

The best results are obtained from streaking through areas providing genteel audiences. Fashionable boulevards, concert halls, places of worship and where organ recitals are in progress, are especially suitable. But avoid altars and sacrilege. And do remember that in any assembly refined onlooking ladies can find fifty charging hard ons rather too much to take.

Perils &
Precautions

Upon Being Stung on the End of Your Prick by a Bee on a Golf Course

Your first shriek will immediately attract the attention of the other players in the foursome who will wonder what the hell's the matter. When they find out, your further wild gesticulations will throw your golf playing opponents into fits of laughter especially as words of your desperate concern for the future well being of your front tail reaches their ears. Take consolation that their game for the day will be ruined by the muscle strain occasioned by their continuous convulsive laughter and take the opportunity to bet heavily upon yourself. And keep your flies closed.

Dealing with the Insane

The nutty, with their minds chockablock with conclusions, can be recognized by the immediate interest they are willing to take in you. Otherwise their dishevelment can sometimes be the key note, but beware there are exceptions and some dress to kill. With spats adorning gentlemen especially. Chaps in abbreviated trousers declaring they have recent naval information should also be immediately suspected.

Although one is cautioned always to be careful, most nuts are benign and usually only given to strong racial prejudices. The major thing in confronting insanity is don't be afraid. Stare directly into their eyes and intimidate them by a supreme demonstration of confidence. In facing a weapon pretend to be mad yourself as the lunatic are usually after the sane. Talk rapidly. Do not give the crazy person time to fit bullets in between your words. Say you hope they are able to take advantage of a weekend you were planning with Dad since he invited you both over. But do not stake your life on this latter inducement which, if you yet have a chance after it doesn't work, the mention of Mom asking you over may have a more calming effect.

In the Elevator

More and more people these days are going up and down in this self consciously tight situation amid the pressing together of bodies and hardening of appendages. In such suspended animation farting or footpath excrement adhering to the shoe can make it most unpleasantly nosy for all. And if someone is fuming or poking where you do not want, the loud statement.

> 'O for God's sake please stop it.'

Will at least improve the silence.

Upon the elevator getting stuck, calmly await rescue and remember those who waste breath complaining usually die first. Be careful never to be just that one extra person who has forced himself on to make the overweighted elevator plummet out of control. Or if you are already on don't hesitate to scream to get off. If nobody lets you, then keep your knees flexed. There is generally some cushioning effect at the bottom of the shaft for your bouncing protection. And you will get there mighty fast.

Angers

Never throw a thoroughly wasted tantrum. When this kind of energy is expended you want an audience. Although explosive outbursts are generally the prerogative of the boss of a privately owned corporation they should be tried now and again by underlings who enjoy toying with being fired. There is nothing more satisfyingly fulfilling than hearing and seeing devastation wrought from your violence. Especially if at another's expense and inconvenience. But fury when intense can quickly become a peril. Be careful striking hard or explosive objects or others which may ricochet back. And always make sure the walls are paper thin before attempting to perforate them with your fists.

Upon Coming upon Two Citizens Engaged in a Fight

It is quite an enjoyable sight watching two suddenly infuriated guys really slam each other around and you must take some pleasures where you find them. However good citizenship insists you do something. But first reconnoitre from behind an abutment and stay there if the antagonists are armed. If it is fists, advance closer and then you might, with appropriate sporting admonitions, make sure that fair play obtains. But on no account part the antagonists. Not only is there far too much peacemaking these days, but combatants will frequently turn in your direction and after beating the bejesus out of you, end up shaking hands and complimenting each other on the good job they did doing it.

Upon Witnessing an Indoor Nuisance Befalling a Lady

Although the well bred gentleman never lifts his head or turns to look at a débâcle in the restaurant, he is permitted, inwardly of course, to be amused. Should however a waiter trip headlong and let slide duck à l'orange from his platter which pitches gravy, wild rice and all down an unpleasant woman's back or bodice, one loud guffaw is permitted. Otherwise you wouldn't be human. She will of course hold this against you for the rest of your life and will try to get even if at all possible and as soon as possible. Some ladies will in fact take the gravy drenched duck itself right off their laps and throw it at you right across the table. Where if you duck the duck and laugh your head off as it hits another man behind you, just one more additional guffaw here could lead to murderous embranglement. Folk really get upset when splattered with victuals or drenched in gravy someone else has ordered or thrown.

Upon People Walking Straight into Pools and Water Filled Excavations and There Being Immersed Headlong

This is certainly an occasion where you may carefully encircle the lower part of your belly with your hands, arch your spine backwards, lift the chin skyward, open up your mouth, and laugh till you are sick, tired, or your emphysema collapses you completely. Should your opponent from the muddy water say in a melancholic manner.

'So you think that's funny.'

It is permissible to keep on laughing. Water has a way of subduing umbrage in the victim and it will be at least a couple of minutes before he can get angry enough to attack you physically. He also will be handicapped by the extra weight of soaked clothing.

However, should you be the victim spreadeagled in the deep puddle it is sporting to shout to your highly entertained adversary.

'Hey you thought that was funny, just watch me this time.'

Thereupon repeat the act by relaxing fully and falling again and again like a felled tree in the water. Your opponent's laughter can then be incited till he's either maimed with rupture or left with a lifetime affliction of bowel disturbance.

Upon Your Spit Landing on Another

Before rushing to your opponent to offer use of your usual beige silk hanky to do the necessary, pause for a moment to size him up. Spitting on someone can infuriate, and a few of your more ill bred chaps will start spitting right back. It is therefore best to be seen demonstrating your sincere regret while standing at a safe distance with your hanky out. Till you are sure your adversary hasn't got the guts to attack. When your first words should be.

'Gee fella I didn't see you standing there.'

Or in pukka.

'I am awfully sorry.'

Accent should be on the am, as well as the awfully. Should your victim be a weak small person without weapons, be compassionate. Warn him not to rub your strongly digestive spit into his fabric, where it shortly will produce glaring holes.

Upon your saliva landing on a lady it is stylish to provide an immediate blistering stream of apologies while your hands are held up high dithering.

'O dear, how tiresomely vile for you and my goodness, how really terrible it is of me, I don't know how I can apologize enough.'

These and similar words will mollify her but in the case of her monstrous, heavy browed gorilla like boyfriend, they will send him into a frenzy of lathered contortions best dealt with by a nimble retreat behind his girlfriend who could, however, be floored with the first punch and deprive you of further protection.

Upon a Fair Fight

These have been made scarce by the use of various methods of unarmed combat. Such as grabbing your opponent by the lapels and swinging him up over your head and back down with a crescendo on his arse or using hand chops to fracture his wind pipe and crush spinal vertebrae. In the days when one gentleman knocked another down for an impropriety he would normally ask his opponent as he lay in the dust if he had enough. But with the advent of these latest grippings and tuggings and choppings, often a knockment to the ground will mean your opponent is opening your shoelaces or trying to flip you on your own arse with an ankle lock reverse lever throw. It is therefore advised to deliver one clean blow to start with and if your opponent is clearly not of the old school, clean out his teeth with your elbow as he falls and give him a belly full of your boot when he reaches the ground. Of course, should he be armed, run in a ducking zig zag fashion.

The Mugger

Although an attacker is a yellow bellied type he can quickly turn you into one too if he is carrying a weapon and has it stuck in your ribs or held across your throat. It is best always to carry sufficient money upon your person to hand over to appease the highwayman. Look at this as an insurance. Courtesy at this time, provided there is an opportunity to

offer it, will often reap rewards. Apologize if you only have extremely large denomination bills or that your jewelled watchband is gaudy and ostentatious. But don't be as in-sincere as you usually are as it will infuriate your assailant who as a self employed man will be quickly intolerant of the mealy mouthed.

To Avoid Attack

Although travelling everywhere by limousine can still put you in jeopardy when you alight between vehicle and build-ing entrance, it is by far the safest transport. With doors locked, telephone or short wave radio at the ready to signal help, and bullet proof windows and body chassis which latter also stands up excellently in collision, you are veritably ready for anything. The awesome splendour and intimidation you present to any would be scoundrel often deters attacks. He is also aware that a man who lives in such triumphant fashion will pull a gun on him without hesitation in order to go on living that way.

Upon Giving Assistance to One Attacked

When suddenly you see or distantly hear a chap or lady being assaulted and if you have the persistent nature of a righteous busybody and don't give a damn if you get a bust in the nose or worse a hole in the head and the person attacked looks or sounds deserving of protection, the proper words upon ap-proach are.

'What is the difficulty here?'

Should the riposte be.

'None of your fucking business.'

Make sure no weapons are present before shouting out your war cry.

'Gung Ho.'

When police arrive on the scene make sure they do not shoot or apprehend you as the assailant since you have laid out everyone around you. This is where your good accent used liberally along with displaying a copy of the city's best newspaper on your person will identify you as a respectable member of the community who would only hurt a fly when preserving the public peace required.

As a Pedestrian

Show some measure of decrepitude when using any public highway on foot. This will in most cases make the motorist pity you and he will steer well clear but always be ready to jump for it. When crossing a street it is permissible to do so in such a manner that other pedestrians cushion you to on-coming traffic. But it is rude to make this obvious. Should a car approach which is clearly going to hit you and there is not sufficient time to go forward or back, go upwards as high as you can. With proper timing and height you can crash feet first through the bastard's windscreen and avoid injury by the flopping onto his roof which harmlessly will carry your body while you hope the vehicle stops. Attempting this with large lorries or trucks can be a real test of your athletic ability.

As a Motorist

Never pull away from traffic lights hoping to outdo your opponent in the next vehicle. He will always give testimony against you should you have an accident further down the road. Of course if he pulls away first and crashes, it is deeply satisfying to later say he was driving like a maniac.

Remember all motorists carry with them heavy personal burdens, unless they be a bunch of reckless kids joy riding whose parents carry the burden. And when under way and no matter how tempted, do not make faces at other passing cars. Folk on the highway these days generate massive hostilities against the outside world and become extremely unstable, isolated as they are in their own little mobile temples of discontent. They may swerve in front of you, force you off the road or even start shooting.

However should you not be able to control yourself and sneer at a passing motorist and his unpleasant passengers, at the first sign of their retaliatory aggressiveness, smile, wave and blow your horn in salute, then display your sign.

TOURIST

Otherwise keep the corners of your mouth well turned down, and your eyes merely slits.

Upon Confronting a Burglar

This is always an impromptu situation which can invite gross incivility since you are generally dealing with a man who is his own boss. If you have decided not to throw caution and courtesy to the winds you may open with.

'I don't mind your taking the material things provided you don't harm me and my wife and I will gladly assist you to get away.'

The trouble with this statement is that most criminals won't believe you, having learned in a hard school. And as you are only one among their many victims standing there in your pyjamas, or god forbid, totally naked pleading for your life, another opening is suggested.

'O.K. shoot us, kill us, but get it over with.'

This makes the burglar feel he doesn't want to be pressed into making a commitment, especially as he is intolerant of taking shit or advice from anyone. But unless the intruder tells you to shut your mouth, keep talking. Although cash and valuables are always uppermost in a professional criminal's priorities, if your wife's figure is astonishingly good and he can see through her nightdress, you may yet get a chance to jump him.

Upon Encountering Incivilities from Taxi Drivers

If the usual comment.

'What's the matter with you.'

Should not suffice to bring about a desistment when a taxi driver is snarling out his window and embarrassing the god damn hell out of you on the pavement of a good area of town or, god forbid, in front of your club and other club members, then, take up an outraged posture, extend a straight right arm, pointing a finger and in your most aggrieved voice yell.

'He tried to kidnap me.'

The more intelligent taxi drivers try to get away. But for those who remain, a water pistol squirted in the eye area generally will quieten him if your propellant is vinegar. Beware however in the more dangerous cities that the taxi driver does not outdraw you, or use the excuse of your pulling your water pistol on him to pull a real one on you. And remember.

'Bang bang.'

Is the sound of bullets.

Upon Helping Ladies Too Fat for Taxis to Get in One

Use the side approach unless your problem is thicker than she is wide. Except in dire necessity it is not done to use your propped up foot to push. But instead get other pedestrians to lend their shoulders. You will find ready help from the majority of city dwellers who are usually curious enough to want to solve such a perplexing situation. Do beware of pickpockets at this time. And be assured your fat lady, appreciative of your gallant assistance, will remain jolly even when subjected to the most bizarre kinds of squeezing.

True dyed in the blue gentlemen will follow such successfully stuffed in a taxi lady in yet another taxi, since getting her out may be even more difficult. When her cab is fully stopped and braked it helps immeasurably if some of the assisting volunteer pedestrians pile onto the roof to hold the taxi in position as the remainder pull. Grasp only the lady's limbs and avoid tugging jewellery or articles of clothing as these will be torn from her in the undertaking. Upon this

unavoidably causing undress, cover her with your jacket and
if this does not apply itself to sufficient area as to prevent
giving the lady embarrassment, a nearby haberdasher or bed
linen supply store ought to have suitable blankets or bed
sheets for the occasion. Should the cabbie get overly over-
heated concerning what he thinks is happening to his cab,
wrap him up too.

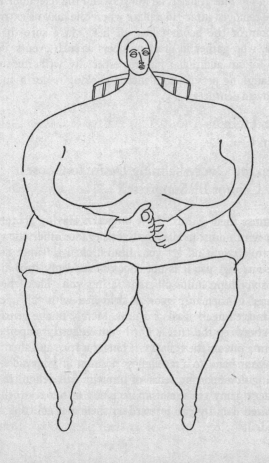

Fat Ladies in Phone Booths

First cross examine the victim carefully as to how she got in in the first place. This will always supply the best clues to getting her out. If needs be the lady and the telephone booth can be removed intact to a place where she may be extricated privately or the booth taken off her. Make sure that the crowd, who gather in great numbers at such events, do not make for an additional hazard, especially with uncontrollably laughing persons accidentally choking to death on their swallowed dentures.

When the Overwhelming Desire to Goose a Lady Cannot Be Suppressed

You must then at least do it properly. Having spotted the target which must in all cases be of elegance otherwise you're going to straight off get your head broken, advance deliberately, making sure it is not about to suddenly turn around with something quite different facing you. Then the well favoured gentlemanly goose is delivered with the upcurled twin index fingers used as a unit. Merely nudge gently upwards between the cheeks until your fingertips experience a moderate pneumatic resistance. Linger a trice and then withdraw your hand to a motionless position at your side. Most ladies with a sporting sense of humour will delight in your confident gamy gesture of appreciation of her rear orbs and will often daintily rise forward on their toes emitting a prolonged.

'Ooooooooooo.'

But. And one cannot be too careful on this score. There are ladies who entirely will object to such licence and may interpret your virtuoso classical goose as an assault upon her person. And throwing yourself immediately upon the lady's mercy can be recommended although the amount of clemency you receive will depend entirely upon how handsome and well spoken you are. And if that's how you are, you will be amazed by the numerous women who thrill to be goosed by gallant debonaire men.

Upon Having without Invitation an Uncontrolled Erection

It is extremely bad manners to stand in prolonged postures with your member prominently bulging in front of strange ladies to whom your temporary enormity means little. And to twitch it is a cardinal rudeness.

Depending upon the size of your engorgement, attempt to sit putting the offending member down the least obvious trouser leg. If you are the witness to whom the tumescence is blatant, be mindful your admonishments avoid enraging or ridiculing the erector. Remember there are few things in which chaps put more pride or take out of, more pleasure. And most chaps in fact expect a standing ovation.

Upon Being Exorcised

Do not allow yourself to be approached by quacks or charlatans. Wear a clean change of undergarments and have a suitable outfit ready to sport as a certified angelic being. And do make sure you want to be dispossessed. Remember, Satan not only allows you to contort and gyrate all over the place but you can scare the shit out of others which is often a lot more useful than voiding the devil yourself.

When an Undesirable Moves In Next Door

As the value of your property plummets, don't feel sorry for yourself. Your new neighbour can hardly do anything further to you because he has already done it all. But in case he thinks of something, it is wise thereafter to prominently display your national flag to make him feel unpatriotic.

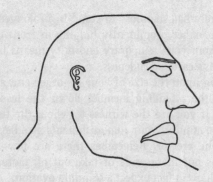

Suburban Boundaries

Sunday mornings are the worst time for these. When you look out over the top of the newspaper and see that goon with his tape measure extending into your petunias which he thinks have been planted on his side. Put down your paper immediately and stand at the window with your binoculars so your opponent can see you. When this scrutiny intimidates him back into his house, go out with your own map or blank piece of paper and tape measure. Upon taking a reading, slowly stand up, face your adversary's windows and shake your fist very slowly back and forth. This means that by god, for unending years in the future you are going to fight tooth and nail, shovel and spade, ashcan and leaves, telephone wires and barbecue pit against your neighbour's insolent effrontery and it would be a lot easier for all if he let your petunias growing on his side, remain.

Plumbing

In strange large houses one must never assume that the door you are about to enter is the gents' and prematurely unzip or unbutton the fly and remove one's private part. One's heated explanations as one appears in this condition through an ante door into a breakfast, dining or drawing room crowded with other guests and even though the exposed part in question is not tumesced in extension, never suffices to quell the rumour which will flourish among those quietly socializing, that you have uncontrollable indecent tendencies.

Hostesses despise it when you pee all over their fittings and carpet. In darkness therefore, make sure at all times that a receptacle you would desire to be there is there and always dip your finger to locate the presence of the toilet bowl. When something is wrong with his flushing arrangements your host will usually be good enough to tell you if he has failed to put up a sign. Do not forget. Not to flush. If you have been told don't. It is always despicably too late when you hear screams from below as a whole bunch of innocent opponents get an unwholesomely unwelcome showering. Made much worse when you rush to investigate and cannot control your amusement.

As a House Guest

Although it is quite proper to use up all the hot water and demand other comforts you are used to, it is not done to blow your nose in the sheets or polish shoes with towels even when invited to do so by the host who says make yourself feel at home. These types usually scrutinize everything after you've left and are always deeply embittered by your stains.

People love to see folk treat even their most humblest possession like it was an heirloom. And if your host lets you get away with leaving rings from your wet glass on his best mahogany always jump in his presence to take your handkerchief and wipe off the moisture. It is the very height of haughtiest particularity if you carry upon your person a special cloth for this purpose. But on no account take out large wash rags or get on your knees in a servile manner.

Treat your host's help well, usually they have enormous resentments built up against him and they will make an immediate ally of you. They will also see to it that you get the best victuals your host usually hides for himself. A little joke concerning their employer scampering round to collect their tips after a guest's departure will often amuse them while they are laying out your clothes and will explain why it seems you never leave a gratuity.

Upon Shortening a Guest's Stay upon the Country Estate

Stayers are those who have been asked to lunch and appear with suitcases ready for tea, supper, a night's sleep and an indefinite number of days' hospitality thereafter based on how soon they can eat and drink you out of house and home. Picking, cleaning and freezing berries is quite effective during summer and autumn as a general ridder of a stayer who resents that you might be enjoying these with sugar and cream or as breakfast jam long after he has gone. Beware of those who may lie between the roses or behind hay bales happily sunbathing.

In order to set the tone when lunch is completed and the stayers are settling in over your coffee and brandy with your latest fashion and movie magazines in the drawing room, the host should stand up and stretch, bringing his arms high and way back at the shoulders and let out a prolonged ahhhh and announce.

'Must haul the boat. Deucedly sorry to ask but it requires all hands.'

If you are without riverbank, lake or seashore for boat dragging on your estate, find something else large to shift over a distance. The host should engineer the procedure and stand over the victims and direct. The following table may be consulted for the various stayers.

Past lunch	Removing junk from attics
Past dinner	Clearing debris from cellars
Overnight	Weeding in the rose gardens
Two days	Wood chopping

Three days	Land clearing
Four days	Hay making
Five days	Roofing work
Six days	Estate road repairs
Seven days	Sludge digging
Eight days	Sewer cleaning

Further incitements to leave can be dreamt up following instructions to servants to leave beds unmade and to turn off both hot and cold water in the guests' wing and by cancelling lunch after your visitors have missed breakfast. Outright violence although being the most immediately effective, should only, as a matter of courtesy, be resorted to last.

Upon Being Required to Work as a Guest

Pretending dizzy spells acts as a deterrent and feigning rupture provides complete immunity. With long moans as you are carried back to the castle. When the doctor is called to examine you it is merely required to wince when he presses in the area you have selected. A discreet phone call to your lawyer overheard by a servant, concerning your injury, assures you of no further chores and comfortably adds another week to your sojourn. Your host may even invite you to invent horrid jobs to help get rid of the other stayers.

The Willing 'Let's Go Gang' Guest

Even before breakfast this early rising chap will, while doing knee bends in his overalls, ask you straight off where the tools are. And further request to be directed to a job the host's been meaning to do for a long time. Such as the demolishment of an old shed. Outside of which the impatient guest will announce with a smile.

'So this is it, just watch me.'

Stand well back as your impresario mounts the structure to give it the works. Remove even further back as he poises there right on the roof smiling down triumphantly. Just before he raises his sledge. And thunderously crashes it down. With the entire roof giving way asunder beneath him.

Let the dust clear first before administering first aid. And remember, even though your worker lies contorted in the rubble, this is a blessing in disguise. Remove him to retire for the week in your best chaise longue, fully contented, and happily injured. Because sooner or later this eager helper would have broken your own arse as well as his.

Upon a Commoner Encountering a Member of the Titled Classes

Be totally calm and nonchalant. Don't stand on too much ceremony. Use a few opening throw away lines but avoid.

'Gee it's nice to meet somebody who really knows their place.'

Instead get straight to the point. Admit that for the time being you are yourself without a distinguishing handle to your name. This is understood immediately by the aristocracy. Indeed they welcome to be surrounded by commoners.

Use his or her title once or twice, then if the conversation is going well, employ the impersonal 'you'. But beware there are some titled people who do not like to be reminded that they have one, and they take immense pleasure at being abroad incognito so to speak. It is ill of you then to call them out of the blue Lord or Lady or other titled address. Instead nudge them quietly in the ribs and shake your head knowingly up and down. This of course entitles you to the privilege of being taken into His Lordship's confidence which can be further deepened should he ask you for a loan. If you are crazy enough to give him one, this will temporarily cement your relationship.

The noble classes are fickle in their selection of friends, always preferring new groups of people who are more easily awed by their rank thus making conversation more amusingly ripe for ripostes. Remember, the titled set, from their long enjoyed positions of superiority, are outspoken and even more so since many deeply resent not having been born normal nobodies. Therefore on no account ask what does it feel like to be a lord, since some aristocracy have rather vituperative natures and his reply may be.

'First perhaps you might tell me what it feels like to be a fuckpig.'

Upon Being a Member of the Titled Classes

Always remember who you are. This is easy provided you accept your lot in life. And freely acknowledge that through no fault of your own, you gain the respect of others without much effort on your part. As a result you will often be more humane and understanding than more ordinary common folk. And the worst that can happen to you is when you marry beneath you.

Before you know it after the ceremony, your newly titled

wife will take to hitting you with the usual curtain pelmets and table sized bronze cast objects of art. And her screams will be heard all over the castle by the servants.

'You mouse, you absolute mouse.'

Don't try to live with this. Commoners always expect far more from a title than it can ever give and their disappointment can frequently make them dangerous. Put Her Ladyship in irons in the dungeons. You will be amazed at how quickly this bitch will then learn between her blazes of anger which side of the aristocracy her bread is buttered on.

The Wife's Disappearance at the Country House Party

Disguise your woebegone depressed spirits. And carry in your search an open bottle of champagne. Knock at the various chamber doors, as it is not done to burst in upon your wife and her companion just to see what filthy minded thing they may be up to. Instead inquire.

'Hey Louise, Louise.'

Or in pukka.

'Are you there my dear.'

Then enter gently. Even when she has denied her presence. If she is compromised, shake the champagne bottle vigorously and with your thumb on top, squirt the contents liberally into your wife's companion's eyes. Then douse Louise and take a good swig yourself.

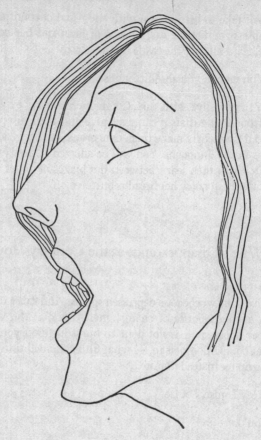

Food Throwers

Begun usually by estranged couples, once this victual flinging starts, everyone will do it. And as the first roll is thrown one should step in to quell matters before they proceed further. Since soufflés and other scalding entrées speeding through space are very splattering. With folk jumping to their feet in some pain and angrily upsetting the place settings around them.

An odd singular piece of asparagus if lashed about lightheartedly can at least be delicately picked off one's dinner clothing by the fingers and should be tolerated by any fair minded host. Or mashed potato which can be removed by knife by scraping. Be cautious with cranberry sauce however, which landing on white garments can in resembling blood, really panic folk.

Should your dinner party have become an out of control concussion match with opponents catapulting croutons and petits pois across the mahogany, don't fight it, go with it. And when you desire to quell the uprising approach the original perpetrator from behind. There, slowly crown her with the contents of the fresh fruit salad bowl. But be warned. Although this immobilizes and rivets everyone's attention it also gives them new ideas.

Upon Encountering Strange and Suspicious Noises

Groans and screams accompanying murder and affray and those emitting from lips enjoying a saucy little game are not easy to differentiate and struggles and thrills in either of those two undertakings can sound exactly the same. Thereby giving rise to a plethora of embarrassing incidents whereupon the enraptured are visited out of the blue by other folk not similarly stirred at that particular point in time.

As a matter of courtesy always confront the enraptured in a gradual manner as they are often, as they lie or stand, devoid of covering with parts or parts of parts flagrantly displayed. To them it is deeply unsettling when burst in upon by folk with pitchforks and drawn guns when all they have are whips, dildoes and handcuffs. But where the protagonists are only naughtily locked in love lower your voice and weapon immediately and announce.

'Holy cow.'

Or in biblical.

'Jesus Christ.'

Upon Changing Your Sex

Dignity along with a suitable christian name are the key words when you do this. But make up your mind it is for the final time. Nothing causes more uneasiness among your close friends than your delight to appear as a man one minute and as a lady the next, unless, of course, all your chums are doing the same. Nor is it becoming to take advantage of your previous gender and if recently male and now female, to be overly coy when the first gentlemen make their advances, or when rejecting a suitor, to suddenly sock or flip the poor guy on his arse. Although provoked to behave otherwise, conduct yourself as a lady at all times.

Women who have become gentlemen should grant all courtesies to their presently opposite sex that they hitherto enjoyed as females. Make sure that those who may have cause to grab or feel your recently added appendages, know what they are in for, if these are not exactly what your normal person would prefer to expect.

Upon Nude Encounters with Servants

Upon a male servant confronting his female employer's stark nakedness he should take no undue notice of her nudity and on no account should he drop what he is carrying. A butler encountering his mistress in the altogether should address madam as if she were fully dressed. And especially avoid being facetious with the remark.

'Madam is looking her best this morning.'

When encountering her master's nudity it is becoming for a female servant to drop whatever she is carrying and then to deflect her glance even when requested to take a closer look or to make comment upon her employer's gifts of nature. Should His Lordship advance upon her person, she ought to withdraw coyly and giggling. In cases where passions become kindled and ignited, do not overly prolong activities or dally to make small talk when the deed is done. And normal formalities of address may only be abandoned during orgasm. Remember there is a household to be run. And insolence lurks but a caress away.

Upon Being of a Colour in an Area Where Such Colour Is Not Highly Esteemed

Keep smiling. If asked what you are smiling at. Keep moving.

Upon Some Guest's Kid Abusing Your Chattels

Close upon the offending little bugger and grasp him firmly by the ear until the kid says.

'Ouch, what are you doing that for.'

Then still attached to his hearing appendage tug him around you in a circle, releasing your grip when his feet leave the floor. Upon the recalcitrant rascal picking himself up, admonish him with your severely wagging finger.

'I'm not going to let some little bastard like you come in and wreck my god damn house. I'll kill you first.'

Should the culprits be a pair of brothers getting up to mischief, take each by an ear and run in a forward direction but beware this pair will later be conspiring to set alight whatever they can find inflammable in your cellar or attic. And indeed should you be a bibliophile they will delightedly fuel your library fireplace with your more ancient first editions.

Upon Suffering Social Descent as a Member of the Gentry to the Lower Classes

Soften this by taking employment in a household similar to the one to which you were accustomed. As a married couple you can work as butler and maid and continue your enjoyment of long corridors, stately rooms and open vistas of parkland. Most likely your new employers will be nouveau riche and insensitive to your past dignities, nevertheless you should be sporting about their failings in not being to the manner born. If you have been slung into basement quarters, remember that your waking day is spent above stairs. And that when the master is away, you can enjoy a brandy and cigar in the comfort of the library without that obtuse money making jerk around.

There will be supremely disheartening moments serving at table. Especially when accosting your previous friends who are taking second helpings of the asparagus and who have not yet fallen upon hard times. Being restrained and spectacularly dignified at such moments is de rigueur. Speak only when spoken to. Later on in the evening in the withdrawing room while you're cutting the cigars and serving the port and liqueurs and when guests are a little squiffy, you may then be a trifle more familiar. While serving the port, it is permissible due to your past elegances to take a sip but remember to comment upon its character and condition thereby still performing your function as a servant of the household. Your cigar sampling should be done in the pantry as it is entirely wrong to blow out your smoke in guests' faces. Which is more or less a way of telling them their days are numbered before they end up like you.

Now and again you will get aggressively drunk and abuse your employer and point up his lack of manners or breeding. Although this is acknowledged and understood as reasonable occasional behaviour consequent upon your fall from grace, don't make a daily practice of it. And above all don't do it in front of other household servants. Although these latter are now your equals, you must continue to lord it over them. Not to do so will produce worse indignities than you've already had in your come down.

The Au Pair

Au pairs are usually possessed of extra large appetites and will shortly after they arrive, suggest to you the brands of food they like. Upon a cake being produced in the kitchen, they will take the first wedge out of it before it reaches your guests and the nerviest may even try on your underwear. If you cohabit with them, they will often embarrassingly pretend to be from socially superior families and as they lie late in bed will offer quite unbelievable exhibitions of brazen impertinence in being requested to get up. And don't be surprised if, encouraged by your familiarity, they even further expect you to play the more demeaning roles in your naughty lewd little games.

Upon Inheriting a Title or Gaining Rank

There are still plenty of opportunities in the bath to behave like the ordinary person you used to be. But make it clear straight off that you are no longer just the same old George you were in your previous status. Exact from those around you the suitable and necessary protocol that goes with your new position. For old times' sake exceptions may be made for your closest intimates to call you in private an arsehole. However, it is recommended not to be too lenient about this, and an occasional reference to your title and rank should be required as well.

Attending the Reading of Wills

This is an awkward time. And on no account slap your thighs and put your head back to roar out loud laughing when you are mentioned as the sole or largest beneficiary under a will and those whom you hate most are the least or are excluded altogether. It is permissible however to assume an air of righteousness and laugh like hell when out of sight.

If the will ignores you or leaves you pathetically entitled, be seen weeping. But do not stand up or bounce around in fury. Instead after wiping your eyes, go into calm consultation with your lawyers near the door where whispers are overheard that there will be an impending legal holocaust with claimants galore.

Upon Encountering Massive Windfalls

Head immediately for the cruise ship. Fully reclined on a steamer chair reading the classics is often where one can best come to terms with mountainous new wealth. It takes time and imagination to groom yourself morally and physically to the enjoyment of spending a fortune. Be patient and sit tight. You'll think of something. Above all do not celebrate or give money away. Thereby you prevent the spreading of the problem you've got.

Upon Being Sued

This is often how you meet your first lawyers, a section of the population who charge only what they hope the traffic can bear. Which is a lot. They are employed by people who desperately don't want to roll up their sleeves and have a fair fight. So get ready for plenty of turpitude and plan for the long haul. It takes time and money to sue you. Before final judgements are handed down your opponent may be crazy, bankrupt or dead. If you can spot a lawyer's letter without opening it and can return it marked deceased, this is a trump card. If you cannot suppress your desire to reply, then state.

Dear sir,
Only for the moment am I saying nothing.

When the World Rats on You

It's amazing how good they are at timing this so that they'll all be together. But before you lose all your faith in human decency, check first to be sure that all windows and other entrances to your premises are securely fastened. Then ask for mercy. This is when they will come at you more eager than ever for the kill. Choose the most unpleasant looking and make sure that he goes with you to your doom. This improves the world. And it is seemly to commit a beneficial act upon your departure. Plus the prospect of going down with you discourages people ratting on you in the first place.

Upon Inlaws Moving In or Trying to Commandeer Your Property

It would amaze you how they think they can present themselves and take over things they decide you don't happen to need at the moment. Have no truck with this kind of nonsense. And with those who find it rather comfortable to take up residence in your house and intend to settle in, don't stand on ceremony. Instead fly into an evening rage giving them notice of an early hour the next morning upon which you require them vamoosed or else. This hysterical manic threat worries and weakens them during the night and by the time it's time to go they're glad to be gone. Especially if you hint at your recent sleep walking tendency for throttling folk in their sleep.

Upon Stabbing Folk in the Back

Although thought despicable, this low down dirty rotten filthy trick is getting more and more popular with nearly everybody. Especially when it's your closest friend sticking in the knife. But no matter how this is done, the guy you do it to is invariably deeply resentful since he always thought you were his pal. Try to make him understand how necessary it was and how reluctant you were to do it. Otherwise he might turn around and bust you one permanently in the face.

Upon Doing the Decent Thing in the Face of Many Juicy and Shoddy Alternatives

No matter how good this may make you feel, it always arouses the scepticism of others. So make sure your ulterior motives are worth it.

Upon Presenting Yourself before an Investigating Committee

Dress soberly in the current fashion and always wipe the dirty looks off your face. Avoid hand wrenching, lip licking and eye darting. At the very beginning of proceedings apologize for any involuntary tremors, facial tics, quakes or quavers. And if you must chew gum to quieten your nerves be sure in disposing of it, to stick this well in under your chair or table. There is nothing worse than when squirming, your knee gets smeared with this viscous matter.

Smile once in a while and don't be afraid to laugh along

with the committee especially when they are laughing at you. Remember fairness, if not forgiveness, is the hallmark of these sessions. When caught in a lie retract and apologize immediately. Unless of course they keep catching you, in which case, absolutely avoid shrugging your shoulders. Instead at your next earliest opportunity demonstrate your eagerness to get at the facts by prefacing your answers with.

'I'm really glad you asked that.'

At all times be polite and respectful. When the committee have you dead to rights it is permissible, in order to gain their understanding and sympathy, to allow tears to well in your eyes. But don't overdo this with outright sobbing. Above all, never stand up shouting and shaking your fist and accusing the committee of being themselves just a bunch of chisellers, frauds, liars and cheats who just happen at that point in time not to be under investigation. It is always appreciated that no one is free of human fault but that some happen to be at certain times freer than others.

Upon Replying to Interrogation

If the dirty bastard questioning you is sarcastic it is always sure damn proof that they haven't got the goods on you yet. In which case be curt, crisp and monosyllabic. This allows your inquisitor little time to dream up any ad lib ways of trapping you. Which if he does, then semantically couch your words with other words, which although meaningful if attached to a fact, will mean nothing when woven into the incredible fiction you're saying.

Upon Committing Perjury

First rehearse being honest in front of a mirror until you absolutely believe yourself. Then upon making sure no one can slam you with contrary evidence, get up there in your best toneless and expressionless manner and spiel off your bare faced lies.

When caught, avoid the sickeningly mealy mouthed excuse that you were only telling the truth as you saw it for the time being. Instead, have ready a list of dire personal tragedies which were plaguing you at the material time of your falsehood and which made you tell such whoppers. Which you hope now makes you no longer sound like a liar.

Upon Bad Mouthing an Enemy

Limit yourself to about seven minutes' continuous ranting and then finish off with about thirty seconds' vituperative scourging. Flavour your scurrilous references, malicious rumours and gossip with a grain of objectivity to make the offending words more effective. This will also make your defence look better in an action for slander.

Upon Being Published in a Debtors' Gazette

Threatening noises to the offending journal is always advised. Meanwhile demonstrate frugality about you. This lessens the bitterness of creditors. Further to combat this most awkward state of affairs, a posture of outrage should be adopted as soon as possible. There will be many non creditors perusing this broadsheet who will smack their lips together with delight and some who will callously get up on their desks and gig all over their bloody mahogany. Besides spelling ruin to your future and being a heinous insult to your good name it is of course also a diabolically unsporting aspersion, being as you are a man who will rise up fit and fighting after having been busted down broken arsed and thoroughly flattened. While nevertheless enjoying the equitable interest rates statutory debt affords.

Upon the Bailiff or Sheriff Arriving to Possess Goods

Although you stamp, holler and brandish cudgels, rarely can these hardened folk be put off the scent. Therefore it is best to have the utmost compassion for their unpleasant job and to treat them with every courtesy. In this manner it is not unknown for the sheriff or bailiff who has come to remove your horses to sell at the auction ring, to instead end up grooming them for you to ride. But don't count on this and hide your valuables.

Upon Doing unto Others as They Would So Treacherously Delight to Do unto You

Besides being accused of murder this would keep you awfully busy.

Upon Being Unflatteringly Dressed in an Emergency

Instantly assert your natural haughty particularity when you appear dishevelled without your usual trappings, decorations, insignia, tailoring and rank which tell folk who you really are. This will let people know that although for the time being you look otherwise, that you really are something. Should they remain unimpressed, burst into tears. Because this really is humiliating.

Upon Letting Your Lawn Grass Grow Long

Nothing starts the looks and whispers from the neighbours accumulating faster. And before they start harassing you, thinking you're a radical about to sell to an undesirable, which of course you are, because you wisely already have, erect a small sign discreetly displayed.

PLEASE DO NOT OBJECT
THIS IS A BIOLOGICAL EXPERIMENT
IN GRASS GERIATRICS

Upon Being Made Aware of an Insult to Your Hotel Companion

When an employee's opinion is heard as follows.

'Gee look at that guy with that red haired tart he's dragging to his room.'

Immediately contact the manager and apprise him of your severe grievance and spiritual maim. Upon his continuing to offer his deepest and most elaborate apologies without undertaking that your stay, with full room and board and the champagne and caviar you and your tart are accustomed to, will be forthcoming with the compliments of the management, keep repeating.

'I demand satisfaction.'

Until such time as this stubborn chap does so undertake.

Upon Paying the Bill in a Restaurant

If the other sons of bitches have through their protestations against your paying, got you to pay, try to be urbane. Although your guests' lip smacking pleasure is no comfort when you sit there ashen visaged and quivering over the bill, this apoplexy can be lessened by scrutinizing your dockets in the most detailed manner possible. And even if you do not wear glasses, have a special pair, or better, a monocle, to elaborately fish out to do this. As enough quarter hours go by in your diligent accountancy, your other sons of bitches will beg to pay.

Upon Inducing Folk to Eat Cheap When You Have Invited Them to Dine

It is amazing that right in front of your face there are some folk, usually those who proclaim it is not chic to talk too loud about money, who will order the most expensive items

they can find on the bill of fare. Therefore it is permissible if
you have lots of nightmare overheads with a town house on
the best side of town and two or three former wives to support, to slam your high priced menu shut after a split second
perusement and announce.

'I'm not hungry.'

Before anyone else has a chance to order, request them to help
themselves without stint to water, rolls and butter. Reach for
these from nearby restaurant tables if necessary and upon the
waiter's appearance point instantly for replenishments.

If the inevitable happens and guests start to mouth demands for real food of the kind listed on menus, allow your
chest to heave in a manner suggesting a possible massive re-
gurgitating. Should your ravenous guest take no notice and
stuff the corner of his napkin inside his collar and signal the
waiter, then don't hesitate, take out your own brown paper
lunch bag. Your guests will, if they have any sense of embarrassment at all, sit stunned, dumbfounded and momentarily
sheepish.

But if the crass bastards still keep vocalizing pricey orders
at the waiter, then forthwith move to another table. Being
that much of a pathological tightwad not only will you have
your guests wondering if you're still paying but other diners
sensing what's happened should be glad of the opportunity
of hearing your conversation shouted back and forth. And
even some, when they hear of your abstemiousness, may invite you to dine with them. But beware you don't end up
with the tab.

Upon Becoming Sick on or Objecting to a Restaurant's Food

If you have the strength and are not permanently doubled up, raise your right hand at once for the manager and clearly gasp out your symptoms. Unless owner run, most eating establishments will be covertly supercilious about your displeasure at the table. Knowing as they do that normally a few hours must elapse before food poisoning gets a real grip on their victims, who will then usually be some distance away yawking on someone else's carpet.

However, complaint, upon reaching a chef's ears, is always instant incitement to these highly temperamental gentlemen who have been known to rush from backstage to slap a face with plaice or slosh antique sauce over customers. But count yourself lucky at such a forthright venting of feelings. For chefs, who remain in the privacy of their culinary castles, and to whom you have returned food, wiping their feet in your steak will be the least of it.

Face Lifting and Plastic Surgery

Contour changing should be done in the winter so that you'll be blossoming in spring. Do make sure your choice of a new set of features befits your social station and also that your recent nose will remain in fashion for a while. Toning up the sloppy loose skin and smoothing over the wrinkles and bags and hacking off excess curvatures can change your expression dramatically. Therefore always steel yourself against an acquaintance's most likely remark.

'Hey what the hell happened.'

And so that this does not make you look even more morbid, never try to explain.

'I was looking for a new body.'

Because your opponent will be tempted to suggest.

'That's not what you need.'

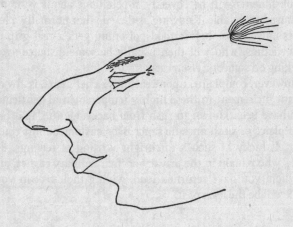

Upon Suing Your Hosts for Injury in Their House

If you still have your brains left having dived deeply into the shallow end of your host's pool, also have the decency to wait at least until the ambulance has taken you away before contacting your lawyer. And when only partially burned and otherwise slightly contused by someone's detonating oven, it is still essential you remove yourself from the premises and do not wait to eat the exploded dinner. When folk attempt to remain friends in the face of their legal action it is a sure sign they are wavering in their affection.

Mischiefs &
Memorabilia

Upon Being Cuckolded

After the years of wearing yourself out giving your wife the adoration the use of her assets required, some sleazy type now manages to forge his way into her favour by exhibiting much swaggering of his boyish hind quarters and showering her with a few second rate compliments. Don't be civilized about this. It is a distinct time for peevishness.

Establish the chap's social credentials straight off, making sure your opponent is not of an inferior sort, since for the sake of protocol you don't want to waste dignified time sassing some fly by night greaseball. And instead of the usual ear fluffing with the usual chamois gloves one should prefer to deliver a good hob nailed boot up your shabby chap's rear end as being the more astonishingly appropriate measure.

Often your better class philanderer will have been your house guest upon occasion. Where he has been taking your wife for walks along your decorative bodies of waters and, would you believe it, spouting poetry. Your first signs of something severely amiss is when he is impatient with your story telling, and looks distinctly sour as you render your most genuinely uproarious jokes. Failure at the table to push the condiments your way is another sign of his increasing insolence. And when dining out the philanderer will make a big show of attempting to pay the bill. Don't give him this sneaky satisfaction. Make your own impassioned insistence upon paying it. Your opponent will confidently retaliate with an equally firm determination. Then let him pay.

Particularly distressing transgressions occur when this ne'er do well encroaches upon your more intimate territories. On no account allow your silk dressing gowns or other personal items to be commandeered. As you will find the bounder trying to wear three pairs of your most elegant town socks on his country hike. And it really is the god damn limit if this upstart starts reading your leather bound first editions in front of your dressing room fire. Especially after he has just rogered your wife in the next room. Together with the shocking thought that she could have, while thrilling, been heard by the house staff. Although, thank god, this is the kind of caper that goes on when you are distantly away overseeing forestry on the estate. Nevertheless the rapid accumulation of flagrant indignities can be quite appalling. But by playing your cards right, you can render the son of a bitch impotent.

Be splendidly turned out for the moment chosen to confront the perpetrator of your cuckolding. This is of course a very tricky period if your wife controls assets upon which, for your own well being, you require to rely from time to time. And some strong line may be required. Which should always be conducted in pukka.

> 'Look here, sir, you are cohabiting with my wife. How dare you.'
> 'Martha and I are in love.'
> 'Sham. Despicable sham. What are your assets dear boy.'
> 'I've got as much as you have.'
> 'Which is, I regret to say, fuck all. And therefore I call upon you in a major manner to desist.'

In accosting this diabolical runt your little flourishes of impeccability will add to your chap's growing inferiority. Particularly your liberal use of gentlemen's talcum powder and the best snuffs. He quite naturally will be sporting some recent fashion craze accenting the casual, as well as his own glaring inanity, of that you can be sure. And hopelessly, he will attempt to imitate you, having been regaled concerning your personal habits by your unfaithful wife. Mostly while the son of a bitch was reading the serial numbers of her bonds over her shoulder. And by now he has settled nicely in.

'Ah how are you and Martha getting on dear boy.'

'Well we have our ups and downs.'

'I understand it has not been up but down.'

'Martha, that dirty bitch told you that.'

'Yes as a matter of fact she did and while you are signally failing to roger my wife I'll thank you not to refer to her as a dirty bitch.'

And don't hesitate to further play merry hell with this bastard by sending little reminders with suitable flowers to the many sneaky bookings into various hotels not to say motels with the accompanying note.

> Hope for the sake of the old bones of my wife that you may yet get it up. You wretched simpleton you. Martha is of course thoroughly used to being rogered in a major manner. In fortissimo spirituoso vibrato, as a matter of fact.

Mirrors

A chap who looks in these in public, thereby practising his phony smile, examining what he thinks is his best profile, or putting what he thinks is his best expression on his otherwise forgettable face, is unpardonable. Always upon encountering a mirror by accident, avert your eyes. But upon entering hotel lobbies there is a permissible moment for a brief glance to flatter the self lightly when a nervous touch may be made to the hair if the wind has been unduly strong outside.

Upon Observing Folk Who Appear So Overly Sure of Themselves

Depressing spectacle though this is, a sensitive gentleman must bear with this rampantly popular affectation. Most of these bastards have the unpleasantly pompous habit of being fully booked up at all times. And upon their rushing to meetings will often be seen referring to their schedules. It helps however, in combating your own forlornness, if you try once in a while to have somewhere to go or someone to meet.

But it could do both you and your victim a lot of good to snatch your man's diary right out of his damn silly fingers right in the middle of the hotel lobby and remind him of the world's starving and dying. Be prepared however for this to have little effect. So many people these days think their own importance is also a matter of life and death.

Facial Expressions

As these guide you through life, it is as well to keep them up to peak performance by exercising them every morning. Begin with glowering and growling. Followed by displeasure and pleasure, nonchalance and discomfiture. And before finishing up with tittering and laughing be sure to give cowardice and inferiority a good workout, just in case your bravery and superiority are not up to scratch that day. Strict privacy should be observed during practice sessions as regretfully these facial expressions in quick combination demonstrate certifiability.

Displaying Your Medals and Decorations

It is simply too self consciously modest to harbour these away in cellars and attics, as it never hurts to let people know how and when you were outstanding. And if such reminders are not presently on your chest, then display them in a glass wall cabinet at the top of stairs or in the hallways leading to your reception rooms.

It is permissible, concerning an award for outstanding valour, to provide martial background music and spotlighting of the medal. But it is extreme bad taste to show a film recording of the event in which you heroically won it.

Upon Walking into Places as If You Own Them

In daily partaking of your pleasures this is a handy demeanour which is best perfected by practising on a place you would not like to own. Choose the worst dump in town. Practise your demeanour there. If you don't get shot, busted on the jaw or arrested then assume this same demeanour back in the best place in town. Where you're damn sure to get shot, busted on the jaw and arrested.

Upon Feeling Out of Place

If you have any finer feelings or dignity at all, this will happen everywhere. But it only means that heinous other people have got there first. Never stick around till you get used to it, or just like the boorish, you will feel thoroughly at home.

Upon Folk Putting Their Feet Up on Your Furniture

People usually take this unpleasant liberty if your house is not fully furnished or if you have said you bought a piece of furniture cheap. But whatever you do in this world, don't let people put their god damn feet up on your furniture. Approach immediately to where their feet are and stand and stare. Should the feet remain, announce in an extremely angered voice.

'Get your god damn feet down offen my property.'

By appending en to off, making the word offen, it will make it sound as if in the heat of the moment, your accent slipped and your opponent will come to fear that another much darker person is hidden by the usually affable you. Upon whom he cannot lightly dare wipe his tootsies.

Upon Travelling in Space

When your fellow passenger's dinner floats away from his mouth with weightlessness, gently push it back in his direction. Be doubly careful at your toiletries and remember, breaking wind in these rarefied atmospheres can be positively dangerous.

Arriving on the foreign planet, do not display your clod

hopping primitive ways but attempt to imitate their modern ones. And don't above all try to get funny by telling a long string of earthy jokes to the first foreigner you see. Nor attempt any carnal linkage or saucy dovetailing until you know for sure where to put your what for into their this is it. Also you better hope to god you can get it out again. As you wouldn't know what the hell kind of magnetics they've got out there in some of them galaxies.

Upon Being a Big Shot

Choose places where there is a sufficient audience. And be sporting enough to ask the small time people present about themselves. Particularly their mothers. Indeed the remark.

'She must have been a remarkable woman.'

Nearly always says enough to your opponent to remind him that he can bet his life yours was.

Upon Ennobling Your Noble Spirit

Enter company shyly. Make it a habit to order the large size of anything. Never walk forth and introduce yourself or heap helpings from your host's sideboard without being beseeched for the second time to do so. Never fear to chat with chaps who have been knocked on their arses by misfortune. Instead of befriending the mighty, be kind to little children. Demand a good price for anything you sell and never pay over the market for anything you buy. Screw other men's wives only when they implore you to.

Upon Being Cultured

Your bowels should move better than those who are not.

Upon Being Unknown

Always wear a miffed demeanour. But for this to matter in the least, someone has got to wonder who the fuck you are. And he could be trying to collect taxes.

Fame and Celebrity

As these come to you, let them go to your head. Among personal friends do not remain just the same old ordinary bloke they used to know. Although the advantages of your notability can suddenly desert you in the middle of a foreign desert or jungle or wherever illiteracy is rife, it can nevertheless be extremely useful in helping you get found when they hear back in civilization that you are lost.

Treat your fans well. But be churlish when they follow you around the clock, even though they like to see you sensational and smiling. And blush if they tend to tear your clothes off. Wear suitable garments which come apart easily and in a manner that your most ardent followers will at least get a handful if not a feel of you.

Upon the Display of Sun Tan

If you are blessed with a little black blood, this leisured look crisping of the epidermis is not a problem. But as the lizard like brown hardens over the years on your sack of haggard old bones, don't smile. As this can make you look like you're grinning out of the grave.

On Tipping

Dropping the foreign coin into the palm causes uncomfortable peering by your opponent into that area as he holds it closely to his side wondering what it is worth. And it is permissible to shout back if you are accused of being a cheapskate, piker or other odious non tipping thing, that your adversary should apply to a charitable institution to obtain his handouts. Most of your better folk anyway would rather receive a sincere smile and a heartfelt thanks. However, the rich get everything they want this way. And the poor, less than they would like.

Upon Being Snubbed

Everyone is snubbed for a good reason. This either firms up the character or destroys it entirely. But as soon as possible let yourself get god damn furious at this inattention. The voids out there in the world where you must drag your feet are windy and lonely and anger is good company. Meanwhile take solace from the fact that it is unlikely you will ever be kidnapped. As your miffed feelings increase to wretchedness, turn it as soon as you can into bitterness. When this is deep enough, convert it into the resolve of revenge. After this is entrenched keep enough energy left over to get rich and famous. Otherwise do not frequent where you will be spurned.

When You Are Laughed At

If you are not trying to be funny this is always a difficult time for your paranoia. But much will depend on the number of people guffawing at you and if the crowd gets uproarious, get yourself a manager, you could be a comedian. On the other hand, should the laughter abruptly subside, grab your hat and get ready to beat it. Jeers and rotten eggs and things much worse are often on their way.

Upon People's Attention Wandering as You Talk

Remedy this damn inconsiderate and infernal cheek by a good shove right on the shoulder and a good loud shout into the ear hole. Indeed don't even stop short of slapping the son of a bitch in the face. It's amazing how fast folk, if they weren't interested in what you were saying, will soon be stunned by what you're doing.

Upon Accepting Prizes Awards and Distinctions

Do this gracefully and graciously. There is nothing worse than to see an overinflated ego thumbing his or her nose at the award committees and hoping thereby with this gesture to increase the publicity. Which by the way it really does.

When giving your acceptance speech wear only your other

superior rewards and medals. It is permissible to hint light-heartedly at why this present distinction hadn't come earlier in your more unknown and needful years. But anyway, you can add, better late than never. Leave a little pause here for the nervous laughter. The audience should find you endearing.

Upon Contributing Money

Always do this out of the goodness of your heart for if you stop to think while you sit there reading the newspapers with these big expensive ads telling you to give, and with photographs of the chairman of these charitable organizations traipsing around in his big limo and private aircraft with luxury apartments all over the place you'd think, hey, where the hell's my money going. It could be less agonizing to remain a confirmed cheapskate and tightwad. However, with lifeboat institutions which effect rescue at sea, you might make an exception, as well as with panhandlers who are charming.

Upon Using People for What They're Worth

First find out exactly how much this is, but beware as you attempt to take advantage. Folk have a devilish way of short changing you, which oft times can only be described as bitterly disheartening.

Upon Living and Let Live

Be sure when taking this attitude your assets or life are not in danger and that your wife is faithful. If someone is being murdered beneath your window, it is not nice to merely say, well everybody has got a time and place when they are going to get theirs. This posture although prudent raises the odds that you are also going to get yours sooner.

Upon Heaping Abuse on the High and Mighty

This is a symptom of knowing you are never going to be esteemed and powerful. In any event it is sporting to give the big guy a kind word once in a while. As everybody is shouting encouragement on the side of the underdog these days.

Upon Being High and Mighty with the Low and Weak Heaping Abuse

It is always a good thing to be away on a trip. But if they've got you to come out on your fortified rampart, try to look reasonable and that you are bowing to the will of the people. Remember if you insult the people everybody with their god damn paranoia rampant is going to think you are insulting them. And of course, since you are, you can have a god damn army around your castle cutting up the meadow and launching assault boats across your moat with ladders to climb your battlements, rocks to bounce off your gun slits and clubs to try to beat back your man eating dogs. Protected the way you are, you could end up with the public maimed all around you. For which you would be further reviled.

Upon Being a Sportsman

This can entitle you to frequent backslaps. And it is a pity that such crass stupidity accompanies this trait.

Upon Accosting Your Trusted Manager or Accountant Who Has Been Cheating You over a Long Number of Years

Since complaint creases the face, bothersome and deuced nuisances should not be dwelled upon. However this is generally an awful occasion which may keep you frowning awhile. Most folk stupid enough to let someone else manage their cash flow, will have no reserves. And this puts you in a vulnerable position upon appealing to your previously trusted chap's honour which will do no good whatever except save you energy wasted in screaming hysterical abuse. Therefore further contain yourself as your opponent sits at his desk silent, letting you do all the talking, since what's there to say when he already has long since spent all the cash and no amount of this sneaky son of a bitch's contrite words will make up for that. And now that you don't have a bean to sue him with also make sure you're well dressed enough so that he doesn't suddenly have you thrown out as a loitering vagrant.

Upon Being Puzzled by the Meaning of Life

Commence fasting till your perplexity is replaced by the desire for food. Should the bewilderment again return upon a full stomach, abandon the roof over your head and give away all your worldly goods until finding a place to sleep occupies your mind. Should puzzlement beset you yet again, it is proof that you have been somewhere sneakily eating and sleeping comfortably.

Upon the Pointy Two Toned Shoe

More grief can be dumped upon you from wearing this apparel than you would believe. Especially when some folk you met last year on the beach say these are not proper for winter wear and look like hell in the snow. With this most exasperating problem it's best to be absolutely lyric in your defence. Because if people think you don't know any better, wow are you going to be way down in their books, with your opponent approaching to archly ask.

'Hey why the pointy two tone.'

Slam back pronto the riposte.

'Because, you objectionable pipsqueak, my soul craves through the barren cold winter some little sartorial nuance to lightly take it a step further towards spring when I'd delight to root the sharp end up your panty.'

Upon the Light Tan Shoe

These as footwear are at all times unforgivable and get to the nearest cow pasture fast to suitably darken them.

Upon Being Done the Tiniest of Courtesies

Always have ready at your fingertips a selection of grateful responses gently intensifying in gratitude. O thanks. Thank you. Thank you very much. Hey really thank you. I mean thanks a whole bunch. Holy cow thanks. Gee that was good of you. I mean to say, how nice can some people get.

Upon Those Who Lack the Basic Human Decencies

While you are well known to be elsewhere, they will ask to rent at an enormous rent your flat or town house you happen to keep at your convenient disposal in a well known sophisticated city. And even further suggest that the resident cook, maid and chauffeur receive extra emoluments. Aside from your wine cellar being depleted and mucho cutlery, Delft and linen missing, they will use more electricity than you ever imagined possible. The telephone bill will be stupendous. And another thing you can be sure of as well. They will not pay. They will never pay. It is even not nice to sue them. Because they have no assets. And tons of itinerant concrete nerve.

On Wielding Disparaging and Chastening Terms Various

Abusive unflattering words are best couched in clichés and delivered with composure which can be nicely accentuated by speaking with one's eyes fluttering closed. But if you encounter someone pulling this on you, don't hesitate, instantly shake the haughty nerve out of them with a non fracturing slap.

The proper insult should contain barbed implications. This makes folk reflect before they think of physically retaliating to your horrid remarks. Popular racial terms such as wop, yid, kraut, mick, bohunk, limey, coon can increase the disendearment as does the addition of god damn. However upon the casual bad mouthing of a pair of established theatrical celebrities ethnic slurs can make way for a generally discrediting reflection.

'He's nothing but a hen pecked fart and she's the most prurient of old hags.'

For emergency gutter use, especially on the pavement with a stranger of obvious repellent qualities, the good old fashioned verbal blast of motherfucker may be preceded by something bitingly choice in order that it heap sufficient malediction upon your adversary.

'You cocksucking motherfucker.'

Or upon your shoe hysterically skidding in a dog's recent steamy befoulment of the footpath, terms from the alimentary canal are suitable.

'You and your bow wow, madam, are both rectums.'

Invectives improve when preceded by the person's colour. And black, white and yellow will be the most common ones you will encounter. Anything else and you might prudently stand immediately away to avoid a disease. Particularly enraged feelings may be expressed in the longer combinations especially to those gentlemen who may hear abusive brusqueries frequently.

'You cocksucking motherfucking ape faced black coon.'

This of course may bring laughter to the lips of one of these elegant pastoral people who might delight in being equipped with so many racy possibilities. In which case instantly address him in pukka as a cad or bounder. However should some red necked whitey pompously so address you, riposte.

'How dare you be unparliamentary with me sir.'

Terms of Reference for Disapproved Folk

Said in a fairly mild offhand manner, your chap may be referred to as of less than average talents, without rank or fortune, does not hunt, shoot or fish and is very skinny in the shank, nor is he a good judge of horse or cattle and since stale biscuits have recently bound his bowel and his wife whom he married for her money has slipped him a purgative, his explosive jet blasts have ricocheted him miles out of good society.

Four Letter Words

Shit is now the proper term for manure, droppings, crap or that stuff. Should you be in extremely polite sophisticated society one may, to show mild impatience, use the expression.

'Fuck this shit.'

When the term is shouted loudly of course, its meaning may be changed. Especially while displaying extreme exasperation at table games when upsetting the whole kit and caboodle. People whose drinks have spilled into their laps in the excitement may exclaim.

'Holy shit.'

The word 'cunt' is still not nice to use in the presence of ladies of riper years, since their sensibilities may be thereby ruffled. And when applied to a chap should be additionally described.

'You unconscionable cunt you.'

Piss as a mild expletive may be used anywhere. It can be made milder still with additions.

'O piss and pother.'

The Unforgivable Insult

List these in a notebook giving the time, place and circumstances. You will be amazed at how quickly your notes will grow and be a potted history of your life. In the case of the more slanderous ridicules these can be reviewed by a lawyer who can also get a working idea of what others think of you in order to assess the amount of damages to be sought.

Handy Sayings

'So nice to meet you like this.'

'Like this' is the simple additive that turns an expression into something quite electrically charming and it can be equally delightful to reply.

'I'm glad you said that.'

In riposte to any double meaning naughty suggestion, 'I beg your pardon' should be used. 'I beg your pudding' is the jocular form.

In showing enthusiasm or shock, have ready rejoinders gradually waxing in crescendo. Gosh. Holy cow. Gee winikers. Land sakes alive. And for ladies confronted by a deliberately exposed outsized engorged gentleman's appendage from which she is not yet sure she wants to run.

'O my god.'

Upon the Proper Haughty Posture for the Delivery of Insult

Rock slowly back and forth on your best leather heels. Keep the upper lip stiff. With the tongue however darting between the lips in the reptilian manner. This rapid moistening of the exterior of the mouth is essential. The eye blink should be given at three to the second at intervals of four seconds. Labial roticism characterized by the defective pronunciation of r in sounding words, should be used especially when pontificating. Hold the head slightly back, the chin up and forward. Remember the recessiveness of the lower jaw was bred for this purpose.

In Extra Ordinary Pukka Conversation

While looking over the speaker's left or right shoulder either at the room's decorations or new arrivals, the repetitive nasal yes should be employed when listening to comments from another and should interpose his conversation at an interval of every five words except where he is approaching the end of making a point when the interval should be dropped to every three words. The word 'quite' followed by Uhmnnnn should be employed in an easy leisurely manner at an interval of every seven words when your phony smile should briefly alight and erase on your face.

Verbal Invitations

In order that these not be accepted too eagerly the brow should instantly be creased in doubt. When the invitation is further pressed, then the blue appointment book is withdrawn and paged through till the appropriate date is reached. A long pause should follow using the word Uhmnnnn and the inviter should then be asked to repeat the details of his invitation. Then purse the lips and in a loud forceful manner announce.

'Yes, by George, I think I may just be able to do it. If I push.'

However, if while you commence pushing, your inviter should lose patience and his temper and riposte.

'Look you god damn tight assed son of a bitch, you can stuff that appointment book up your hole.'

In haughty manner one may reply.

'I beg your pardon but are you addressing me.'
'You bet your god damn life I am. You stuffed shirt, you.'

To reassert your posture of aloof dignity and also to get another chance of being reinvited do not hint that your adversary's background may not be of the best but reply.

'Dear me you are in a tizzy, aren't you.'

Trembling Your Lid before Flipping It

This gives folk a courteous chance to get the god damn hell out of your way.

Handshaking

This courtesy provides a handy connection and sublimates the outright grabbing of each other so that folk upon being introduced can get a chance to form their strategies on how to make the best use of each other. Your handshake should be firm and brief. If held overlong neither of you may wish to be the first to let go.

The tarzan grip comes from the chap who wants but never gets the biggest piece of the pie. The limp handshake can often be taken as a sign of early betrayal while the hard grippers will usually plan to leave the treachery till a little later. In any case the skin has a natural enzyme which is bactericidal, which helps in case you could catch a disease.

Bowing

It is much appreciated by ladies of riper years, and if this is accompanied by a smart clicking of the heels, it rates a smile. In the case of a dazzling younger woman, a slight genuflection of the head will suffice, as it is understood you will bend over plenty later.

Upon Introduction

'Gee I just can't recall your name.'

Take this as warning of inescapable grief ahead. Therefore should you be unable to remember a person's moniker, blurt out.

'I can't get over how good you look.'

Folk to whom this is said are only concerned in their disbelief to replying.

'Really.'

Name Dropping

This is essential to do to let others know whom they might get to know if they get to know you. In order to warm up, bring out your minor names first, slowly increasing their importance till your adversary quakes with the sound of the majors. If you are a big name yourself, you will of course be deprived of dropping it, unless you can momentarily pretend you are someone else who knows you personally.

Gatecrashing

Come well dressed for this heinous social offence. And give folk a chance to like you. If 'go home' is openly suggested, smilingly enunciate with your best vowels your willingness to do any little jobs to make the other guests happy. If 'go home' is again mooted, be bold enough to come back again. And don't knock, use an axe. The next time after that you will be let in. But nobody nice will tell you where the party is.

Upon Doing Surreptitious Damage at Your Host's Party

It goes without saying that your opponent upon whose pastel walls you leave your greasy hand prints, is rich and also well known for hiding his best drink and victuals while shoving at you all the old stale contents from his larder. Which ingredients should, just as they pass your lips, be exploded back out onto the carpet for starters.

Canine befoulment carried liberally on your instep and wiped off somewhere where it shouldn't be, is a really lousy ill bred dirty stinking trick. Which your host may deserve for his stinginess. But the more serious destructions should be wrought approaching objets d'art backwards with your hands behind you snapping off a leg on all the Tang horses you can find. Beware of bronze specimens of other dynasties, as busting these can lead to your detection. Especially when you grunt, struggle and sweat wielding a hoof off one of these exceptionally strong ancient works of art.

Dancing

Don't get up and continue to hoof about wildly, unless onlookers are clapping and cheering you on vociferously. Folk have been closeted in strait jackets for less. Always ask old ladies to dance, they enjoy this inordinately. If they happen to be extremely rich old ladies you could finally end up enjoying it.

Should your partner encourage you on when stepping upon her toes, it is then permissible to step on her toes but it is not proper to get caught up in the folds of her dress, trap her foot under yours or trip her on her backside unless she too is learning to dance.

The Telephone

This is an instrument a lot of folk use to pretend to be important. So never, by lifting the receiver up too fast, show the bastards that you are sitting beside the god damn phone all the time waiting for it to ring. If the call is obscene, listen carefully as some of these people exhibit really impressive imaginations with their dirty suggestions. In making a call don't say who you are until people get curious thereby providing a little passing entertainment in this soulless method of communication. Always talk on your phone as if it were being bugged and try once in a while to be amusing. This is always appreciated by those who have to spend long hours eavesdropping, taping all the boring things you have to say.

Receiving Letters

Having mail delivered to some address other than at the one where you live can give post a chance to accumulate before you collect it, thereby improving the chance of getting some good news with all the bad. After some preliminary scrutiny to assure that it contains no letter bomb, use a letter opener in case your hysterical fingers tear up a cheque inside made out in your favour.

Feeling bumps running your fingernail over your opponent's letterhead will indicate if it is engraved. This does not always mean that he is big time. But does mean he's concerned with the world's first impression of him and has spent money for expensive printing. In which case if he's looking for investment backing don't give him money to do any more.

The nasty letter should not be replied to. But if someone's intelligent insult has you really boiling out of your mind with rage it is permitted to write.

Sir,
Shame shame shame and so sad for you to still be so shabby.

Letter Writing

Following the exercise of expressing yourself on paper to another there can always come the time that the words so said can be unpleasantly held against you. Therefore be careful putting your libellous thoughts of another into print unless you say you heartily believe them to be untrue.

Upon Writing the Annual Mimeographed Dear Friends Letter

Aside from pointing out your grossly pompous smugness, the form letter also makes you really appear like a publicized asshole. But since such overdone conceits abound, the following is a permissible example in unexpurgated form.

Dear Friends,
It seems such a long time since I last wrote to you. The year has flown by and boy has it been full of nightmarish days for us. January started off with some lousy creep on Bill's staff trying to get him fired (which Bill was in June). This house we bought, thinking we were going to live it up and lord it over the numbskull neighbours awhile, is really for the birds. The lawn sprinkler couldn't sprinkle the tip of my arse. And while on that subject just let me say that my figure is shot to hell since John John. Bill used to say he liked a little tit droop but the way his eyes keep busting out of his head over the local drum majorettes, I know this is hogwash. It takes a double feature showing now of an oral suck sequence and mixed combo daisy chain for him to get it up and it's down for good soon as we get home. We went to the big championship football game and Bill's firm were supposed to pay for everything but our reservations got lost and we had to spend a week in a crappy dump and now even have to pay the bill after Bill got fired. And as if this wasn't enough, when we got home we found sewerage leaking into the swimming pool.

Although fall means football, Bill has had to spend all his free time trying to get spare parts off the derelict cars on the highway. This supplied the year's only real highlight when Bill found a brand new chrome hub cap that fitted our car. But even that victory was dashed a week later when some cop stole it as we parked a second to look at a scenic sight. Then our patio we built when we moved in, is now sinking and cracking up with something like quicksand or something worse underneath it (venomous snakes used to live on this site before it was reclaimed). This blow finally rendered Bill impotent even when I try to relieve his anxiety with a hand job at the local porno flick. Our New Year's resolution is to find out who the hell our real friends are. Please don't plan on visiting us this year. But we hope that you have a very happy holiday and a really prosperous New Year. If my figure was better I'd try to sell ass out of the motel down the highway, I swear it. Instead, I've taken up meditation and masturbation. And Bill is studying Eastern philosophy to see if it will help him get a hard on. It doesn't.

Fondly,
Bill, Barbara, Carol, John John.

Upon Replying to an Unexpurgated Form Letter

Dear Bill and Barbara,

I really laughed like hell when I got your letter this year. I know it sounds terrible but it really made me feel good. I mean you and Bill, if you don't mind me telling you, were always a couple of prize jerks. As you know I was thrown out of high school and when I see a couple of big time college grads like you getting a few slams up the whammo scalammo, it don't half make me feel there's a future for all of us yet. Watch out for them snakes, they like to come back to their old haunts at night. And by the way, why don't you try a mixed racial gang bang for senior citizens, some of them fusty old cats really have a few new fangled novelties up their senile sleeves. And further by the way, while you're at your form letters, why don't you both show a little humility once in a while, all you ever talk about is yourselves. I'd really like to see you libel someone in one of those damn things and then get the shit sued out of you. Also by the way, although this looks like a personal letter I am having copies of it sent to everyone we mutually know, maybe they might know some remedy that could wise you up.

Fondly,
Your form letter friend.

PS   The local movie house suck show has every housewife in town gasping.

PSS   I'm also returning enclosed prints of the nudie photos of you and Bill which I feel must have been mistakenly sent. You're damn right, Bill does look deader than a doornail.

Christmas

In addition to the hurtful beastliness of folk sending you cheap christmas cards or returning yours you sent them last christmas, this is the most vulgar and vicious time of the year for any true lover of the human spirit. And when you are forced to arise on this morning to witness all the god damn money spent on all the crap that lies around gift wrapped under the tree, control yourself. Have a nip of port or sherry as you sit there glum in your dressing gown. As this will be a time of family squabbles and recriminations. When insults stored up all year are unleashed. It is also when litigations are launched to catch the unwary bastard stupidly counting his blessings.

Servants

Since it is now especially tough to find suitable aristocracy, these devoted and biddable people are dying out. And are being replaced by a lot of layabouts who throw up their feet with a six pack to watch colour television in your panelled library, that is if they're not using the pool, sauna or billiard room. Nevertheless it is still unbecoming for the master of a household to be peeved upon staff taking the cream off the milk or nipping the filet mignon out of the steak. And such a sorry state of affairs has come about from employers whose own moral fibre is no better and who do not know how to keep servants honest, happy, loyal and proud to serve.

On Being a Good Butler

You will, of course, upon a visiting Colonel being served his drink and being made to feel thoroughly at home, be able to discreetly recall, after begging sir's pardon, the time when the Colonel gave the order to his troops out in wogland to un-scabbard their swords in such a manner that the sunshine threw a blinding glint upon a mob becoming unruly and riotous and who were with that dazzling tactic quelled.

Remember your master often is a busy man. Avoid giving him botherations. Keep in mind that his success and welfare is yours. Be sure his socks and linens are kept suitably pine scented in their mahogany drawers. That the whisky is at his bedside, shoe horn by his shoes, toothbrush by his toothpaste and his newspaper crisp and freshly ironed. Do not abuse your trust in the wine cellar. However, to keep your hand in and your palate up to scratch it is permissible now and again in your own chambers to light up one of the better cigars accompanied by one of your master's ready to drink vintage ports.

The pantry is the nerve centre of your household. From here proceed elsewhere with a quiet military manner. As the senior in staff, keep those below stairs where rumours and gossip abound, in their place. Never be unpredictable. Keep to prescribed routines. And never, unless summoned, confront the master in the music room, conservatory, library or where he may be earnestly engrossed in a hobby. Especially never divulge details learned of your master's personal oddments, unless fired without reasonable cause. Then exposure in the right magazine or newspaper at the right price is permissible. The auction is the method which gets the best price. Remember there are volume rights, and serial rights. And thank god, for your master's sake, rarely film rights.

Upon the Conduct of Business Negotiations

At the end of it all someone is going to be left holding the bag. Therefore in buying and selling, couch your position carefully in words which may, when a lot more words are put together, say a lot of things to your future advantage as well as provide someone with assets to go after when things go wrong. Especially if you've sold your two favourite pigs for a new wife.

Never assume that people know you are tough. Even when they think your reasonableness is only an attempt to momentarily appear really endearing. Although shouting, stamping your feet and banging the table with your fist makes others uncomfortable at business transactions, it is necessary to demonstrate that your usual easy friendly manner can be instantly and without warning exhausted. Always have ready at your fingertips the following ominously growled statements.

'I'm not going to put my neck out on a limb for anybody.'

And when ratting would appear to be on the horizon.

'And no god damn son of a bitch is going to get away with a thing like that.'

Your position in any deal descends as follows.

> The Lion's share
> A Lion's share
> A Mouse's share
> The Mouse's share

Upon Being Interviewed

If photographs are being taken as well, use one of your better reception rooms and dress in your medieval armour with cross bow if this little flourish bespeaks your present image. Remember the public want to know as much as is intimately possible about you even to having a peek under your steel cod piece. Therefore beware instantly of the interviewing fucker who starts telling you about his or her life while using up your valuable time. Drum your fingers rapidly and loudly on some drum like hollowness near at hand. If this does not make them reach for their note pad to take down your profound remarks but they keep bending your ear. Firmly say.

'Shut up.'

Upon Hiring a Secretary

Never mind the typing, shorthand and assuming of responsibilities, see if they can lift half a hundred weight two handed over their heads. Next look for a pleasant strong leg. These latter are best tested by checking their speed running over a two hundred and twenty yard distance in under thirty seconds flat. You never know when you may have to vacate somewhere fast with your files.

Duties as a Citizen

Remember some people are not as good citizens as others. The common good eludes them completely and most of their daily lives are orientated in the abysmal direction set by their financial advisers for their own comfort and well being. You will recognize many of these chaps in any mirror. And the least you can do is present yourself as a cheerful chap on the pavement each morning and assist the elderly. Plus remain good humoured when they think you're assaulting them.

Vacating Your Seat on Public Transport

Choose a lady of riper years. A smile and a nod is all that is necessary. She will adore this chivalry. Of course when a sly fucker makes a rush and gets his arse right into the space you have just left, you are obliged not only to pin his ears back but to send his bicuspids scattering from his wretched insolent skull. Meanwhile your lady will of course implore you that it doesn't matter all this fuss, that she will gladly stand. For the sake of other passengers' comfort seize this opportunity, especially if the guy is big, to announce. Just before you get off.

'Louts like that make the world lousy for the rest of us.'

Upon Glances at Ladies

If you are in attendance at a dinner party where the seemingly brainless ladies' tits are pouring out of their dresses, keep calm. There will be lots of opportunities between soup and pudding to stare. Meanwhile channel such feverish inclinations as you may have into animated clever ripostes which will provoke laughter and giggles. This should not only make the ladies' items you are perusing shake, but your eyes goggle without compare.

In public the fleeting glance is called for. Or the frequently darting glance if the lady is really something to look at. However, if you can't help the lingering glance and it continues unreasonably, cover your eyes with your hands. Ladies who are beautiful know it. And although they like to be reminded of this, it will please them even more to see you fall off your seat dizzied by your darkness, or if perambulating, walk smack bang into some obstruction. Which always saves them giving you a sock on the jaw.

How to Prevent People from Detesting You

Don't try.

Calling Cards

Upon leaving and bending your calling card, it could, but does not mean I'll break your god damn ass for you. It instead informs those upon whom you have called who do not happen to be at home that you are going away and will not be immediately available and also, that meanwhile, you fervently believe you both move in the same social circle.

Living in Your Own Little Enclosed World of Privilege and Liking It a Whole Bunch

Chuckle generously when observing those who don't but watch out even more.

On Taking Free Reads of Newspaper Headlines

This habit is thoroughly disliked by newsvendors and may be defended by the phrase.

'It's a free country.'

Should the vendor get further angered, add.

'And it's people like you who are making headlines what they are today.'

Upon Fouling the Footpath

What people say about your dog they are saying about you, therefore be ready for a thorough defilement when someone treads in your dog's fresh leavings and when backing away to have a good shout at you, stamps hysterically in even more.

It is permissible when strolling, if a strange doggy comes up and lifts a leg on your latest style newly dry cleaned trousers, to wait till you catch this damn mutt alone and in order that the owner doesn't hear the terrified yelps of agonized canine pain while you kick it in the ribs, hold its mouth closed.

Upon Ordering Kit

Into the shop enter. Deliver the operative word by opening the mouth and hesitating. Then in a higher pitched tone than you ordinarily use, state in a commanding voice, hat, gun, shirt, cane, whip, binocs, et cetera. The assistant will ask the necessary qualifying descriptions, such as top, shot, evening and so on. And in the case of the whip, inquire sadism or masochism, and concerning binocs, racing or peeping tom. Come clean if you are a novice by stating so to the attendant.

'I am a novice.'

The assistant will then supply the necessary fortifying conversation like well sir, there is a first time for everything. A little knowing chuckle from you both will make this pleasantly risqué. Should the unexpected happen and the attendant haughtily view you down his nose, stand silently and still. Let the hurt sink in till globules of tears descend the cheeks. Then in lowered voice inform.

'How could you be so cruel to make me go through all the wretched take over bids I must make to control this store and fire you, you wretched fucker you.'

Upon Robbing a Bank

Although this is among the more respectable forms of crime, always try to make clear to yourself if not others that if it weren't for the world being consistently horrid, resulting in terrible desperation in your own personal life, that you wouldn't be doing it. In any event do not be overtly rude when requesting the cash. A firm precise voice with a slightly evil smile should be used along with the teller's christian name if known. And beware that a lot of your chaps and gals behind counters might want to be heroes by giving the alarm without allowing you a sporting chance. Therefore if you stammer, slip your message across in legible writing.

FREEZE
THIS IS A HOLD UP

And be careful not to leave your name, address and phone number.

If shooting starts courtesies should be instantly suspended. Try to fire over employees' and customers' heads. Remember, a ricochet or whistling bullet often can scare more hell out of folk and keep them in order than anything. But when severely outnumbered, surrender. The sympathy the surrounding public will offer as the police escort you away will amaze you. They know that you've got worries and that they themselves have often passed the same bank with the same thoughts of robbing it. Should you see someone actually mourning on your behalf, comfort them.

Having Successfully Robbed a Bank

Remember you now have, with your newly acquired assets, responsibilities. Deposit your untraceable unmarked bills in a reputable bank. If you want to have a bit of a fling, do it modestly. Do not overtip nor give your wife or girlfriend cause for jealousy. As she can frequently be a source of betrayal. Do good but modest works in the community. And openly complain that you wish others would do as much.

Philosophy

These are thoughts affecting the long term view which one is forced to get in sudden big troubles which come from rain, wind, flood, volcanoes, earthquake, fire and lightning and the

people who wouldn't be human if they weren't out to get you.
And such thinking should come naturally.

Blowing upon Soup

Always do this if it is too hot.

Upon Opening Your Stately Home to the Public

Undertake this begrudgingly and for the money. Since they
will want to get a look at and find out all about your most
private and intimate things. But by dressing in a suitable
manner as a guide and employing further necessary disguises,
you can really have a ball spreading the most wonderful
rumours about ancestors and yourself.

Upon the Nearby Arrival of a Flying Saucer

Immediately offer the comfort of your toilet facilities and just
hope that these foreign bodies can or need to make use of
them. Tea can be mentioned later. But give the chaps a chance
to debark and get their earth legs before burdening them with
a lot of questions. Especially that irritating one concerning
are they really real. In answer to which, flying saucer pilots
are quite liable to wonder if you are.

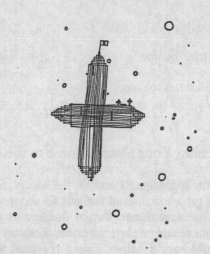

Wife Beating

It is chivalrous to use your least favoured arm keeping your slaps firmly on the jaw. Most wives learn their lessons quickly but in cases of a wife's protracted intractability your favoured arm may be employed. The trouble with spanking is that many wives may not, after a few samples, regard it as punishment and indeed might incite this form of chastisement. Upon the wife fighting back or protecting herself with a weapon take instant precautions as frequently she means business. And above all don't remind her that a discharging shot gun at close quarters or piece of heavy glass sculpture landing on your head could make her a widow.

Upon Being to the Manner Born

This is awfully nice, occasioning as it does much fresh country air, wet nurses when necessary and a doting nannie. Your playmates will be found in similar circumstances in other castles across the meadows. Or if you are a sad lonely little boy there will be an abundance of toys. At school your teachers and masters will regard you with certain courtesies and you will rarely be unpleasantly trifled with. As you inherit your father's fortune, title or both, a path will be laid for you to follow in your ancestors' previous comfortable footsteps and eccentricities and you will always commit your most unforgivable rudenesses with the most stylish of manners. But early in life you will be told as when to appear in the dining room, or take leave of your elders. And mommie will sometimes talk to you in the nursery after she dresses for dinner. Savour such times.

When Blackballed from a Club to Which You Have Desperately Tried to Gain Admittance

Absolutely refrain from writing letters as follows.

Dear Members,

It is with some relief I learn of my not being accepted as one of you, having upon occasion or two been present in your high ceilinged lounge in that pile of masonry down that dark shadowy whorey street watching some of you self importantly reading high brow magazines while peering over the tops of them to see if anyone 'Important' was around. Well I'm not around and if you are the last word in exclusivity, god help us all. Meanwhile you can shove all your marble staircases and brass candelabra which is what you may be doing anyway in those cosy club rooms where you spout your inanities while intoxicating yourselves.

Upon Having Your Picture Taken with Famous People

Get close and throw your arm around your victim's shoulder and smile. Do this at the very last second before they have a chance to jump away from you.

Hotels

These are at best homes away from home and at worst a lot of other things when they have fucked up the reservations. Stand patiently waiting in silence until the clerk thinks you have accepted the matter with good grace. Then in a slightly raised voice.

'I fear, my good man, that this will not do. Aside from my lawyers and advisers taking it to the highest court in the land, which we always do as a matter of course, of course, I will also make a scene in this lobby. Should you be so foolish as to call the police, a gentleman waiting outside the building and my body guard presently sitting over there, will inform the international press agencies to get the story out on their wire services immediately. In addition to that, I will make the next fifteen minutes of your life extremely distasteful and miserable. I suggest therefore that you evict the necessary folk from rooms and suites already occupied so that I may take my pick.'

Beware, usually when you get to the end of such a long spiel, the house detectives grab you on both sides from behind.

Upon a Lady Exhibiting a Motion Picture of Her Saucy Antics

Advanced ladies will quite often exhibit themselves privately on screen in action to gathered guests. And gallant gents present should show a suitably enthusiastic response. Otherwise she may keep rerunning her flick all night thinking you missed something really good. Therefore, during her most tumesced moments, murmurings of bully, goodo, my my and hear hear, often early content madam to rest upon her obscene laurels especially at the end when you all stand up with an heart felt ovation of erections.

Upon Encountering Happiness

Be wary at such times since most of life's blows fall then.

Upon the Untoward in the Pissoir

First, unless serving the public in a personal way, wash your hands before and not after peeing. And then care should be

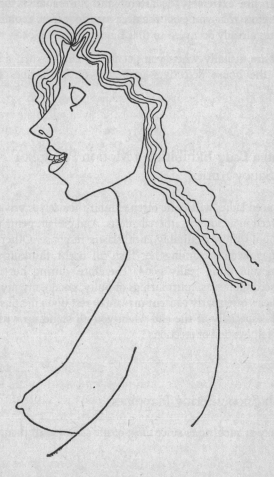

taken in public conveniences not to give offence. Nor to take
any. If you have entered a gentlemen's latrine where the in-
mates are pulling hell out of their appendages don't stare
unless you intend joining the group. Better to retreat as if
you need to make a sudden phone call or if you are desperate

to take a pee, stare straight ahead like you were struck dumb.
To remarks addressed to you from a nearby puller, the simple
phrase.

'I know that my redeemer liveth.'

Will make him wonder what the fuck you're talking about
when jerking off is the immediate subject at hand.

If you have by genuine mistake entered a female public
convenience when you are not clearly garbed for that, be
ready to shield your eyes from any sharp corners of swinging
ladies' handbags.

Upon Being Old

It's not nice but take comfort that you won't stay that way
for ever.

Upon Disappearing

This is the usual method adopted when trying to start a new
existence free of creditors or enemies who want to end your
life. Therefore it is rather required you do this without trace.
And this is not easy, even when a plastic surgeon has changed
your scars, height, face and fingertips. Especially if a wife
looking for support is after you.

In leaving behind your clothes and wallet on the beach or
at the edge of active volcanoes to pretend you are dead, be
sure folk don't find your footprints where you were standing
around climbing into another suit of clothes. In your new
life be courteous to your new friends and don't get caught up
in a lot of tall tales about your past life that you can't

correctly tell twice. Lies really travel fast and you'd be amazed at how they can make some people remember you.

Upon Exercising a Realistic Thought

Little people don't matter where big countries are concerned.

The Psychologist

This smug son of a bitch.

Upon Biting the Hand That Feeds You

First find out why the hell it's feeding you. If it's for a really damn good reason, instead of taking nibbles you can then take out chunks.

Forgiveness

Be careful, those getting this then do the unforgivable. Which is frequently a lot worse than the first lousy thing they did to you.

Upon Expecting Fair Play in High Places

You'll get it if enough folk are watching.

When Some Supercilious Cunt Asks Is There Anything Wrong

'Yes, you evil little man, I'm looking at your tie.'

The Old School Tie

This will, when worn in far off parts, give you some solace when recognized by another. If challenged in cases where you are not entitled to wear this representative garment, state to those inquiring who are so privileged, that you merely wanted to meet persons who have such right to do them the courtesy of directing them away from you towards the other bores so entitled.

Charm

Although this gets you going that way it can keep you from the top.

Upon Various Races Venturing Abroad

The Chinese keep quiet
The English get embarrassed
The Germans start pushing

The Swiss go home
Frenchmen get scared
Americans get stupid
And the Austrians open a boutique
Which the Hungarians finance.

Upon Being Down and Out

This is, if you've recently taken a shower, the same as being up and active except that you wonder what the hell happened when you weren't looking to slam you there.

Meditation

Make sure you really need this on top of the worries you've already got.

Religions

Many fly by night religions, although flashes in the pan, can offer more laughs than the more established ancient ones. Most of these specialize in spiritual contentment and offer adherents music and speeches in return for money donations. Choose a good one and ask to see an audited account of their activities. If they fool around with venomous snakes, don't take these seriously and you will enjoy them all the more. Far Eastern religions are very popular as these are thought to harbour deep truths which are hidden by the modern civilized world. Be careful however, when they ask for a lot of your modern civilized cash. Religions which call upon you to give up all your worldly goods will often supply food and shelter but the wise man will keep a little nest egg by the by in case of prolonged emergencies when God doesn't provide.

Caution

It is awfully bad for the conscience to go out to get laid with another woman while wearing a shirt washed and ironed by one's wife plus she may upon laundering this again, get suspicious.

Shabby People

These throw the smaller party frequently termed intime and they collect guests from a mixture of recent friends right up to the brand new. Informality is the key note. And your host often is without a tie. He may in fact even dare to wear a turtle neck garment. Upon entering such parties raise your eyebrows.

Shabby Shabby People

Always throw bigger parties than shabby people. Some scruffiness will be evident with louts and a gold digger or two freely kissing asses among the guests. Upon entering such parties repeatedly sniff your nostrils.

Shabby Shabby Shabby People

As you ascend by lift to their spacious apartments, someone recognizable from stage, screen or even radio will be waiting in the private vestibule to descend as the doors open. If they are known to you they will instantly make it a habit of calling you by the wrong christian name as well as leaving syllables out of your surname. Upon entering the shindig two large rooms will be in action crammed with more celebrities, some singing duets and two perfectly different bands will be playing. Less famous guests will feign serious conversation in corners where there is a prevalence of books and cultural artifacts. Upon entry smile and slowly shake your head up and down with a big yes if these are the people for you.

Upon Good Manners Honour and Duty Getting You Absolutely Nowhere

This is disheartening. But if anyway you can sit at your hearth with an evening cocktail and the light gently playing on your newspaper with the wife not bitching from the kitchen and your kids growing up to be like you, say to yourself, what the hell, I got some of the good things even though those rude pushy ruthless bastards have got the best. And maybe that's the reason you're still alive.

Ingredients for Survival

There are so damn many of these that you first want to make
sure you have the money to afford them.

Epitaph

Tis as well
To be wise and know
That so goes other people's lives
So goes your own
Alas
And ere long

More about Penguins
and Pelicans

Penguinews, which appears every month, contains details of all the new books issued by Penguins as they are published. It is supplemented by the *Penguin Stock List*, which includes around 5,000 titles.

A specimen copy of *Penguinews* will be sent to you free on request. Please write to Dept EP, Penguin Books Ltd, Harmondsworth, Middlesex, for your copy.

In the U.S.A.: For a complete list of books available from Penguins in the United States write to Dept CS, Penguin Books, 625 Madison Avenue, New York, New York 10022.

In Canada: For a complete list of books available from Penguins in Canada write to Penguin Books Canada Ltd, 2801 John Street, Markham, Ontario L3R 1B4.

J. P. Donleavy

THE DESTINIES OF DARCY DANCER, GENTLEMAN

His future is disastrous, his present indecent, his past divine. He is
Darcy Dancer, scion of the gentry, youthful squire of Andromeda
Park and rider of horses and housekeepers to hounds and to bed.
His adventures as a vagabond across country and in bohemian
Dublin in search of the lost glories of his youth are ferociously
comic, hilariously sad.
And what else did you expect from the great Donleavy? This is
one of his finest novels, brim-full of zest and life.

'Truly and uniquely life-affirming . . . an almost magically potent
blend of the vulgar and the elegant, the grotesque and the lyrical,
the archaic and the lewdly up-to-date' – *Listener*

'Tender, sexy and tough by turn, it is always easy, conversational,
constantly ruffled by surprises . . . [it] is one of his most ambitious
odysseys and his most enjoyable yet' – *Vogue*

J. P. Donleavy

THE GINGER MAN

'In the person of *The Ginger Man*, Sebastian Dangerfield, Donleavy created one of the most outrageous scoundrels in contemporary fiction, a whoring, boozing young wastrel who sponges off his friends and beats his wife and girl friends. Donleavy then turns the moral universe on its head by making the reader love Dangerfield for his killer instinct, flamboyant charm, wit, flashing generosity – and above all for his wild, fierce, two-handed grab for every precious second of life' – *Time Magazine*

'No one who encounters him will forget Sebastian Dangerfield' –*New York Herald Tribune*

The Plays

THE GINGER MAN

Presented at the Fortune Theatre, London, in 1959. Presented at The Orpheum Theatre, New York, in 1963.

FAIRY TALES OF NEW YORK

Presented at the Pembroke Theatre, Croydon, England, in December 1960 and then transferred to the Comedy Theatre, London, in January 1961. Winner of the *Evening Standard* 'Most Promising Playwright of the Year' Award in 1960.

A SINGULAR MAN

Presented at the Cambridge Arts Theatre, Cambridge, England, in October 1964 and at the Comedy Theatre, London, later that month. and

THE SADDEST SUMMER OF SAMUEL S

J. P. Donleavy

THE BEASTLY BEATITUDES OF BALTHAZAR B

Balthazar B is the world's last shy elegant young man. Born to riches in Paris and raised in lonely splendour, his life spreads to prep school in England. There he is befriended by the world's most beatific sinner, the noble little Beefy. And in holidays spent in Paris Balthazar B falls upon love and sorrow with his beautiful governess Miss Hortense, to lose her and live out lonely London years, waking finally to the green sunshine of Ireland and Trinity College. Here, reunited with Beefy, he is swept away to the high and low life of Dublin until their university careers are brought to an inglorious end. They return to London, there to take their tricky steps into marriage, Beefy in search of riches, Balthazar in search of love.

'Donleavy at his best, eloquent, roguish and at last at one with his world and the terrible sadness it contains' – *Newsweek*.

THE SADDEST SUMMER OF SAMUEL S

'It can't be, you're not, are you?'
'Not what.'
'Samuel S.'
'You don't know me.'
'You are. Gee, I mean I've never seen a picture of you, but somehow I wouldn't miss you anywhere. You know a friend of my uncle who's a professor at NYU, he knows you. He said you were one of the points of interest in Europe.'
'Despair is the word.'
'Gee it's true, that's just, ha ha like what he said you might say ... by the way, I'm Abigail.'

J. P. Donleavy

MEET MY MAKER THE MAD MOLECULE

'In this book of short pieces Donleavy has given us the lyric poems to go with his epics. They are almost all elegies – sad songs of decayed hope, bitter little jitter-buggings of an exasperated soul, with barracuda bites of lacerating humour to bring blood-red into the grey of fate. These stories and sketches move between Europe and America, New York and Dublin and London, America is always the spoiled Paradise, the land of curdled milk and maggoty honey. The place that used to get you in the end, but that now does it in the beginning' – *Newsweek*

'The stories are swift, imaginative, beautiful, and funny, and no contemporary writer is better than J. P. Donleavy at his best' – the *New Yorker*

A SINGULAR MAN

His giant mausoleum abuilding, George Smith, the mysterious man of money, lives in a world rampant with mischief, of chiselers and cheats. Having side-stepped slowly away down the little alleys of success he tiptoes through a luxurious, lonely life between a dictatorial Negress housekeeper and two secretaries, one of whom, Sally Tomson, the gay wild and willing beauty, he falls in love with.

'George Smith is such a man as Manhattan's subway millions have dreamed of being' – *Time Magazine*

'A masterpiece of writing about love' – *National Observer*

'... an utterly irresistible broth of a book' – *Daily Telegraph*

J. P. Donleavy

THE ONION EATERS

On a grey cold day in a damp gloomy city Clayton Claw Cleaver
Clementine of The Three Glands descended directly in the male line
with this medical rarity intact sets off westwards to take up
residence in the vast haunted edifice of Charnel Castle. Clementine,
a polite unknown unsung product of the new world and recently
recovered by a miraculous cure from a long decline, alights at a
empty crossroads. Standing lonely on its windswept hillside the
great turrets and battlements rear in the sky. Clementine destitute
but for his monstrous dog Elmer and a collection of toothbrushes
enters this ancient stone fortress. Bedevilled by rats and rotted
floors Clementine stands unbelieving as an unpaid staff assembles
out of the woodwork and guests appear barefaced on the tiles of
the great hall with their equipment of audiometers, waterpipes,
onions and other venomous reptiles. Bills run up, debts
accumulate, confusion mounts and the Army of Insurrection
threatens while the definition of clarity is ringingly declared as
'that force given to a fist sent in the direction of a face that when
hit has no trouble seeing stars'.

Madness triumphs over love, beasts over man, chaos over reason and
for the moment life over death.

A FAIRY TALE OF NEW YORK

'Fantastically inventive ... madly funny. He is an original and
almost irresistible writer' – *Sunday Times*

'Cornelius Christian is J. P. Donleavy's new hero, person,
protagonist, figure-head, creature. He struts and weaves and shrugs
and punches his way through the pages of *A Fairy Tale of New
York*. I think he is Mr Donleavy's best piece of man-making since
Sebastian Dangerfield in the good old ginger days. The book is
fast, funny and addictive' – Robert Nye in the *Guardian*

'Irony, farce, satire and lyric' – *Spectator*